WILDERNESS AMBUSH

"Come out and talk!" he called.

The third shot followed on the heels of his call. It flicked his Stetson, hit the rocks behind him and whined off in ricochet. Plain sense made Jim yank his horse around and rowel it toward the bank from which he had come. As the horse hit the shore and lurched up the bank, Jim rolled out of the saddle, staggered and landed sprawling on an upjutting of shore boulders.

The shooting, stubborn and senseless, continued. Jim worked his way over the broken ground toward it until he was very close. It seemed over the next low ridge. Pulling off his Stetson, he bellied down on the loose gravel and carefully edged up to the hump and peered over.

There, on the near side of the slope toward the river, the rifleman was bellied down, methodically putting shots across the river. Jim looked closely and then swore softly under his breath.

The rifleman was a woman.

Books by Luke Short

GUNMAN'S CHANCE

LUKE SHORT

A DELL BOOK

Published by
Dell Publishing
a division of
Bantam Doubleday Dell Publishing Group, Inc.
666 Fifth Avenue
New York, New York 10103

The trademark Dell® is registered in the U.S. Patent and Trademark Office.

ISBN: 0-440-20950-1

Reprinted by arrangement with The Frederick D. Glidden Estate

Printed in the United States of America
Published simultaneously in Canada

September 1991

10 9 8 7 6 5 4 3 2 1

RAD

1

It was a sorry camp, a misery camp, that Jim Garry made at dusk up in the rain-pelted aspens. He couldn't help it because he and his two horses were too tired to make it down to real timber.

He thought he'd fall on his face before he got a fire started on the short strip of grass beside the stream. The aspens that mounted steeply out of sight on either side of the creek gave him some shelter, but not enough. When he'd staked out his horses downstream on the only grass he could find he plodded back to fix his camp. As he was rigging his tarp lean-to as shelter for himself and his gear a blob of wet snow fell from the crease of his sodden, dun Stetson.

He pulled his boots off, sticking them upside down on sticks in front of the fire, and then warmed his half-frozen feet. The aspen branches clashed in the wind, and cold rain was runneling down his back inside his sheepskin, and still he sat there, stupid, tired.

He heard it before his horses did. It was a sound he knew and couldn't believe a kind of clattering, thick-muted earth trembling. He rose, stood motionless a second to confirm it and then lunged for the slope. He had pulled himself into the first aspens when they hit—about a hundred mad, stampeding cattle. They boiled out of the dusk down the creek bed and funneled through his camp with the annihilating force of an avalanche.

They were gone in about twenty seconds, taking, Jim knew, his two horses with them. With the dismal, uncursing despair of a man whose present misfortune is past immediate calculating, Jim slid down into his camp.

His fire was gone, of course, and while his eyes were focusing in the dusk he felt his sock feet sinking in the churned mud left by the cattle. Nothing was left of his camp except the muddy hump of his saddle. His tarp and blankets were sodden tatters; his boots had disappeared, and perversely enough, there was the smell of fresh coffee in the air.

Jim heard a horse coming toward him from upstream. It hove into sight, snorting, and its thick-bodied rider was outlined against the lowering night sky.

For a few seconds neither man spoke, and then the rider said cautiously, "Who's that?"

Jim didn't answer.

"Put a match on yourself!" the rider ordered curtly.

Jim looked toward him and said in weary and savage disgust, "The hell with it. The hell with you too."

For some reason the rider seemed mollified by the retort. He rode closer and dismounted, his half-frozen slicker creaking like tar paper in the cold rain and smothering the sound of his rifle leaving its saddle scabbard. When he saw the remains of the camp in the half dusk he said softly, "Man, man. I didn't know that."

"I had a fire," Jim said bitterly.

"I couldn't have stopped 'em if I'd seen it," the rider said in a matter-of-fact voice. "Let's build up another."

By the time Jim, still in his sock feet, had rounded up some wood the rider had a fire going. He kept his rifle by him. When the fire had started enough so that its light was a help he rose and confronted Jim.

Jim Garry was a sight that might have made the man smile at another time and place. It was the sock feet, deep in mud, that were so out of place. But even without boots Jim Garry was a head taller than the other. There was a taciturn unfriendliness in his bleak eyes that warned a man he seldom smiled. A week's growth of dark beard stubble softened the sharp planes of his weather-browned face, giving him a tough look the rider thought rightly was not wholly spurious. The rider wasn't sure, but he didn't think he liked Jim Garry.

"Come over the pass today?" he asked.

"With an outfit."

The puncher flushed a little. He was not such a wide man, now that there was firelight to see him by. His thickness of body was due to a blanket wrapped around him under his worn slicker. He had a weathered, sober, faintly overworked look about him that men who work cattle for wages always have.

"Let's find your boots," he said. Without speaking Jim turned and began the search for his boots outside the circle of firelight. He was wearily aware that the puncher was examining what was left of his outfit under the pretense of helping in the search. He was also aware that the man carried his rifle and was careful not to let Jim near him. The rain pelted down, and Jim began to shiver.

The search didn't take long. Jim found one boot buried in the mud; the other, with its top cut to ribbons, was half lying in the stream some thirty feet below his camp.

He went back to the fire, sat down, clawed the mud off his boots and put them on. When he looked up he found the puncher watching him, an expression of bafflement in his face.

"I wisht I knew who you was," the puncher said, his tone not unkindly.

"You don't though."

"Come in with one of the reservation trail herds?" the puncher asked shrewdly.

Jim nodded.

"What are you doin' over here? This ain't the way back to Texas."

Jim said with an expressionless face, "I'm waitin' till you get out of camp. Then I'll roll in—if I can find my blankets."

The puncher didn't smile. He said doggedly, "It's a dirty cold night. Let's see how much clothes you got on under your sheepskin."

Jim didn't move, only said, "No gun."

They watched each other a long ten seconds, Jim with hostility and stubbornness in his tough face, the puncher with indecision in his. Finally the puncher seemed to come to a judgment.

"You can't stay here without horses or grub or blankets. Our camp's down in the pine timber. We can make it double that far."

A kind of stiff pride kept Jim silent a moment. He didn't like it but, after all, he had no choice.

He rose and said surlily, "Whatever you say."

When they mounted Jim noticed the puncher was careful to give him the saddle, mounting behind him. He was also careful to keep his hand on the butt of the carbine in the saddle scabbard.

Jim thought, "Then the trouble has broken wide open."

They followed the stream down into pine timber, and the rain still held on. There was no sign of his two horses, and he knew tomorrow's hunt for them would be a dreary job.

A half-hour later, where the timber broke away for a mountain meadow, they saw the light of a fire, and Jim heard his companion grunt with satisfaction. A half-dozen horses grazing out in the meadow's darkness snorted at their approach.

It was this that sent one of the men around the fire out into the dark trees, a rifle in his hands. Jim noted it idly, thinking how trouble always ran to the same pattern.

His companion gave a shout, and the rifleman stepped back into the firelight. They dismounted, and Jim was the first to walk toward the fire, a tall, tired man with a quiet arrogance that ignored these men and their puzzled, hostile glances.

Against the cold drizzle a big slanting tarp had been rigged between two trees, facing the fire. Under it three other men were now coming to their feet, their movements made awkward by the clutter of gear and bedrolls around them.

Jim held his hands out to the fire for warmth and then regarded these men with a kind of brash curiosity. Two of them he pegged as punchers, like his friend of the aspens. They were ragged, unshaven, alert men. The third was a camp cook and poacher. The fourth man was not of their kind, and it was he who stepped out into the slow rain now, inquisitive glance on Jim's companion.

"I dunno," Jim's companion said in answer to an unasked

question. "I was shoving my gather down the creek, and they cleaned out his camp, outfit, horses and all. I brung him along."

"Good," the fourth man said. His voice was low-pitched, quick. He turned his head and cooly regarded Jim. There were many things Jim could read in those dark eyes—implacability, a swift, hard judgment and little patience. The man was about fifty, spare and of medium height, with a skin weather-blackened to swarthiness. His thin saber of a nose was high bridged; his mouth was hidden by a soot-black mustache, although his hair was turning white at the temples. His clothes were even more careless and shoddy than those of his men, and yet he contrived to look like their leader.

He stared at Jim with an insolence that wasn't aware of itself.

"Come over the peaks?" he asked.

Jim nodded

"But not the pass. Why?"

"There's no law says a man has to stick to a wagon road, is there?"

The older man didn't answer for a moment, as if adjusting his judgment.

Then he said, "Your horse is branded Flying W. I don't know it."

So they'd caught his horses. They'd probably broken away from the herd at the meadow.

Jim said, "Don't you?"

One of the punchers made a low noise in his throat and stepped toward Jim.

"Wait, Ferg," the older man said.

The puncher stopped just outside of the tarp's shelter. The other puncher walked around him to the other side of the fire. They regarded Jim watchfully, fight in their eyes. It was up to Jim to talk or be made to talk.

Jim looked at the older man. "You go to hell," he said quietly.

The punchers started for him, but they stopped as the older man waved them back.

He said, "All right. My name's John Lufton. That's a fair exchange. A month ago nobody would have asked you any questions. It's different now. Who are you?"

Lufton had provided a graceful exit, Jim saw, and he considered it. His name would mean nothing. None of these men could know that a letter written two months ago and read five hundred miles south of these mountains had summoned him here. And his ignorance of what this reception meant wasn't put on.

"Jim Garry," he said. "Flying W is a Nations' brand."

"Come up with one of the reservation trail herds?"

Jim nodded.

Lufton hesitated and then said, "This isn't the way back to Texas."

"I'm fiddle footed," Jim drawled. "I don't like wagon roads either. A Ute told me there was a town called Sun Dust over the mountains. I was on my way to it and through it. What else?"

"Know anybody in Sun Dust or the Basin?"

"No," Jim lied.

"I apologize," Lufton said curtly. "We've got your horses. We can outfit you with blankets and grub too. Step in out of the rain." To the cook he said, "Joe, rustle up some grub for them."

Jim went to the far side of the tarp and gratefully sank down on a bedroll. He took off his sodden hat and with his neckerchief he scrubbed the water off his face. His black hair, ragged at the neckline and temples and lying in a crooked, awry part, was the only wholly dry part of his body.

The cook raked the Dutch oven out of the coals and served him biscuits and meat and coffee. Jim wolfed them down, staring at his plate. The talk of the men was constrained at first, but soon the crew was questioning the slickered cowboy. Jim was ignored. This, too, was the pattern of a thousand campfires, and Jim seemed to expect it.

The talk was cattle talk, and Jim was able to piece together only a little of it, for it was guarded and wary. John Lufton was the owner, and his beef was being pushed down out of the mountains and off the reservation, he gathered.

Jim finished his meal and leaned back on the bedroll, a frugal cigarette pasted in his lips. Nobody paid him attention. He stared at the fire, out of the conversation, an aloof man whose face, now that he was left alone, settled into a taciturn melancholy.

Like all shy men to whom friendliness does not come easy, Jim Garry was both aware of his loneliness and powerless to change it. He had been fifteen days alone, and now his first contact with men had been a snarling anger that walled him away from them. It was always thus. Five years ago he wouldn't have cared, because then he was too absorbed in his life to notice it. Nothing else had mattered then except the long gamble of the drovers' game in the Indian Nations. In those days he had driven himself mercilessly, bringing up herds from Texas to stock the leases of the Cheyenne-Arapaho reservation and going back for new herds the day he was paid off. After three years of it he had found himself one day with a herd that was his own, representing every dollar he had made. And he had seen this herd two weeks later strung along the bottom lands of the Red River, dead of Texas fever.

He guessed it was after that he began to care about what men thought of him, but it was too late then. He was friendless. What had happened to him in the two years since he didn't like to think about. The riding jobs and the fights, because nobody liked a sour man. And then the dishonesty, the small brand changing, the whisky to the Indians and, finally, the running of small herds into Kansas through the fever quarantine. Men got the habit of coming to him, always at night, not to hire him for crime, but to pay him for the small dishonesties they themselves were ashamed to commit.

And then the letter that brought him here: the letter from Tate Riling in Sun Dust. He'd been with Tate in running the quarantine until it got so hot for Tate that he had to leave. That was six months ago—no, a year. And now this letter. It was brief, and Jim remembered its wording: "There's trouble due to break up here, and I need a man I can trust if I'm to make a stake out of it. Drift into this country quiet and look me up. There's money in it, Jim, for us both—big money."

Crooked money, Jim knew, and he didn't care. He was here, and the trouble was here, and he was alone, watching a fire not his own and sleeping in the blankets of men who would like to fight him.

"A rotten night."

Jim glanced up to see John Lufton kneeling beside him, peering out into the slow rain.

"Yeah," Jim agreed. Lufton had seen his loneliness, wanted to be friendly.

Lufton glanced at him, and his eyes were kindly. "I'm sorry we had to be so rough with you, Garry. But you're a loose rider, and we've got to watch them."

"Why?" Jim asked.

Lufton paused to consider his answer, regarding Jim thoughtfully.

"It's pretty easy said," Lufton said softly. "If you came from the agency you likely heard of me."

"I was paid off and rode out. No."

Lufton said wryly, "I've contracted beef for the agency for five years and never had a complaint. This year they've got a new agent. He didn't like the weight of my beef or its count after I'd brought my herds up from Dodge. He refused acceptance."

"I thought that was Texas beef that took out my camp," Jim said with grim humor.

Lufton almost smiled. "It was. That's the part of the stuff Pindalest rejected. He not only rejected my beef, but he trumped up a whisky-peddling charge against me so he could kick me and my beef off the reservation grass."

Jim pondered this, and still it didn't satisfy him. "That don't explain about the loose riders."

"No, not in itself. But, you see, I haven't got any grass to move to except what I used to claim down in the Basin. I've got a brand down there, the Blockhouse. It was there before Sun Dust, before there was a white in this country."

Lufton was talking slowly with a kind of relish that held a bitter humor for him.

"Five years ago," he went on, "I started to contract beef for the agency, buying my herds in Dodge and Abilene. I'd turn them over to the agent, and they'd winter on reservation grass. I couldn't use my grass, except for a scattering of horses, so I didn't pay much attention to the homesteaders that drifted in."

"Ah," Jim said. This, too, ran to a pattern, an old and dismal story.

Lufton nodded grimly. "That's it. Now that I'm kicked off the reservation I need my water and grass; it's taken. I'm moving back."

"They'll fight?"

Lufton rose, a faint smile moving his mustache. "I reckon they will. They say they will now that they've been told they ought to."

Jim was puzzled, and his face showed it. Lufton made an impatient gesture. "Just a jackleg hard case that come in this summer. He's organized them to fight me. Name's Riling, which"—he smiled wryly—"is what he's doing to me."

Jim didn't speak, not trusting himself. For a panicked moment he wondered if his name had given him away, and then the moment was gone. For so many months his name and Tate Riling's were linked in men's minds, as they soon would be again, that he thought all men knew.

He said calmly, "About the loose riders."

"He's bringing gunmen in."

This was what Lufton was getting at. Jim could tell it from the way the crew looked at him, from the way Lufton waited, from what had gone on before.

Jim's cigarette was dead. He tossed it into the fire and then said equably, "Nobody can blame you for being careful."

"You don't get it," Lufton said.

Jim looked squarely at him. "Get what?"

"This: It's work for Blockhouse, for me, or ride on out of the country. That's your choice, Garry."

"And what if I don't?"

"I'll give you time to get a shave and drink and night's sleep in Sun Dust, and then you better drift."

Jim's glance shuttled from Lufton to his men. In their faces was the same iron challenge. If they could prevent it no man would stay in this country unless he was a Blockhouse man.

Lufton said mildly, "Sleep on it, Garry," and left him.

Morning brought a cold sunrise, but no rain. After a hasty breakfast the crew rode off. Bart, Jim's companion of last night, left to pick up his yesterday's gather and shove it down to the herds that would move into the Basin. The crew didn't talk much, and Lufton didn't give any orders. The men seemed to know their job and want to finish it quickly, so they could face the real job.

Jim borrowed a rope, caught his horses and led them back to the camp. He fashioned a hackamore for the saddle horse, and when he was finished he came over to where Lufton was saddling up.

"Much obliged," he said.

Lufton nodded. "Working for me, Garry?"

"I don't reckon. I'll ride on through."

"It's your choice," Lufton said. "I take it you're heading for Sun Dust?" When Jim said he was, Lufton went on, "Mind leaving a note at my place with the women-folks? It's on your way."

"I'll leave the rope too," Jim said.

Lufton went over to the fire, tore the label off one of the cook's cans and wrote a note on the back. He handed it to Jim, gave him directions, said, "Good luck," and watched Jim ride off, leaving his pack horse. There was an expression of grim and sardonic humor in his eyes as he watched.

It was an October mountain morning, and Jim had found his camp of last night, salvaged what he could of his outfit and was below the Blockhouse camp before the chill was really out of the air.

By midmorning he'd tied his sheepskin behind his saddle and when, around noon, he slanted down into the dry canyons that let onto the Massacre River the sun was hot on his shoulder blades.

He picked up a wagon road on the flats between the river and the canyon mouth, and before it had taken him to the river he had a long look at the yellow-stippled rolling reaches of Massacre Basin to the east. Unless his directions were faulty, the patch of green far across the river and to the south against the white-hooded limestone outcrop was the Blockhouse, Lufton's spread. The river was the east boundary of the reservation. According to Lufton, the left-hand one of the forks in the road across the river would take him the five miles across the Basin and to the rim below which, on the Basin floor, was Sun Dust.

At the river Jim's pack horse was already drinking. He rode out into the river, shallow and wide here at the ford and fringed with the willows of the dry country, and let his horse drink.

He stretched in the saddle, feeling the welcome sweat that replaced the chill of last night. And now he faced the decision he had been postponing all morning. He was carrying a note from John Lufton to his ranch, and it might well be that this note held information valuable to Tate Riling. He would read it, and if it contained orders that affected Lufton's plans he wouldn't deliver it. Otherwise he would, since it would insure the day of grace in Sun Dust Lufton had promised him.

His hand rose to his shirt pocket and then paused. A faint stirring of shame halted him, the memory of eating a man's grub, of sleeping in his camp, of violating a trust, of all the shabby dishonesties of these past years. And then his hand moved on to his pocket.

The hard, unechoing crack of a rifle exploded the stillness, and a geyser of water leaped up beside his horse.

Jim sat motionless, hand half raised, his glance searching the thicket of willows for the telltale wisp of smoke.

He located the place in the willows from which the shot issued, but he didn't move. His horse stood alertly, and the sound of its slobbered water alone broke the stillness.

Jim called out, "Put it up. I'm ridin' through."

The second shot at his horse's feet sent water in his face. His pack horse turned and sedately retreated.

A slow anger narrowed Jim's attention. Whichever faction was stopping him, Blockhouse or nester, he had a passport if he could only speak.

"Come out and talk!" he called.

The third shot followed on the heels of his call. It flicked his Stetson, hit the rocks behind him and whined off in ricochet. Plain sense made Jim yank his horse around and rowel it toward the bank from which he had come. The horse lifted sheets of water in its flight, while Jim yanked his carbine out of its scabbard. As the horse hit the shore and lurched up the bank, Jim rolled out of the saddle, staggered and landed sprawling on an upjutting of shore boulders. His horse stopped immediately, missing the weight in the saddle.

Levering a shell into his carbine, Jim laid a sight on the far trees opposite and then fired. He shot six times, fast, laying them two feet apart and at the same level. Whoever it was across there had chosen a fool's shelter, for he was screened only by trees. The rocks were above and behind him up the slope.

When his hammer clicked on empty Jim reloaded, his glance searching the shore. He heard a snort over there and again he raised his carbine. This time he widened his aim, searching patiently along the shore.

At his fifth shot he saw a horse break out from the trees and lunge up the far slope. On its far side the rider was holding onto the horn, running bent over, shielded from sight by the frightened horse.

Jim didn't wait to see more. He vaulted on his horse and put him into the river at a lope. By the time he had lost sight of the lone horse and runner over the ridge he was in the shelter of the screening shore willows and coldly angry.

He reined in and turned his horse upstream at a slow walk, listening. Presently from downstream the shooting began again —at what, Jim didn't know, since it wasn't at him.

He hugged the willows for a quarter mile, then put his horse into them. He rode through the thicket, reined up and peered out. The rocky lift of the ridge screened him from sight. He ground-haltered his horse, patted his coat pocket to make sure he had shells, took his carbine and then moved downstream again in the willows. Presently he crawled up on the ridge and dropped on its far side.

The shooting, stubborn and senseless, continued. Jim worked his way over the broken ground toward it until he was very close. It seemed over the next low ridge. Pulling off his Stetson, he bellied down on the loose gravel and carefully edged up to the hump and peered over.

There, on the near side of the slope toward the river the rifleman was bellied down, methodically putting shots across the river. Jim looked closely and then swore softly under his breath.

The rifleman was a woman.

Her hair was the giveaway; it lay with the sheen of wheat down to her shoulders, where it was caught by her Stetson, which had been lost in her retreat and now hung down her back from the chin strap. Otherwise, at this distance she could have been mistaken for a man with her worn levis, flannel shirt and man's coat.

Jim's gaze narrowed and his eyes grew oddly hard. She was shooting methodically at something—at him, she thought—as if this were sport. His gaze shuttled to her horse ground-haltered behind her, and he saw the Blockhouse brand on the left hip. One of Lufton's womenfolk playing at being a man.

Slow wrath stirred within him as he watched her. She'd kill a man, and gladly, it seemed. Shoot first, ask questions afterward. It didn't matter to her if she killed a man; it wasn't worth the trouble, apparently, to find out if the man she was killing was friend, enemy or U.S. marshal.

He glanced down at his Stetson. There was a notch bitten out of the rim, fraying the felt, where her bullet had touched. His mind was suddenly made up, the result of a stubborn conviction he did not even put into words to himself.

He crawled up to the ridge and laid out his cartridges on the ground beside him. The girl was still shooting as fast as she could lever the shells into her gun.

Jim calculated the distance to her, his eyes hard and cold and wicked, and then drew his bead. He held his breath and made it careful and fired.

The heel flew off her boot as if expelled by a spring. The girl whirled to a sitting position, and Jim shot again. The dirt beside her leaped in a little geyser of dust. He shot again, and on the other side of her, closer yet, leaped another spurt of gravel. She came to her feet in panic, and Jim laid a shot at her feet. She started to run for her horse now, stumbled missing her heel, fell sprawling. Jim laid a shot not six inches from her head that plowed dirt into her face and hair.

When she rose this time she had given up the idea of reaching her horse. She turned and ran for the rocks she had been hiding behind, and Jim laid three shots behind her close enough to hurry her. When she disappeared over the ridge and down the slope to the river he moved with her and put a last shot beside her as she made the willows.

He came erect and slipped down the ridge to her horse. Swinging into the saddle, he rode over the ridge and picked up the trail he had come afoot. At his own horse he dismounted and found that his hands were shaking, his knees oddly unsteady. The backwash of a tension he hadn't understood had its way with him for a minute as he slowly realized what he had done. What if he had hit her? In that momentary anger he had forgotten that she was a girl and remembered only that she deserved a rough scare. And scare her he had, heedless and unthinking, in the same way he would scare a man in a reckless and savage brawl.

Standing there in the willows, he had a rare, blinding moment of self-judgment that comes to a willful man, and it turned him sick with loathing of himself. When it was gone and pride had come back he knew he wasn't going to try to remedy what he'd done. It was finished, gone, like all the other mistakes.

Soberly he mounted and headed away from the river, leading the Blockhouse horse. He had no intention of riding back to pick up his pack horse and run the risk of meeting the girl.

Swinging south and east, he was soon in a rolling, open, grama-grass country; hummocks of sage broke its rich golden monotony. To the east, running southeasterly, was a low rim with more of the broken grasslands running off into mountains that were barely visible in the blued distance. Autumn haze touched the land, and off below the rim he could see the square sear patch of a homesteader's planting. When he reached the road he turned the Blockhouse horse loose and kept south, and presently the bright yellow flag of the autumn cottonwoods pointed out the Blockhouse.

It lay, when he at last saw it, at the heel of a low thrust of limestone that spilled in a five-mile tongue from the rim to the east. A stream, following the edge of the limestone, now took off for the distant Massacre, rearing this thick stand of cottonwoods at the parting. They were old and thin leaved and a gaudy yellow now.

The house itself, a one-story, flat-roofed stone affair with a long, deep veranda, squatted under the big trees. Off closer to both creek and the shelter of the limestone there were clustered the barns and corrals and sheds that made up the working ranch. It had the rich, worn look of something used and old, and as Jim rode into it he understood why Lufton supposed this country was rightfully his. No raw nester shacks could ever lay the claim to this land that this place could.

He rode past the house, judged a second stone building midway between house and barn to be the bunkhouse and headed toward it.

A girl's voice at his back called, "Don't go over there, please."

Jim reined up and turned in his saddle. The girl was standing on the edge of the veranda, leaning against a pillar. Dutifully Jim swung his horse around and rode up to her, touching his hat as he pulled up.

"The men need sleep," she said. Her voice was careless,

slurred, indifferent. He noticed first that a rifle was leaning against the veranda railing beside her, and then his gaze lifted to her face. He was immediately aware that this was a woman who knew she was beautiful. Everything about her told him so —the cut and the stuff of her dress, which was a strange green color that matched her eyes, the searching arrogant stare that summed him up, judged and dismissed him. It was the look of a woman who could afford to hold men in gentle contempt. Her auburn hair, thick and silky and alive as light, had been pinned up off her neck in back. She had that drowsy and impatient look about her of a bored woman who has been waked from sleep only to be bored again. And yet Jim Garry thought she was the most beautiful woman he had ever looked upon, and he knew she thought so, too, and was not interested.

Jim climbed stiffly from the saddle and brought the note from his shirt pocket. He handed it to her, suddenly aware of his shoddy appearance.

"From your father."

The girl took it, asking indifferently, "You're working for us now?"

"No."

She read the note. Her expression didn't change, and yet the way her long lashes were shadowed on her cheeks as she read the note seemed to Jim something to admire.

"Will you eat?" she asked.

"Much obliged. I'm on my way to Sun Dust."

"Did Dad say when he was coming down?"

"No ma'am."

"Thank you," she said.

That was all, and he was dismissed. He touched his hat again and reluctantly turned toward his horse.

"Stop right there!"

Jim's gaze whipped around to the rear corner of the house. The slim yellow-haired girl of the river shooting had her rifle trained on him. Behind her was Jim's pack horse. If he needed any more proof of her identity the heel on her left boot was missing.

Jim drew a long breath and waited, his attention narrowed on this girl as she came two steps closer to him. She was in the grip of a fury that made her lower lip tremble. That and her dark eyes that were black with anger were the first things Jim noticed.

Noting, too, that she cradled her carbine against her hip with the unconscious negligence of a person used to guns, Jim had a fast, hard intimation of trouble.

"You're the man that shot at me at the river, aren't you?" she demanded.

Jim thought: "Slow her up or there'll be hell to pay." Under the golden sun brown of her face she was pale, and Jim could even see the thin dusting of freckles across the bridge of her small nose. The malevolence in her brown eyes jolted him and made his speech mild and without expression.

"I reckon I am."

"I'm going to show you how it feels."

The girl on the veranda said sharply, "Put that gun down, Amy!"

Amy fired. The shock of its swiftness held Jim motionless, at once surprised and incredulous.

The auburn-haired girl screamed, and Amy said wrathfully, without looking at her, "Keep quiet, Carol! I'm going to do it again!"

Jim began to sweat. Behind thought, he knew he'd have to bluff this out. If he didn't move she couldn't bring herself to shoot him. If he lunged for the house and shelter he knew she'd hound him clear to the river, as he'd hounded her.

She started to raise her carbine to her shoulder, when the pounding of running feet made her turn her head. This was the time for him to break if he wanted to. He only stood there, watching the three men running toward them from the bunkhouse, the man in the lead calling, "What is it? Who shot?"

Amy turned back to Jim, her face grim and its expression urgent. She raised her gun to her shoulder, and Carol screamed again. Amy shot again. This time Jim's hat was lifted from his head and fell in the dust behind him. Amy levered the gun frantically and was lifting it to her shoulder again when the first man reached her. He batted the gun down, and it went off at her feet.

She fought frantically for a second and then saw that struggle was useless. By the time she had relinquished the gun Carol had reached her.

"Amy, Amy, have you gone crazy?" Carol asked. She put her hands on Amy's shoulders and shook her.

Roughly Amy shrugged her hands off and looked bleakly at Jim. There was a wildness and a pride in her face that burned passionately, a kind of fierce exaltation that made her at that instant more alive, more beautiful, than her sister.

Jim stooped and picked up his hat and looked at the hole in its crown and then at Amy.

"Ask him!" she said furiously, pointing at him. "I was doing to him what he did to me."

The man who had seized the gun laid his curious, truculent glance on Jim. He was a middle-aged man, heavy chested and thick jowled, with a blocky, bulldog breadth of body. His thin saddle of sandy hair was awry, as if he'd been wakened from sleep.

He said to Jim, "What about this?"

"She's right."

The man turned for confirmation to Amy.

"After I spelled you, Cap, those rocks got hot, and I moved down into the willows. Then he came along and stopped in the river to let his horse drink. I put a warning shot close to him, and he didn't turn back. I put another closer, and he went back to the other bank and started shooting at me. I didn't have any protection there, so I went back to the rocks. I don't know how he got across, but suddenly he started shooting at me from behind. He almost hit me too! And stole my horse!"

Her words poured out in bitter and outraged anger, and when she finished there was utter silence. The man she had called Cap slowly turned his head to regard Jim. The other two punchers came over closer to him.

"What about it?" Cap said.

"That's the way it happened."

"You knew it was a woman?"

"Not till I got behind her."

There was another silence while the men looked at each other. Cap said unbelievingly, "You mean you tried to hit her?"

"Scare her," Jim said stubbornly, anger at last in his voice in spite of his efforts to keep it out. "A woman's bullet kills you just as quick as a man's."

"You deserved it, Amy," Carol said sharply.

Amy Lufton said hotly, scornfully, "Why has Dad kept a man at the river for a week, if it isn't to keep riders from crossing?"

Cap came over to Jim. The other punchers moved in closer, watching Cap for a clue to their behavior.

"What are you doin' here?" Cap growled.

"He delivered a note from Dad," Carol said.

Jim said dryly, "That's what I was goin' to tell her, but she wouldn't stop shootin'."

Cap was plainly baffled. He looked from one girl to the other. Amy had settled into sullen and smoldering silence. Carol was regarding Jim with quiet interest now, a fresh curiosity. She said lazily to Cap, without looking at him, "At least he's one person who'll give Amy as good as she gives."

Cap waited, and nobody spoke. He nodded at Jim and tilted his head sideways and said, "Get out of here. Quick."

Jim walked over to his horse. Amy turned and strode around to the back of the house, her back ramrod-straight. Jim swung into the saddle, looked at Carol and touched his hat. She smiled at him and watched him ride out.

2

Sheriff Les Manker put a bony shoulder against the doorjamb and fished aimlessly in his vest pocket for a match. He took careful note of the man riding down the center of Sun Dust's main street, an unsparing shrewdness in his gray eyes. He noted the condition of the horse, which was jaded, and the brand, which he did not know, and then he looked again at the rider. Sheriff Manker's opinion of him, which he did not express, was summed up in one word: tough. He watched him pick his way, courteously enough, through the nester wagons and the scattering of hands from the ranches up on the Bench who were crossing and recrossing the road on their way to their sundown drink. At last the rider turned into the archway of Settlemeir's feed stable and was lost to sight.

Manker raised a match to his mouth, but before he put it between his thin lips he said, "That him?"

The man in the office, the man who had been looking through the window at the same rider, said, "That's him. What do you think?"

Manker didn't speak. The setting sun threw long shadows on the street, turning its deep dust to silver. It was a harsh light, unkind to the gray, weathered store fronts, the tangle of corrals and homes and sheds that rose up to abut the base of the rim to the east. The narrow, dug road crawling the four hundred feet to the rim slanted away to the north, and the dust motes of the last riders in still left a fog clinging to the slope.

Manker said dispiritedly, "Maybe."

"Maybe hell!" Milo Sweet said bluntly. "You got to get hit on the head with it? Lufton threatened to get one, didn't he?"

"You ain't sure it's him."

"I cut his sign goin' into Blockhouse, and I cut it goin' out. He's a stranger."

"John Lufton's got a right to hire a range detective."

"Not to watch me, he ain't," Sweet said flatly. "Range detectives mean framed evidence. Evidence means court. And I seen too many judges bought to let it get that far."

Sweet shouldered past Manker and stopped on the boardwalk. He was a two-bit rancher out in Massacre Basin, one of the men John Lufton had first tolerated and was now fighting. A brusque little man, with reddish close-cropped hair and an intense face, he had a wire-edged temper that Manker didn't like. Manker wished it had been anyone but Sweet who had seen this stranger, and he said, "Let Riling handle it. And no shootin'."

"He ain't here. This man is likely talking to Settlemeir right now about Basin cattle stealing. That's the way evidence starts."

He started to walk away, stopped, came back and faced Manker. "Who the hell elected you? Remember?"

Manker shifted the match in his mouth and said nothing. Sweet turned and angled across the street, and at that moment Manker felt an odd stirring of tired hatred. He was a nester sheriff, and he knew it and he didn't like it.

It was so unnecessary. Ten years back John Lufton had spent three weeks at the capitol, and when he came back there was a new county, Lufton County. Its seat was Sun Dust and its boundary was the rim, so that it excluded all the Bench ranchers to the east. John Lufton had gone that far to insure himself protection against rival ranchers and authority—and then sat back and watched these nesters and small ranchers fill up his county and bully his sheriff. Trouble was, Manker liked John Lufton a lot more than he did most of his other constituents.

Sweet hit the boardwalk in time to see the rider leave Settlemeir's and cut down his way. He lounged against a store front and was suddenly concerned with fashioning a smoke, but he had noted with rising interest that the rider was now wearing a gun and belt which he had probably brought in his war bag.

The rider passed him and went into the Fair Store, and Sweet pondered that. Fighting down a rising impatience to hurry over to the Bella Union and spread the word, he waited. When the rider came out of the Fair he had a package in his hand. Sweet dropped in behind him, traveled three doors downstreet, and the rider turned in at the barbershop.

Sweet turned back then, sure of where his man would be, and went upstreet to Settlemeir's. The sun had fallen behind the Three Braves, and the town was in immediate dusk. A chill wind riding off the Basin lifted through Sun Dust's streets on its climb to the rim. Lamps were lighted now, the signal for some of the wagons to pull out for home.

Old man Settlemeir, feeble and deliberate in his movements, was hanging the night lantern in the archway when Sweet approached him.

"Who was that just put up his horse?"

Old Settlemeir had been John Lufton's first blacksmith and he had small use for the way things were shaping up now. But Sweet, while against Lufton, was a cattleman and not a farmer, and Settlemeir was civil.

"Flying W is the brand. I don't know it."

"He say anything?"

"Asked where he could find Tate Riling."

Sweet stood transfixed with amazement. Then he murmured, "Ah," wheeled and cut across street for the Bella Union. His suspicion had turned into conviction now, and the thing that colored it was a fierce outrage. The detective had come straight from his boss to see Riling. Sweet shouldered through the door of the Bella Union and tramped on, his hot glance raking the bar. There were two drummers there and an army man on his way to the reservation, talking to a couple of the Bench punchers.

At a back table were the men he was after—Big Nels Titterton, from out by Chimney Breaks, and Bob Paulsen, the wild nester who let his wife farm while he gambled away the money he got from selling stolen Basin beef over in Commissary. There was Anse Barden, an old Blockhouse man and the best head in the bunch, and his boy Fred. They were playing poker for next to no stakes. Mitch Moten, a thin, taciturn man who grazed a small tramp herd of culls across the Basin all summer and traded them to the Indians who had offended the agency and lost their beef ration, stood watching the game. Against the wall was Chet Avery, with his black hoe-thickened hands folded on the lap of his bib overalls, the only man in the country who farmed because he liked it and not because he didn't own cattle. These men were waiting.

Sweet hauled up beside Barden and ignored the greetings and said, "Lufton's watcher just drifted in, boys. I saw him leave the Blockhouse."

Barden put down his cards. "Cattle detective?"

"What else? He's looking for Riling."

"Riling!"

Sweet smiled thinly. "That's it. Riling. He asked Settlemeir where he could find him."

The men looked at each other. Chet Avery said, "You sure he's an association man?"

"I cut his sign goin' into the Blockhouse and comin' out. No stray rider is goin' to find his way to the Blockhouse without he follows the wagon road. He didn't. He was sent for."

There was a baffled silence as Sweet looked challengingly from one to the other. They'd been expecting this for weeks, since it was one way Lufton had of fighting them. But the rider's request for Riling was puzzling, and Barden asked, "What do you figure he wants with Tate?"

"Let's ask him," Mitch Moten suggested dryly.

Sweet looked up at Mitch, stared at him a second, and then his face broke into a smile.

Chet Avery said cautiously, "We better wait for Riling."

"Riling's here," Sweet murmured.

"Where?"

Sweet pointed to Big Nels. "Right here."

The idea met with only Chet Avery's objection. Sweet said

sardonically, "All right, maybe you'd like to send him over to Riling, Chet. Tell him where Tate is. Tell him he's waiting to knock hell out of the first Blockhouse herd that crosses the river but that he'll have time to see an association man."

Avery's broad face flushed, but he kept silent. Sweet said, "What about it, Nels?"

"Sure," Nels said slowly. "Sure. Better warn Barney."

Jim Garry, his new shirt stiff against his skin, came out of the barbershop into Sun Dust's night and paused on the edge of the plank walk. The hot bath had soaked the stiffness out of him; in his nose was still the pleasant reek of the bay rum from his shave. He watched the traffic of the main street, heard the cheerful talk shouted from boardwalk to boardwalk and eyed the restless ponies racked in front of the two saloons. A housewife, a sack of sugar under her arm, left the Fair, gathered her skirts and ran past him in her hurry home to a late supper.

It was all homely, all familiar. He fashioned a cigarette and reached in his shirt pocket for a match. He had none, but the memory of this afternoon, when his similar gesture had been interrupted by the gunshot, was conjured up, vivid and alive. He wondered idly if Amy Lufton would have shot him if he had elected to cross the Massacre instead of retreat. This thought would not leave him alone; it, and the memory of her fury there at the Blockhouse, had nagged him all afternoon. Nor could he forget the expression on Cap Willis' face when he admitted shooting at Amy.

He was suddenly restless and dissatisfied and put these thoughts from his mind and turned downstreet. Presently he remembered his unlighted cigarette and threw it away. There was Tate Riling to find yet, a fact he faced with a lack of enthusiasm that puzzled him. It wasn't because John Lufton had warned him out of the Basin and Sun Dust, either.

A slight, wiry puncher, about to pass him, hauled up and said "Got a match, mister?"

"I haven't," Jim replied.

The puncher said in an altered voice, "Looking for Riling?"

Jim peered at him in the half-light of the street, suddenly suspicious, trying to place him as one of the three men at the Blockhouse this afternoon. He couldn't and yet he wasn't satisfied.

"Riling?" he murmured. "I'm not looking for anybody."

The puncher seemed puzzled. He hesitated and then said, "He's over at the Bella Union," and walked away.

Jim watched him until he was out of sight, and then he peered across the street, his attention narrowed. He remembered asking the stable hostler for Riling's whereabouts. He thought, "News travels fast here," and wondered if this was a Blockhouse attempt to trap him into admitting he was here.

He swung under the tie rail and passed behind the ponies racked in front of Ben's Gem, reading their brands. Then he swung across the street and by the light thrown from Bella Union's big windows read the brands of the horses tied there. Blockhouse was not among them.

He came up on the plank walk in front of the Bella Union and for a moment considered what to do. As always, his leaning was toward the bold move—and then he smiled to himself. Why suspect anything? He'd asked for Tate, and the puncher told him where he could find him.

He shouldered through the doors of the Bella Union and walked up to the bar, immediately aware of the number and location of the men here. He watched the army man in the back-bar mirror, and when the bartender approached Jim asked, "Where can I find Riling?"

"Back table."

Jim shoved away from the bar and tramped past it and hauled up at a table where a poker game was in progress. Riling wasn't there, and yet this was the only occupied table. He'd walked into something and he had a choice to make, he knew immediately.

The bartender had lied, so he was against him, and the army man and drummer didn't count. Without turning Jim knew the small puncher was already posted at the door behind him.

"Looking for someone?" It was one of the players, a gray-haired man, who asked.

"Play it out," Jim thought, and he drawled, "Tate Riling."

The gray-haired man nodded toward the man on his right—a big blond moose of a man who wasn't Riling.

"Riling?"

"That's me."

Jim studied him a brief moment, feeling something gathering inside him. He wondered if these were Blockhouse men and he really didn't care. "I'd like to talk to you."

"These are my friends."

The man had no intention of moving, which was wise. They had Jim whipsawed, and it showed on the face of the youngest Barden. Jim shifted his feet a little, moving closer to old Barden and bringing the door into sight. Sweet was there. Jim said, "I'm after a riding job."

"Who said I was hiring riders?" Big Nels said meagerly.

"I heard it."

"You hear what I'm hirin' them for too?"

"I heard that too," Jim murmured.

Big Nels looked at the others with triumph in his eyes and put both hands on the table edge, ready to rise. "Why, yes," he said, and that was as far as he got.

Jim whipped an arm around the neck of Barden and hauled him roughly backward out of his chair and toward the back of the room. In the same motion he unholstered his gun and then confronted the players, Barden sagging in front of him and kicking wildly against Jim's armlock.

Sweet pounded through the front door, headed, Jim guessed, for the rear alley. Jim said, "A dumb play, boys."

They were standing, caught flat-footed. The drummer hurried out, leaving the bartender facing the army man. Jim called, "You stay set, army," and then moved toward the front door, Barden still in front of him. He saw the big blond man calculating the chances of cutting him off, and they were bad. Any gunplay would get Barden, who had ceased struggling now against Jim's hold. He had both hands on Jim's arm, pulling it away from his throat.

Jim backed toward the door, caroming into a table and knocking a chair over in the thin silence. When he got abreast of the bar he said to the army man, "When I get to the door you walk out."

The army man started to protest and then was under Jim's gun. Jim hauled up beside the door. The four men moved slowly out from behind the table into the center of the room. Barden had ceased to struggle, waiting for the break. Jim rammed his gun in Barden's back, released his hold and then lifted Barden's gun from its holster.

He said to the army man, "Get out of here," and the lieutenant stepped gingerly out the door. Jim put his foot in the middle of Barden's back and shoved him crashing into a nearby table.

Then he dodged out the door.

From across the street behind a spring wagon Milo Sweet opened up. The first slug boomed against the dry boards of the doorjamb, and Jim cursed softly. Sweet had outsmarted him, and now he was caught between Sweet and the rest of the crew in the saloon. It would be impossible to get on a horse under Sweet's fire.

Jim drove two shots toward Sweet, and then, stooping low so as not to silhouette himself against the saloon window, he ran downstreet. Sweet's fire searched him out, and ahead of him a store window collapsed in a jangle of glass at his very feet. And now Sweet's shooting was echoed by the first shots of the crew in the saloon. A slug boomed into the plank walk and caromed up past him in a long whine.

He found protection two doors down—an opening between two buildings. He turned down it and heard Sweet shout, "The back alley!" Somebody was pounding down the boardwalk toward the opening. Jim lunged noisily through the litter of cans and weeds and bottles cluttering the open area. Once he turned and threw a shot back through the opening, and then he burst out into the alley.

It was pitch black, save for the square of light on a shed thrown by the rear window of the saloon. He turned down the alley, his boots pounding on the cinders. Suddenly from ahead of him came the sound of a running horse. It was on him, riding him down, and he lunged to one side, sprawling in the cinders.

He rolled to his knees, cursing, and looked back. For a brief instant the rider was in the light of the saloon's high window, and in that time Jim saw the rider hurl something through the window, shattering the glass. He also identified the rider by the thick auburn hair glinting in the light. It was Carol Lufton.

He started down the alley again, the dim cross street far ahead. Before he had reached it two men rounded the corner of the building and started to shoot down the alley. He flattened against a shed and looked back in the other direction. The back door of the Bella Union suddenly yanked open, flooding the alley with light. Two more men, the phony Riling and the boy, piled out into the alley, and a man from the street end yelled, "He's between us."

Jim faded around the corner of the shed, searching for shelter. He found a door, opened it and stepped inside. The gloom here was profound, smelling of dust and fresh resin. He judged he was in somebody's woodshed. He worked toward the rear of it and was finally against the alley wall. The shouted talk now was muffled somewhat, but he heard enough to know they were arguing hotly, shouting directions. Calling for lanterns, probably, he thought. None of them wanted to close that dark gap of alley that they were sure held him.

Jim's breath slowed down and he listened. His mind was searching for some way out of this yet everything that occurred to him was soon discarded. If their search was thorough he was cornered. He wondered objectively what they would do with him when they found him and debated on the wisdom of fighting.

He was aware now that the talk had died down, and he moved slowly across to the door.

Halfway across he heard a shout that he couldn't mistake.

"Here's Tate!"

Tate Riling? What would a Blockhouse man be doing mouthing that name, except to curse it? Jim was puzzled, and he listened.

"Tate! Tate! Careful how you come up!"

There it was again, this time from the street. Jim moved over to the door, puzzled, and opened it gently. Through the crack of the door, past the corner of the adjoining barn, he could see two men—one of them the phony Tate Riling—talking animatedly, gesturing with a gun to a man Jim couldn't see.

Jim gauged his chances and stepped outside. The big man hadn't seen him. He moved swiftly across to the barn and in the sheltering wedge of darkness worked up to the corner of the barn. The talk out there came into focus. He heard: ". . . and wanted a job ridin' for us. But he saw how it shaped up and made the first play."

"Then get him, get him!"

It was Tate Riling's voice; Jim couldn't mistake it. He didn't understand this, yet he did understand that these men were looking to Tate for orders, and he was safe.

He stepped out from the corner of the barn. The boy saw him first and yelled, "There he is!"

Jim stood motionless on the outer fringe of the lantern light. They wheeled and split, lifting their guns, and then he was looking at Tate Riling.

"Jim Gurry!"

The words exploded from the lips of Tate Riling like an oath, and then his booming laugh lifted into the night. He was a massive man, tall, with tremendous shoulders, built solid, with great thick hands and long arms. The lantern on the ground lighted his face from below, giving it a depth of jaw that almost hid his neck. Close-cropped pale hair that burred out even at the temples widened a face that was long jawed and had a quality almost mastiff-like. He just missed being ugly with a nose that was broad with thick volutes, but the humor in his face saved it. He smiled often, as now, and it hinted at the tremendous vitality and drive of the man. He would command or die; everything about him suggested boldness. Only his eyes, quick and a burning blue, held the reserve of a slyness and cunning that Jim knew.

Riling turned to the men. "That's Jim Garry, dammit—the man I sent for! He's no range detective."

He strode over and grabbed Jim's hand and almost mashed it in his grip and flung an arm over Jim's shoulder. He said, "What went wrong, Jim? Who started this?"

Jim said thinly, "Ask these buckaroos, Tate."

The men at the end of the alley now came up. They were all here, along with a couple more that had come with Tate. There was a wicked dislike in their faces as they eyed him.

But it took Milo Sweet to voice it. He said suspiciously, "If that's Garry what was he doin' at the Blockhouse?"

So they'd seen him go into Lufton's place and thought him a Lufton hand. Jim almost smiled at that, thinking how simple it would be to put things to rights. A couple of spoken sentences and it would be clear. Yet some cross-grained stubbornness held him silent. He didn't like these men, not even if he was going to work among them.

"Blockhouse?" Riling echoed. "Jim went into Blockhouse?"

"I seen him," Sweet said.

Riling looked at Jim now, and Jim's face was bland, faintly curious. "That's right," Jim said. "I delivered a note from him to his women. What about it?"

Riling scowled. "But Blockhouse is the outfit that's tryin' to run us out of the country."

"Am I supposed to know that?" Jim countered.

And then Riling's face broke into his brash, friendly grin. "Why, hell, no, Jim. I'd forgot." He turned to the crew. "I never wrote Jim about our fight. I told him I needed him and to come up, and I never mentioned Blockhouse. So quit chewin' leather, boys, and go in and get a drink. Me and Jim will be with you in a little while."

When the crew had drifted into the Bella Union through the back door Riling regarded Jim with an amused affection. "Same old Jim. When lightning strikes you're there."

"Wasn't a fair test," Jim drawled, but he grinned too.

Riling took him by the arm and they turned up the alley, and Riling asked questions about the journey, and Jim knew Riling was glad to see him. Jim answered and then inquired about Riling's affairs. He didn't get an answer immediately.

They were at the mouth of the alley now, and Riling paused. Across the street was Sun Dust's hotel, the Basin House, and Riling contemplated it thoughtfully.

"How am I doing?" he asked, echoing Jim's question. "I won't tell you; I'll show you, Jim." He pointed to the hotel. "We'll go over there, and you sign for a room and we'll go up. I've got a piece of business to do."

Jim was curious now, but he knew Riling wouldn't talk until he was ready. They went into the lobby of the Basin, and Jim signed the register at the desk under the stairs and was given a key. Several men were idling in the lobby chairs, but neither Riling nor Jim paid them much attention.

Upstairs Jim unlocked the door to his room and went in and lighted the lamp. Riling, however, stood in the doorway, looking down the corridor. Presently Jim saw him lift an arm and wave and then step back into the room, a faint smile on his bold face.

Soon there came a knock on the door, and a man stepped quickly into the room, closing the door behind him. He turned, and when he saw Jim a look of petulance crossed his face.

He was one of the lobby sitters downstairs, Jim remembered, and was curious. He was the sort of man that Riling, or any man who worked with cattle and horses, would take an instinctive dislike to. Of medium size with a comfortable paunch, he wore the old-fashioned frock coat and flowing tie of a politician. His watery blue eyes were close set to a narrow nose, and his full pursed lips were cherry red in a sallow face. He wore his sparse sandy hair long at the back, and he wore a full black Stetson that was wide brimmed and well brushed. He was carrying a small black valise, which he did not put down.

There was a faint note of amusement in Riling's voice as he

said, "Jim, this is Mr. Jacob Pindalest, the United States agent for Ute Indians over on the reservation."

Jim put out his hand, and Pindalest tentatively gave his. His hand was soft and damp, and he looked curiously at Riling, waiting for an explanation of Jim's presence. There was a sour whisky reek about him.

"This is Garry, my partner," Riling said.

"Partner? You didn't tell me you had a partner, Riling."

"I am now."

Pindalest looked distressed. "Before we go on I'd like to have it understood how he'll figure in this."

"You mean money," Riling said dryly. "I'll share with him, so you don't need to worry, Pindalest."

The agent seemed relieved. He came over and put the valise on the table and said, looking obliquely at Jim, "There's the—uh—item we were discussing the other day, Riling. I think you'll find it satisfactory."

"Gold eagles are usually satisfactory, aren't they?" Riling asked dryly. He was amused by the pompous circumspection of the agent, and now he smiled openly. "I told you Garry is my partner, Pindalest. What I know he knows."

"To be sure," Pindalest said. He was uneasy now, and when Jim shoved a chair toward him he shook his head nervously. "No, I can't stay, thank you. I must be going."

"Scared?" Riling asked.

Pindalest flushed. "I am merely being cautious, Riling. If we were discovered together our whole plan might be jeopardized."

"That's right," Riling said. "Now all you have to do is sit back and wait for me to swing it."

"Exactly. I'm counting on you."

"And on your money too," Riling observed. He put out his hand and Pindalest took it.

"Good luck," the agent said. "If you need my help let me know." He shook hands with Jim and went out, first peering up and down the corridor to make sure he wasn't seen.

When he was gone Riling looked at Jim and made a wry

face. "That," he said, "is our partner, Jim. He's a cross between a rabbit and a very timid snake."

He went over to the valise and hefted it and said, "And that is our working capital—courtesy of the United States government."

Jim was frowning, not understanding, and Riling laughed. "Sit down and listen to a story."

They rolled smokes, and then Riling perked his thumb at the black bag. "There's ten thousand dollars in there, Jim. With it I'm going to buy twenty-five hundred head of Lufton's Texas beef at a little over three dollars a head." He grinned. "Cheap enough, isn't it?"

"Too cheap," Jim said, puzzled. "Where's the catch?"

"There isn't any." Riling put a foot on the chair and shoved his hat off the back of his forehead. "You met Lufton, you say?"

Jim nodded. "Camped with him last night."

"Did he tell you he was shovin' his beef across the Massacre River into Massacre Basin here?"

"That's right. Said the Indian agent had refused his beef, framed a whisky-peddling charge against him, and then denied him reservation graze."

"True. Did he tell you that the army from Fort Liggett has orders to seize all his beef that's still on the reservation by the first of November?"

"No," Jim said.

Riling smiled. "Well, that's the layout, Jim—the neatest scheme a man ever rigged—and I'm proud of it. It's my own."

"But what is it?"

"Just this. I've organized these nesters—a dozen of 'em—to fight any move Lufton makes to shove his herd across the Massacre into the Basin. They're mad and they'll fight, because they figure they're fightin' for their range. They're not; they're fightin' for me. Because if they can keep Lufton out of the Basin he won't have any graze for his herd after November first. He'll have no range to move on to. And if he's caught on the reservation on the deadline, his herd is seized by the army at Pindalest's request. So what does he do?"

"Sell?"

"To me. Cheap, because he'd rather get a little money for the stuff than lose it all to the army." He paused. "Once I've got 'em, I sell them to Pindalest for less money than the government contracted to pay Lufton in the beginning."

"And how much is that?" Jim drawled.

Riling laughed softly and said, "These are the figures. The government contracted to pay Lufton through Pindalest over a hundred thousand for the herd. The money is banked here in Sun Dust. But Pindalest refused the herd. So when the deadline comes I take this ten thousand that Pindalest advances me and buy the herd from Lufton. I sell them back to Pindalest for sixty thousand." He spread his hands and shrugged. "I make fifty thousand, and Pindalest makes the difference between sixty thousand and a hundred thousand, or forty thousand." He paused. "And your share of that, Jim, is twenty thousand, two fifths of my loot. Did I lie to you in my letter?"

Jim was silent a moment, considering this, and then he asked idly, "What do I do to earn it?"

"Fight," Riling said bluntly. "Lufton's tough. These nesters aren't. You'll make up the difference."

Jim stared thoughtfully at Riling. This scheme was like him, daring and bold and unscrupulous. He'd organized his small army into a weapon with which he could blackmail Lufton. There was a wry admiration in Jim for Tate's scheme, and he thought of the money. It was more money than he'd ever seen, and earning it wouldn't be hard.

"Well?" Riling said.

"Why not?" Jim murmured.

Riling grunted with satisfaction and picked up the valise and tucked it under his big arm. "Your first job," he said, "is to get on the good side of these nesters. You better start now. So come along."

They went out into Sun Dust's main street and into the Bella Union. The nester crew was loafing idly, waiting for Riling, Jim understood then how completely Riling had done his job. He'd won their loyalty enough to be undisputed leader.

Riling put the valise on the bar and said to the bartender, "Lock that up in the safe, Barney."

The bartender took it, and Riling turned to go back to the men.

"Wait a minute," Barney said. He reached down under the bar and brought up a rock, around which was tied a note. He handed it to Tate.

"Someone fired that through the back window during the ruckus," he said.

Jim had a sudden memory of Carol Lufton riding past him and flinging something through the saloon's rear window. He watched Tate unfold the note and read it and saw the slow smile that came over his face.

Riling went back to the table and said, "Saddle up boys. I know where Lufton's crossing tonight."

Milo Sweet came over and said, "How do you know?"

Tate grinned good-naturedly and handed him the note. "I know the writing. Saddle up."

Jim knew then the reason for Tate's confidence in his eventual success. Carol Lufton was willing to betray her father to him.

3

Amy Lufton rose before daybreak, threw a wrap around her and padded in bare feet out to the kitchen to light the lamp and make a fire in the big range. There was a chill in the air, and when she looked out the kitchen window toward the mountains she could see the golden sunlight touching the very tops of the distant Braves. It was a melancholy sunrise, as all fall ones are, with their promise of winter coming. When the wood began to snap in the range it was more cheerful, and Amy put on a kettle of water.

Afterward she started back down the long corridor toward her room. Passing the door of Carol's room, she debated whether or not to waken her now. This day would tell them if Blockhouse could force its way across the Massacre in the face of the fighting nesters. Already it was decided, for they had made their drive in the night at Ripple Ford up by the Chimney Rocks. That's all Amy knew, learning it through her father's brief note to them yesterday, and she was tense and excited.

She'd slept little the night before, so that she had heard Carol come in late. She stood irresolute for a moment outside the door, slim in her worn wrap, her arms folded across her breasts. Her attitude was solemn, her face grave, pensive, faintly excited. It was a slim face, serene for a moment, and her full, wide mouth was almost smiling in mockery. Carol always hated to get up early, yet today was a day she must.

Amy opened the door and stepped into the dark room and walked slowly toward the bed where Carol was sleeping. Amy put a hand on Carol's shoulder, and Carol roused, shook it off and buried her head deeper in the blankets.

"Roll out, Red," Amy said mockingly. That name usually roused Carol fighting.

Carol opened her eyes and closed them again and said, "My lord, it's the middle of the night. Go away."

"But we're riding."

"I'm not," Carol said.

Amy sat down on the bed and said, "Remember what day it is?"

Carol lazily opened her eyes to regard Amy thoughtfully. "No."

"Dad either crossed the Massacre last night or didn't. Don't you want to know which?"

Carol sat up in bed with an abruptness that made Amy smile. "I'd forgotten!"

"Then hurry."

Amy left her dressing and went back to her own room. It was small, simply furnished, with a kind of happy-go-lucky and not-too-neat carelessness about it. She dressed in yesterday's levis and shirt, ran a comb through her thick light hair without looking into the mirror and went back to the kitchen.

When Carol came out, sleepy eyed and dressed in a divided skirt and corduroy jacket, breakfast was ready.

Carol tasted her coffee and then looked at her sister. "Over your sulk, baby?"

"I feel fine," Amy said.

"But you can't forget it."

Amy countered with a show of spirit. "Could you, if you'd been shot at?"

Carol didn't answer her question but said slowly, "I wonder who he was?"

"Somebody riding through," Amy said bitterly. "He wouldn't have dared to do it if he were staying around here."

Carol put down her cup and laughed. "You didn't like him, baby? He stood up to you as if you were pointing a potato masher at him."

Two spots of color showed at Amy's cheekbones. Carol, watching her, felt a sudden rush of love for her, mingled with a feeling of self-pity. She called Amy "baby" with a kind of mocking irony that wasn't explained by the two years' difference in their ages. It was because Amy was so impetuous and wild and untamed, like a young and unbroken horse. Amy was twenty-four and yet she hardly understood the obligations of womanhood, had never known what it was to love a man or to suffer because of him. In her motherless childhood she had been more boy than girl, and in her womanhood she was still like that, Carol thought. Her generosities were magnificent; her angers were rages, her manner as simple and direct as a man's. Men adored her and loved her, and Amy neither welcomed it nor understood it. Carol, with that dark intuitive knowledge of a desirable woman wise in the ways of love and men, knew there was heartbreak ahead for Amy. It made her feel old and exasperated.

"Darling, if you shoot at some men they'll shoot at you," she said simply. "Guns aren't playthings—not in these times."

"It's not that," Amy said angrily. "It was—well, the humiliation, I guess."

"Then don't be such a perfect spitfire," Carol said crossly. "Come on and finish your breakfast."

Amy said, "In a minute," rose, went to the door and whistled shrilly through her teeth. A halloo at a far corral answered her, and Amy shouted, "Saddle up two, Ted!"

Carol winced, yet there was something so natural in Amy's act that it was laughable. Amy finished her coffee standing, seized her Stetson from the peg behind the door and went out.

Carol cleared the few dishes off the table. Her hand was unsteady, and she paused by the table and shut her eyes, fighting for control of herself. Now that she was alone, bit by bit the appalling knowledge of what she had done last night came to her. Last night she had made her choice. The Bible said for a woman to cleave to her man, and Tate was her man—or would be, when this mess was over. She had betrayed her father, but for what reason? So that she and Tate, once they were married, could be secure in the knowledge that their little piece of range and their few cattle would support them. It wasn't as if her father would miss it, for Carol believed him wealthy. Last night, then, Carol had made her choice. She would go with Tate.

She blew out the lamp and went out. At the corrals Ted Elser, holding the reins of two saddled horses, was talking with Amy. When Carol approached he yanked off his Stetson and said, "Mornin', Miss Carol."

Carol gave him a careless greeting. Elser was a man close to thirty, a lean, inarticulate man whom few of the Blockhouse crew knew well. He'd drifted into Massacre Basin a year ago, and Cap Willis signed him on. He knew more about horses than anybody at Blockhouse, and both Cap and Lufton had come to depend on him. He had a pleasant, almost homely face with deep, friendly brown eyes, and he was always soft spoken.

He was unutterably and deeply in love with Carol. He said, "I picked Monte for you, Miss Carol."

"But he's got such a hard gait, Ted."

"He's got speed," Ted said.

The way he said it made Carol turn her cool green eyes on him. "I'm not out for a gallop."

"You're likely to need speed," Ted said doggedly.

Carol looked at Amy, who was grinning, and then at Ted. "What do you mean by that, Ted?"

"I wish you wouldn't go, Miss Carol," Ted blurted. His thin browned face was flushed dark, but his eyes were beseeching.

"Why not?"

"Startin' this mornin', there's goin' to be trouble in the Basin," Ted said grimly. "If any stray rider will shoot at Miss Amy, I reckon Tate Riling would like to get a shot at you too. And I can't ride out with you because I've got to stick here."

Carol's cheeks turned darker, and she said angrily, "What absolute nonsense! Turn Monte out and get me a horse I can ride! And I can do without advice from you too, Ted!"

"Yes'm," Ted said docilely.

He led Carol's horse back into the corral, and Carol waited, furious and unable to say anything. These stupid, stupid cow hands. A man who would fight for his rights against them was both a criminal and a killer of women, according to their thinking. She noticed Amy watching her, brown eyes quizzical and intent.

"You'd think I was six years old," Carol said resentfully.

"He's in love with you," Amy said simply.

"I know he is. That doesn't excuse his insolence, though." Carol said it matter-of-factly, with an absence of emotion that puzzled Amy.

Ted returned with a big bay horse, and Amy and Carol mounted and rode off. Ripple Ford lay to the north, a hard three hours' ride. Somewhere on the way, Amy hoped, they would meet a Blockhouse rider who would give them news of the crossing. Ted Elser, she thought, was right. Trouble would break today. For a month now Blockhouse riders had kept out of Sun Dust except for urgent business. There had been wild talk, and trouble had been averted only by her father's iron insistence that his men give no provocation. The nesters, led by Tate Riling, had given their warning, however. No more Blockhouse cattle in Massacre Basin. And Agent Pindalest had given his orders too: no Blockhouse cattle on the reservation after the first of November, or the army would impound them. This was the twenty-second, and last night her father had moved. Massacre Basin was fifty miles long. Blockhouse riders had been patrolling the river on the reservation side, just as the nesters had been patrolling it on the Basin side. Somewhere along those fifty miles, at Ripple Ford, her father's note said, Blockhouse would break through into the Basin. After they succeeded the nesters would fight. Blockhouse would fight back.

They were riding now into broken land that lifted to the Chimney Breaks. The chill of morning had worn off, and Amy was beginning to be worried. The first thing Blockhouse would do after they made the crossing would be to scatter the cattle and send riders ahead. They were close to the ford now, yet there was no sign of Blockhouse cattle or riders. Had her father changed his mind?

Amy glanced at Carol and caught her at an unguarded moment. Carol was worried and, beyond that, frightened. Faced now with the consequences of her smuggled message to Tate, she was afraid. Of course there had been a fight, Carol thought, a fight in which her father might have been hurt. She glanced at Amy and saw her watching her.

"Where are they?" Carol asked.

"Let's ride on to the ford."

They were in the clay dunes now that were on a slope toward the Massacre that was so gentle they could see nothing beyond except more dunes and the distant mountains. Amy watched for tracks as they wound in and out among the dunes, and she saw none. That meant Blockhouse had not crossed here.

Presently, two miles beyond, the dunes broke away, and in the V of the break she could see the flats by the river. There were no cattle there.

And then Amy saw the tracks coming out of a gut to the north and heading toward the V. She pulled up her horse and studied them. Horsemen, and many of them. As she lifted her gaze to Carol's face she saw a look of quiet panic there.

Amy pulled her horse around and put him into a trot. She saw a sudden and imperceptible movement on the north hummock of the V, and it puzzled her. She lifted her pony into a lope.

The trail wound through the last of the dunes and took off across the flats. Amy, however, swerved sharply around to the north of the dune, Carol behind her.

A hundred feet away, against the last dune, were a dozen men, all dismounted, their horses bunched behind them.

Amy hauled up sharply and let Carol pull up beside her. There was Tate Riling, still hunkered down on his haunches and half turned to them, an amused expression on his big face, as if he had been interrupted in the middle of an explanation. Amy knew the others, too, the whole crew of nesters and small cattlemen banded to fight her father.

And then she saw Jim Garry. He was standing aloof from the others behind Big Nels, who was also squatting. His face was taciturn and unsmiling and calmly watchful.

Amy walked her horse closer, and Riling rose to his feet. "Looking for someone, Miss Lufton?"

Amy didn't answer immediately. She was looking at Jim Garry, her first bafflement giving way to a slow understanding. She said to him, "So you're one of them?"

Garry didn't say anything, just looked at her. Now it came to Amy with a sudden rush of certainty—the knowledge of why these men should be here at a place where her father had planned to attempt the secret crossing of the Massacre.

She swung out of the saddle and came up to Tate Riling. Carol, behind her, dismounted, too, remaining by her horse.

Amy said, "Get out of the way, Riling. I want to talk to your new gunman."

Tate looked quizzically at Jim and stepped aside. Big Nels drifted away, leaving Amy facing Jim. He had been fiddling idly with the reins of his horse, his feet planted wide, Stetson shoved back off his forehead. His hands stopped moving now; otherwise he didn't move.

There was malicious triumph in Amy's brown eyes now as she regarded him. "I guess Dad wasn't so wrong about you after all, was he, Garry?"

"Wrong?"

"I haven't talked to him; I don't have to. He had you spotted for one of Riling's saddle-tramp gunmen the moment he saw you."

Riling laughed softly, and Amy wheeled to face him. Her smile was wicked. "It's funny, isn't it, Riling?—but not to you. Right now Dad's across the Massacre, while you wait here with your crew to throw him back."

"Is that why we're here?" Tate drawled in mock innocence.

"Isn't it? Simply because Dad was smart enough to give Garry a note to us that Garry was sure to read. That note told us Dad was crossing at Ripple Ford. He knew this saddle tramp would tell you and decoy you over here."

She looked around at the uneasy men, and her gaze settled on Anse Barden. He'd been in Blockhouse when she was a little girl, and they'd been friends ever since. There was something in Anse's rugged face that belied dishonesty, and it hurt Amy to see him and his boy here. She said jeeringly, "And how do you like it now, Anse? Why, you aren't even being led by a smart crook."

Anse shifted his feet, and then his glance fell away. Sweet was looking hotly at Riling, and Amy saw him.

"How do you like it, Milo?" she taunted.

Sweet said thinly, "This is only the first move, Miss Amy."

Riling, meanwhile, had turned his head and was studying Carol. His face was unreadable to anyone watching, and yet Carol knew what he was thinking, and her eyes were pleading. She had been idly drawing circles in the dust with the toe of her boot. Now she looked down at her feet and up at him and down again. Riling was briefly puzzled, and then he nodded imperceptibly.

But Amy wasn't finished. The irony of the situation was broad enough to be obvious to them all, and she used it unmercifully. She picked out one of the strange punchers, a tough, slant-faced man named Riordan, and said with a maddening politeness, "I don't believe I've seen you around here. Are you fighting for your own graze too?"

"No'm," Riordan said uneasily.

"And you?" she asked another. She didn't wait for his answer but shuttled her glance to Anse Barden. "I thought you were all old-timers fighting for land you'd settled on, Anse."

Milo Sweet said hotly, "Your Blockhouse hands are bein' paid to fight!"

"And you're paying these men to fight," Amy countered. "At least it's in the open now—gunmen against working punchers."

And now her gaze settled on Jim Garry. His indifference was a goad to her, for among all these men she held him in the most contempt. And he didn't care.

Amy said, "Even an Indian wouldn't betray a trust, Garry. Think it over."

"I have," Jim murmured.

"And it doesn't bother you?"

"Nothin' much does, except talk."

He was baiting her, Amy knew, and she resolved not to lose her temper. But she had a wild desire to corner him, to make him confess. "You did read the note, didn't you?"

"No."

"You're a poor liar," Amy said quietly.

"Yes'm."

Amy wanted to argue, but she knew she'd said enough. A look at Tate Riling told her that; the muscles along his jaw line were corded with the effort to control himself. More talk might spoil it, but she couldn't resist a last gibe.

She said to Riling, "Better luck next time—old timer."

She swung on her horse and waited for Carol to mount. Not until they'd walked their horses around the dune did Riling's crew cease looking at them.

Then the men looked at each other. Amy Lufton's gibes had hit the mark with the Bardens, Sweet, Big Nels and the other Basin men. Since Riling had bought Fale's old place and stocked it with his handful of cattle a month ago, he had been their leader. He had voiced their fears, organized them, made their threats and brought in his own friends, the last of them Jim Garry. It had taken Amy Lufton's tongue-lashing to show them how far they had come from a group of unimportant local men who feared to lose the little they had, how they depended on a man who had been a stranger to them a month past.

Tate Riling saw it, and for a moment his anger flared. "Damn her," he muttered. "Damn her tongue too."

Barden said dryly, "Well, Lufton's across the Massacre." He looked bleakly and pointedly at Jim. "Lufton's not a fool, mister."

Tate said, "Garry didn't bring that note."

"Where'd it come from?" Milo Sweet asked abruptly.

Riling looked at him, speculation in his cunning eyes. Sweet was the rebel, the maverick. If trouble came it would come from him, Riling knew. Sooner or later would come a showdown with Sweet, and Tate didn't care when. Now was not the time for it though, but on the other hand, he couldn't show weakness. He had too much at stake to be gentle.

He said quietly, "None of your damned business, Sweet."

Sweet's rash temper fled across his eyes, and Riling didn't give him time to speak but went on boldly, bluntly.

"I got a wrong tip. I won't get another. If it sticks in your craw, Sweet, ride out."

Riling understood the way to crowd a man; too, he understood that this was too trivial for Sweet to make an issue of. He saw Sweet's rashness judge it slowly and put it away and then subside. Sweet said sullenly:

"All right, only Lufton's across the Massacre with that herd."

Riling had won. He turned away and said agreeably, "Sure, sure. But steers have got legs, and they can be driven back." He looked at Barden. "The thing to do is spot his herds—the one

that crossed, the two that are still on the reservation. After that
we can move."

The men agreed and soon settled how they were to split up
and what they must do. Tate pointed out that if they could find
and stampede the held Blockhouse herds across the river,
Lufton would have to draw most of his crew back to the reservation to gather them up again in time for the deadline. Once
that was done it would be easy to drive the shorthanded Basin
herd back across the Massacre.

The crew agreed, broke and went for their horses. Riling
spoke for Jim, Riordan and Joe Shotten to side him, for he was
wise enough to know that from now on he must keep them out
of the nesters' way. As Riling went for his horse he detoured to
where Carol's pony had been standing. He glanced at the
ground, not pausing in his stride, and then got his horse.

With the memory of last night still fresh in his mind, Jim had
watched Carol, and he had seen the same thing Riling saw. He
stepped into the saddle and rode his horse over that same piece
of ground. Drawn in the dust was a broken arrow. Jim filed
that away in his memory as he joined Riling.

Tate's face was set in a scowl, and he eyed Jim sardonically.

"My first slip," he said. "We'll have to hit him hard."

"Before he hits you," Jim murmured.

Riling looked at him closely. "How's that?"

"He must be tough," Jim mused. "He's got a tough daughter. He was smart enough to spot me."

Riling grunted, "Not only you. He spotted Riordan and Joe
Shotten in town before I knew they were here."

"A couple of beauties," Jim murmured. "Who are they?"

Riling smiled faintly. "It don't matter who they are, Jim.
When this thing shakes down to a fight, Barden and his friends
will get scared. These boys don't scare."

"It's pretty crude," Jim observed.

"Not so crude," Riling contradicted, grinning. "I've made
everybody like it but Lufton, and I'll make him too."

Jim didn't say anything, and Riling went on easily: "I want
you and Riordan and Joe to drift into town now. Keep out of

this from now on until trouble breaks. That damned girl saw the setup, and she's got Sweet and the boys to thinking. Give me time to cool 'em off and make them think they're doing the work."

Jim said softly, "Me and Riordan and Shotten, hired gunmen."

Riling looked at him intently, hearing both the irony and the protest in Jim's statement. He said, "What did I write you?"

"That you needed a man you could trust and that—"

"That's far enough," Riling said calmly. "I meant it too. And the difference between you and the other two boys is that they're paid in gold eagles. You'll get paid in thousands, Jim. Any kick?"

"No kick," Jim said mildly.

Riling rode over to Shotten and Riordan and spoke to them. Most of the others had gone in groups of two and three. Sweet was with the two Bardens, and when he reached the end of the long slope to the river he turned in his saddle and looked back. Riling, Jim, Riordan, and Joe Shotten were angling south along the river, heading for the cottonwood motte that lined the river for miles to the south.

Sweet watched them out of sight and then spoke to Anse. "Notice how them four stick together?"

"Why not?" Barden murmured. "Riordan and Joe work for him. Garry's a friend, come in to help."

"I can buy that kind of a friend for seventy-five a month and no questions asked," Sweet said sardonically.

Barden knew what he meant, and he said gloomily, "Maybe we'll need 'em, Milo."

"But how did Riling know that a month ago? Tell me that." Barden couldn't answer him.

When they had ridden a mile or so Riling said, "All right, cut for town, boys, and stay out of trouble."

He watched them go up and over the ridge, Jim Garry riding in the rear. Then he drew out his sack of tobacco and rolled and lighted a smoke, afterward pulling his horse deeper into the

cottonwoods. He didn't dismount there but quietly sat his
horse, waiting for everyone to ride out of sight. The midmorning sun slanting through the cottonwoods touched the yellow
leaves scattered beneath the trees in a bright harlequin pattern
that would have pleased him at any other time. But not this
morning.

Lufton had tricked him smartly, and the thought of it both
galled him and pleased him. He was pleased because he saw
that Lufton underestimated his intelligence. If, as Lufton probably thought, Jim Garry had read the note and told him, Riling
would have seen through it. But coming from Carol, he
doubted it. His slow, thorough mind considered Carol now. He
had read that look in her eyes back there as pleading for understanding; in another hour she would be telling him why she'd
failed, although he knew. He must be careful with her if she
was to be of any use to him. Today she'd been afraid of what
she'd find there at Ripple Ford and thankful that the plans had
misfired. He'd have to win her back again, give her the courage
she lacked, reassure her.

Presently he put his horse out of the cottonwoods, back-
tracking to the V and going into the dunes. He was a solid man
on a horse, carrying his arrogance even to the saddle. He rode
with one big hand on his thigh, elbow a little outthrust, back
straight. His face was thoughtful during that hour that he
crossed the dunes and dropped down on the other side of them
onto a long reach of alkali flats that lifted in dun steps to the
base of the distant Bench. Carol remained in his mind, put
there by the happening this morning. Again the choice confronted him, as it had all this past month since he'd known her.
He couldn't remember when it first came to him that she could
be his to use. It must have been after that dance at the Roan
Creek schoolhouse the week he'd bought his place. He'd been a
stranger then, a big, smiling man who was sure of himself,
friendly, new to the country, eager to meet people.

He'd met Carol and Amy Lufton that night, along with
twenty other girls. Carol had cornered all the men, as she always did with her beauty, but Tate had seen it was no pleasure

to her. She was restless and bored and a little desperate, and when he'd been introduced to her that night she had looked at him with a rising, provocative interest. Tate had wanted her on sight and had set about getting her in his own, always oblique way. He had not danced with her that night. The whole evening he ignored her, dancing with all the other girls and the married women, and because he was a stranger, he took the party away from her.

Two days later she'd ridden up to the sorry shack he'd bought as his excuse for being there. Tate had seen her coming and sent his men to the barn, and when she rode into the yard he greeted her coolly.

"I came about that," Carol said and explained. "The way you spoke, I mean—so unfriendly. The other night too. Why?"

"I never bother with a beautiful woman," Tate had said bluntly.

The flattery drew the sting from the offense, as he knew it would. Carol had laughed and asked him why.

"You can buy them in honky-tonks," Tate drawled. "I like a woman who doesn't want the world, doesn't expect it, wouldn't take it."

"And you think I want the world?"

"I think you've got it," Tate said bluntly. "Why bother with me?"

Carol had ridden off in anger. Two days later in Sun Dust, Carol had met him on the street, and she smiled almost shyly. Tate stopped and was pleasant to her. At parting he said, "That's the last time you'll have a smile for me, Miss Lufton. I think I'm going to fight your father."

That had done it. Carol had ridden over next day. Tate, curious, wanted to see if he could kiss her, and he tried and succeeded. The easy way she came to him puzzled him. She wasn't trash, and he knew it, and he knew also that he was probably the first man who hadn't groveled before her. It explained much about Carol, and he saw that as long as she couldn't get him she would be his.

The choice was put up to him then, as it was put up to him

today. He could marry Carol and talk softly and walk into a share of the Blockhouse. Or he could play out his hand as he'd framed it.

Tate Riling was a shrewd man, and he knew himself, and he made his choice with a faint regret. Carol was nice, but the nicest things palled—except one, money. That was his choice.

Billings' place, the Broken Arrow, lay between a couple of bald hills above the alkali flats, and when Riling cut past the hill he saw Carol's horse in the weed-grown yard. Carol was sitting on the ruin of a porch, and when she saw Tate she rose.

Tate rode into the weed-grown yard and stepped down, and Carol was in his arms. He kissed her indifferently and walked with her to the shade of the stone house and squatted there. She sat beside him, her eyes anxious and a little afraid.

"Did I do wrong, Tate?"

Tate shoved his hat back off his forehead. His short blond hair burred straight up and, together with the look of worried bafflement in his eyes, gave the impression of a small boy hugely puzzled.

"Wrong? Wrong how, Carol?"

"I didn't know it was a trick, Tate! I swear I didn't, until I heard Amy say it."

"How could you?" He put a big hand on hers. "Forget it. It's done, dammit, and now we've got to fix it."

"But I'm glad, Tate, in a way," Carol said in a low voice. "I couldn't bear it this morning when I thought that maybe you and Dad were fighting."

"It's not pretty," Tate conceded slowly. "It's not easy for you. But I do what I have to do, Carol. You can see that?"

"Not—quite," Carol said hesitantly.

Tate held her hand and fixed his clear, bland blue eyes on her, his face utterly sober. "I'm a poor man, Carol. Money has come hard to me, and what little I've got is sunk in a handful of cull cows, a jag of grass and a shack that I bought from a homesteader. Your dad wants that grass, and he's got the men to take it. Do I tuck my tail between my legs and run, or do I join up with men like myself and fight for what little I've got?"

"Is it that simple?" Carol asked.

Tate made a rough, flat-palmed gesture with his hand, a gesture of dismissal. "To me it is. Your father has got his truth, and I've got mine. I've got to stand or fall by it."

Carol hung her head a moment, so he couldn't see the tears that were making her eyes glisten. "I've got to accept this," she thought; a woman has always got to accept her man's truth, or he isn't her man.

She said gently, "Now what? He's across."

"We'll shove him back."

"But how, Tate? He's got as many men as you have, and he'll fight."

Riling snapped off a weed stem and chewed thoughtfully on it, looking out at the blue fall distances of the alkali flats.

"I want to know first," he began doggedly, "if you've made your choice, Carol. I've got to know that. Is it me or is it your father?"

"It's you, Tate!" Carol said swiftly. "It's you!"

"I won't ask you to risk your father's life," Tate said stubbornly. "You'd hate me for that. But I'm asking you to help. I need you."

Carol nodded, misery threaded through the happiness she felt at his words.

Tate said bluntly, "Then ride back and find out where the herd he crossed is being held. Ask him where. When he tells you, pretend you're worried. Then confess to him; tell him you circled back and watched us this morning, and we lined out to find his cattle, like we meant to drive them back."

Carol was following his words with close attention. "And did you?"

"No. But he'll fear a raid and draw the reservation crew over to help him."

"But I don't understand," Carol said slowly.

"That'll leave his other two herds under light guard. We'll stampede them from hell to breakfast, and he'll have to call every available man back to round them up again. That's when we'll drive the Basin herd back across the Massacre."

Carol considered this slowly, with a kind of breathless attention. She could see no fighting here, no threat to her father's safety. And when she couldn't she felt a vast and rising relief.

"I can do that, Tate! It won't harm him."

Tate rose, and she rose with him, and he folded her to him. He kissed her then, and he had his moment of doubt again. She was beautiful and she was his and she was desirable. She put a spell on a man that was a drug and made him want to forget everything but her. But that distant coolness in his mind, a kind of gray-and-iron knowledge that he wanted more than this, checked him, and he moved her gently away from him.

"I'll want to see you soon, Carol."

"Shall I come to the rock tomorrow?"

"There, or if I'm not there come to my place. Good-by, darling."

She watched him ride out, and she was utterly and completely happy.

4

After skirting the dunes they dropped down into the Basin level, and inside of an hour Jim Garry knew enough about the two men with him. He knew about Joe Shotten when they jumped a band of antelope. They didn't see the antelope, but the dust funneling up beyond the low ridge to the south and the faint rataplan of quick hoofs were the giveaway.

Joe Shotten touched spurs to his horse and galloped toward the ridge. He was riding a bay with four white stockings, and it was a pleasant sight to watch the horse run. Shotten had drawn his rifle from its scabbard on the way over. On the back of the ridge he slipped from his saddle, bellied down and presently fired. He shot once and came back, smiling a little.

"Can still do it," he bragged with pleasure.

He was a plain hard case, Jim thought. His hands were rope calloused, and he chewed tobacco with a patient violence. It bulged the left cheek of his concave face and seemed to draw his small eyes even closer together by widening his face. He stank of horse sweat, and its sweet, acrid smell, mixed with the even sweeter smell of the chew, clung to him like a sickening aura. A man of average height, he had narrow slanting shoulders that set his big head in bold and ugly dominance.

They crossed the ridge, and far ahead on the amber flats Jim saw the downed antelope blending almost imperceptibly with the grass. It was three hundred yards, he calculated, and he knew that Joe Shotten knew he was calculating it and he said nothing.

Tom Riordan didn't even look up. A decade of hard living had frozen his slanted face into a vicious indifference. He had a cough that he was constantly trying to smother. It started softly, like low gears meshing, and he seemed to be shaken with silent laughter. At these times he would put his bright feverish glance on anyone watching, and there was a murderous dare in them. Two circles of color stained his cheekbones above the stubble of his beard, helping the illusion of doll-like delicacy that was in his slight frame and thin hands. It was when they pulled up at the antelope that Jim learned about Tom Riordan, the consumptive.

Shotten had killed a doe. It lay formless and deflated, the long grace gone from its legs, its eyes smeared with death.

Joe said placidly, "It was a hard shot," and contemplated it with quiet pride for a moment and touched his horse with his spurs.

Riordan said in a soft voice, "Take a quarter, Joe."

Shotten looked at him and laughed. "Hell, we're headed for town."

Riordan said with deceptive gentleness, "God damn a man that leaves game to rot! You'll eat some of it. Get down!"

He had braced Shotten as easily and gently as a woman talks, but it was deadly. Jim stayed silent, watching Joe Shotten weigh his chances and immediately refuse the fight.

"I like a tongue," Joe muttered. "Why not?"

He dismounted and cut out the tongue, and Riordan seemed satisfied. Shotten put it in his pocket and mounted, and in a few moments he was whistling, the incident forgotten.

Jim had his hour of bleak disgust after that. In Tate Riling's eyes the only difference between Jim and these two was the price he was paying for each. Jim understood that and the reason for it. These two were unstable as the weather. At another time a sudden flare-up like this would bring gunplay that might leave them both dead. Tate Riling needed them, but he needed judgment, too, and it was Jim's job to have it, to keep these two apart and think for them. He was like Riordan—only with brains. It was a new picture of himself, and Jim pondered it with a gray and bitter distaste. Amy Lufton had not been very wide of the mark: she had named him truly—a gun hand.

They came afterward to a dry lake bed where a half-dozen seeps still held the grass green. Beside one of these, off to the south a half mile, was a log shack. Its grounds were barren of trees, and it stood stark and sun-baked in the noon heat.

Shotten said, "I'm thirsty," and pointed his horse toward the shack.

"Whose place?" Riordan asked.

"That big one—Titterton."

They rode across the yard to the well frame by the seep and dismounted. Shotten had his drink and then stood aside, hands on hips, regarding the shack. It presented a windowless wall of logs at the back. The plank door was closed. Beside it, hanging over a bench, a tin washbasin glistened brightly in the sun.

Shotten viewed it with rising interest and then pulled his gun. He shot without aiming, and the basin boomed and leaped off its nail and clattered to the ground.

"Chase it," Riordan challenged, and he was smiling.

Shotten emptied his gun. By the time he had finished he had chased the basin around the corner of the house. Riordan nodded mild approval and lifted his gun from its holster.

"Let's leave a card," he said.

"What kind?"

"Blockhouse, right on the door."

He raised his gun and shot five times. Four of his shots made a square; the fifth was above the square. "There's the top half and the ridgepole," he said softly. He looked obliquely at Jim to see if he was watching.

Shotten had reloaded by now. He lifted his gun and now he shot four times in swift succession. Below the big square and joined to it was a smaller square. The Blockhouse, as Lufton branded it, was outlined. Shotten now looked at Jim. "It needs a door, don't it?" It was both invitation and challenge.

"You mean like this," Riordan drawled. Again he fired four times, rapidly and seemingly without looking. His four slugs picked out a small rectangle in the lower square against the base line. He had outlined the door. At this distance it was shooting and he knew it and Shotten knew it, and they both regarded Jim, sly elation in their faces. They were feeling him out, impressing him, and behind all lay the implied threat of their expertness.

Jim walked beyond them, so he was clear of the horses, and lazily, almost indolently, pulled his gun. The interval between the gun leaving the holster and the shot was imperceptible.

"There's the latch," Jim murmured. To the right center of the smaller rectangle that was the door was the mark of Jim's slug.

It was the kind of cheap bravura that these two understood, and Jim watched their faces. Riordan regarded the door thoughtfully, looked curiously at Jim and walked toward his horse, indifferent again. Shotten was more transparent. His mouth opened slightly as he studied the door and then it clamped shut. He spat, said, "Sure, sure," approvingly, and went over to his horse, not looking at Jim.

The ride into town brought no further comment from the two. They rode into Sun Dust in midafternoon and went straight to the Basin House.

Jim tramped downstreet and ate alone and afterward returned to the hotel porch. He dragged a chair to the rail and slacked into it, putting his feet on the rail. As he watched the sleepy street his face settled into moroseness. Presently he lifted a cigar from his pocket and fired up. He stayed with it for a dozen drags, and then it went sour for him and he tossed it away. Across the street, in front of a saloon, Riordan and Shotten lounged idly.

Jim felt the gray depression settle on him, and he hunkered down in his chair, a long, restless man with defeat in his gray eyes. It was the old pattern again this long waiting for trouble out of which he would profit. For what? A few hours at the tables and the old driving restlessness that pushed him into trouble again. He watched Riordan across the street, back to the wall, hot eyes raking every passer-by, every interplay of movement, interpreting them only as they affected his ultimate survival. That was himself in a few years, when the edge of his conscience had blunted even more. A hired gun hand, who balked at nothing that would pay for his whisky and his taste in horses or women and his pride. A man with no roots, who could know the lifetime of a town and its people in a few hours and reject its ways and theirs. A man with no stomach for anything except trouble.

He knew now that he would have to leave here, but his mind did not answer the question of when it would be. "That will come, too," he thought bitterly; "I'll be having a drink and see myself in the bar mirror, and then I'll walk out and get on my horse and ride out, sick of myself and what I am, but with a little hope for what I'll meet over the next hill."

He was thinking this when he saw the buckboard stop in front of the hotel and John Lufton step down from it and come toward him.

John Lufton rode into Blockhouse with one of his crew around noon. Amy saw him and ran for the horse corral. The three men left to guard the place were already there when Amy reached him.

Her father was dismounted, beating the gray dust from his

clothes when Amy came up. Even his mustache was gray. He looked up at Amy and grinned swiftly.

"Dad, what's happened?"

"Nothing. We've got cattle in Massacre Basin again."

Amy waited impatiently while he inquired of Ted about things at the ranch, and then he joined her. He took her elbow lightly and squeezed it and said, "I could eat."

Amy knew she wouldn't hear much about it until after he was fed, but she was happy. John Lufton wouldn't admit it, but this had been riding him for the last month, had been riding them all.

While he washed in the kitchen Amy put the meal on the table. There was little talk between them, and it had always been like that. With Carol and her father it was different. In Amy's place, Carol would have learned all there was to know before she left the corral. With Amy, there was a man's patience, a knowledge that news would keep until a man's hunger was worn off, a kind of thoughtfulness. She demanded little, and because of it John Lufton was apt to give her more consideration than he did Carol.

When the first edge of his hunger was gone Lufton began to talk. He told of moving the cattle across the river this morning. It was unexciting; they were primed for trouble and it didn't come.

"And I know why," Lufton chuckled. "Did a loose rider drift in here yesterday with a note to you?"

"Garry? Yes."

"I pegged him for one of Riling's gun hands," Lufton said dryly. "I think I'm right. I think he read the note, like I hoped he would, told Riling, and Riling was waiting at Ripple Ford this morning."

"I know he was," Amy said. She told her father about the morning ride. He listened attentively, eyes alert and curious. She didn't tell him about Garry shooting at her at the river; she was afraid of what he would do.

"So he's joined Riling," Lufton murmured. He went on eating then, but his mind worked carefully. He saw here the excuse for which he had been hunting, the excuse to take the fight to Riling and take it hard. Garry had been warned; he'd been given a choice of joining Blockhouse or riding on through, and he had done neither. Lufton arrived at his decision with a somber reluctance. He didn't have any gun hands and he was asking his men to go up against some. But it was root hog or die, even for them, and it had to be done. It had better be done by himself, he thought.

"Another thing," he said to Amy. "I don't want you girls to ride out alone. That's orders."

"All right, Dad. Carol's out now, you know."

Lufton nodded and pushed his plate away, drew out his pipe and packed it thoughtfully. Amy watched the absent-minded, expert way his hands went at it. It was one of those small male rites that, if seen a thousand times, still hold a curiosity for a woman. Her father was still troubled, she knew; she could read it in his saturnine face.

Lufton grimaced. "What's this damned country comin' to? And the men that'll run it." He looked darkly at Amy. "There's that Garry. I can't shake him from my mind. A nice-seeming man, but snarly." He clamped his teeth on his pipe and drew smoke deep into his lungs. "In my day there were two kinds of bad men. One was a dirty, tough, drunken killer. You knew it, and he knew it and he bragged it. Then there was the river-boat gambler—pretty as a snake and just as deadly. Point is, you knew them. Nowadays a man acts and looks like a thirty-a-month puncher, but he's just as apt to brace you and shoot your ears off as not. It was simpler then. I liked it better."

"You think Garry is a killer?" Amy asked. She didn't know why, but it seemed very important to know this. She did know why too. It was because she, like her father, would have been misled at another time by Garry's looks, just as she'd been misled by Riling's. Jim Garry, in looks, was like the men she danced with at the schoolhouse, the men she grew up with.

"I think he will be soon," Lufton said meagerly. "Only he won't get the chance."

The sound of a horse coming into the yard made him turn

his head to listen. The horse stopped, and soon the door opened and Carol stepped inside. Lufton smiled at her, thinking she was the prettiest thing he'd ever seen, and she came over and kissed him.

Amy got up to get Carol's food, and she listened to Carol asking her father how things had gone. He told her, and she asked where they had pushed the cattle. They were scattering them in the scrub piñon and cedar hills to the west of Avery's patch, Lufton said.

"Avery? He was with Riling, wasn't he, Amy?" When Amy nodded Carol said, "You know, I went back and watched them this morning after I'd left Amy."

Lufton was disapproving but amused. "To see what they'd do? And what did they?"

"They were heading south toward Avery's," Carol said. "I wonder why?"

"They didn't split up?"

"They sent a man upriver and another down, and then they headed south. But before the two men left Riling called them back, and they gave him their rifles."

Amy brought Carol her dinner, and they talked about the ride. Carol talked on nervously, speaking to Amy now. She said the scrub-oak thickets up by the Chimney Breaks, where she pretended to have ridden that morning after she left Amy, were one mass of red foliage. Improving on that, she said the slope looked like a forest fire from a distance. While she talked John Lufton was looking out the window, his eyes musing, speculative. Carol wished she knew what he was thinking.

Presently he rose. "I'm going into town. I'll take the buckboard, so there's room for you girls."

"I'll go, Dad," Amy said.

Carol demurred, and Amy went into her room and changed from levis to a dress. It was a ceremony that she had retained from childhood, out of some dim loyalty to her mother's custom. She remembered how her mother used to corral them, make them wash their ears, rebraid their hair and put on dresses before they went into Sun Dust.

When she returned to the kitchen she was wearing a blue dress with a white collar, fichu style, that seemed to turn her skin a deep golden tan. John Lufton was slowly pacing the floor when she came in. He stopped and almost glared at her.

"You didn't tell me that damned Garry shot at you," he said accusingly.

Carol was still at the table, and Amy looked at her reprovingly. "There wasn't much to tell, Dad. Nothing happened."

Lufton started to speak and then checked himself, but he was cursing under his breath as he took his hat and went out. Amy and Carol followed him. At the barns Lufton ordered Elser to hitch up the team, and Amy went over to watch him. She liked to watch Tel Elser work with horses, liked the slow, soothing way he swore at them, as if it were a caress.

Carol stayed with her father, who was now joined by Cap Willis. Her father was scowling darkly. Twice he was about to say something to Willis and twice changed his mind. The third time he spoke, and with decision.

"Cap, we're going to cross those other two herds tonight."

"Tonight?" Willis echoed blankly.

Lufton nodded decisively. "Carol here saw Riling and his crew this morning, and they were heading south in a body. It looks to me like they'll make a try tonight at the herd we crossed if they can find it. All right, let them make it. Nobody will bother 'em. But while they're trying to round up that herd and push it across we'll be crossing the other two. How does it sound?"

"Risky."

"Suits me. Now get along and tell the boys."

Carol couldn't think: the fear that had dissolved this morning at sight of peaceful Ripple Ford was back again, only stronger. Tate had counted on the Blockhouse crew being pulled away from those two herds. If they weren't there would be the fight that Carol had been dreading. She'd have to get word to Tate to stop the raid.

On the way to Sun Dust Amy took over the team while Lufton hunched sleepily in the seat. He noted Amy's handling of the horses with a quiet pride and approval. Her hands were brown, strong. "She should have been my son," he thought and then knew that wasn't right. But she was close to him, like a son. And yet, to him, she was more of a woman than Carol. John Lufton had a high opinion of women, set by his wife who was dead these ten years. Their occasional vanities and featherheadedness amused him when he noticed it, and he did because he had raised two daughters. He looked beyond those things, however, searching for something in them that was in his wife. In Carol he had not found it. It was all surface emotion and weakness with her, and he forgave her, as a man will a beautiful woman, simply because she is beautiful. With Amy, however, it was different. He had watched her and shaped her when he could, giving her a free rein to make her own blunders. But even as a child she judged those blunders, grave and troubled and stubborn, something Carol never did. The things he liked most about her were odd: she put a man's value on words; they counted, like money, and they were sound as money. She loved work for work's sake, not for reward. Another man's trait, he supposed. The streak of humor in her was his own— gay and tolerant and sometimes sardonic. That was the salt. It was his ego, and he knew it, that made him think it would take a rare man, a simple man, to understand her and love her. If he did he would have the world, as John Lufton once had the world. The rest of it, her clean-lined face with its wide, grave mouth, her honest eyes, the sunburned, streaked hair that a man always wanted to touch, the young, slim, quick body—all that was frosting, and nice frosting too.

Amy felt his scrutiny and glanced obliquely at him and gave him a slow smile. "I know. I look like Mother, don't I?"

"Did I say so?"

"I can tell," Amy said gently. "I hope I do."

Lufton grunted. "You can tell too damned much." He smiled too.

Sun Dust was in its midafternoon drowse as they drove in. The shadeless street simmered in the overhead sun; a hawk, wings motionless, coasted out over the rim, peering at the town below, and then wheeled north, uninterested.

John Lufton glanced at the sheriff's office. The door was open and Les Manker was in, so he could get his business over with. He was going to tell Manker of what he'd done, what he would do, and warn him that if he was against him, then he could expect the same treatment Riling was going to get.

First, though, he would leave Amy at the hotel, which always kept a room open for him and his family's use when they were in town. No use to trouble Amy with this business further.

"I am going to get a new hat," Amy announced. "I feel like one."

Lufton said, "I never felt like that, myself," and idly observed the street. On the hotel porch he saw a man sitting with his feet on the rail.

Something in the attitude of the man jogged his memory as the team drew abreast of the Basin House. Then he recognized him.

It was Jim Garry.

Lufton knew it was time, and he reached over and pulled the reins. He stepped down into the street, saying without turning, "Drive on to Settlemeir's."

His boots scuffed up faint risings of dust as he walked. His attention was narrowly on the man in the chair. When he hit the plank walk he crossed it and came up to the railing by the post and said mildly, "I thought I told you to ride on through."

Jim Garry came slowly out of his chair. His face had been relaxed, somber; now wariness came to it, now the eyes grew oddly chill.

"So you did," he murmured.

"Your time's up," Lufton said. "Get your horse."

"I reckon I'll stay."

John Lufton was aware of two things at once. One was that a man about to walk past him suddenly stopped, sized up what was happening, turned and retreated. The other was that Amy had left the team in the street and was coming up behind him.

He said without turning, and he said it sharply, "Get out of here, Amy!"

"No."

Jim Garry had seen Amy leave the buckboard. Beyond her, beyond the stopped team, he saw Riordan and Shotten come to sudden attention. Then they moved, Shotten upstreet, Riordan down, both heading for the middle of the street.

He heard Lufton say angrily, "Amy, leave us. Go into the hotel!"

"I won't do it."

Shotten had crossed the road now at a long lope and was on the plank walk upstreet. Riordan had stopped in the middle of the road. Jim Garry knew with rising panic that this was wild luck for these two, that this was the chance they had dreamed of and that they assumed he was in on it. He knew with cold and terrible certainty that Lufton was a dead man if he turned.

Jim said quietly to Lufton, "Don't move, Lufton, or you'll never move again."

He took the one step to the porch break, putting himself in the open, and he looked at Shotten. "You drift," he said.

Shotten was standing in the middle of the walk, hands at his side, ready. A look of puzzlement fled across his face, and he said thinly, "Get that girl out of there."

Jim stepped down to the walk and headed toward him slowly, putting himself between Shotten and Lufton. "I said drift," he repeated.

"What are we waitin' for?" Shotten asked hotly. "There he is!"

Jim was closer now, and Shotten backed up a step. He couldn't size it up with that slow brain of his, and now he protested wildly.

"But Riling wants it! He said so!"

Jim was six feet from Shotten now, and he lunged. He slashed savagely at Shotten's face and missed and followed through with his elbow that caught Shotten in the mouth. The man staggered back, and now Jim drove a smashing blow in his face that knocked him sprawling on his back. He leaped on him

as Shotten clawed blindly for his gun. Jim landed on his chest
with his knees, driving the wind from him in one coughing
grunt. Jim grabbed his vest lapels and twisted them in his big
hands and came off Shotten, dragging him to his feet. And
when Shotten's knees took the weight a little Jim hit him again
in the face. He hit him with a long, looping overhand smash
that caught Shotten on the shelf of the jaw and turned his head
abruptly and tore him out of Jim's grasp. The tie rail caught
Shotten across the small of the back. He arched his back, and
then the tie rail split with a sound like a gunshot, and Shotten
fell through to the dust of the road. He lay senseless, not moving.

Jim looked up at Riordan, wondering why he had waited.
Riordan stood in the middle of the road, small and wicked and
cocked to move. From the corner of his eye Jim saw that the
girl had backed away from Lufton, putting herself between her
father and Riordan, and there she stood, facing Riordan.

Jim said, "Riordan, that's your horse in front of the saloon.
Get on him."

He started to walk now. He came through the break in the
tie rail toward the middle of the street, and when he was beyond the prone Shotten he paused, facing Riordan across fifty
feet of dusty street.

He said, "Crawl to him, Riordan. In the dust."

The sick man's face was shadowed now. He'd been puzzled
up to this point, held motionless by what Garry had done.

And now, like the sudden change of the wind, it was on him.
He was faced with it and he knew it, and a quick and dismal
flash of temper mounted to his eyes. It had gone wrong, and
Garry had braced him.

He had his moment of judgment, which was what Jim
wanted and which he allowed him in the silent street.

Then he said, "Make up your mind, Riordan."

"I never crawled for any man," Riordan said softly.

"Any time you want it, start it," Jim said gently.

Time stopped. Riordan heard the sick blood pounding in his
ears. He kept remembering that last shot in the door at Big

Nels's place, and then his decision froze. He could haul it up to that point, but not past it. For one wild and reckless part of a second he thought he had it. Then he knew he was beaten. Nothing was left but the rage and the fear, and the fear was stronger.

"I won't wait," Jim prodded gently. He stood there in the middle of the sunny street, tall and still and barely patient now.

Riordan cursed wildly. Then he fell to his hands and knees and crawled on all fours through the thick, hot dust toward his horse. He reached the tie rail and almost decided to make his stand there in the shelter of his horse. But his nerve was gone, drowned in anger. He yanked the reins loose and vaulted to the saddle and roweled his horse savagely. He lay flat against his horse's neck for a half block and then sat erect and quirted the horse with full-armed slashes.

Afterward Jim walked over to where Lufton was standing and watching him.

He said, "You won't be that lucky next time, Lufton."

John Lufton's face was drained of blood, and his eyes were blacker than night. "I don't get it, Garry," he said slowly. "I don't get it at all. Why did you do it?"

"A man can change his mind, can't he?" Jim asked mildly. His glance shuttled to Amy, who had been watching him with an unblinking, breathless concentration. He touched his hat then and wheeled and went across to Settlemeir's, skirting Shotten on the way.

When he rode out through the long gangway ten minutes later Amy Lufton was standing by the arch on the plank walk, and he reined up beside her. She regarded him a silent moment and with a child's grave and troubled expression.

"You're riding on, aren't you?"

Jim nodded.

"I am glad," Amy said. "Not for us, but for you. I want to thank you for this, and I want to apologize, too, for what I said to you."

"No," Jim said bleakly. "You were right. Don't let a man's whim fool you."

"I haven't."

Jim looked at her sharply, feeling the blood crawl up into his face. Then his glance fell away, and he touched his hat again and rode out, turning upstreet toward the dug road and the rim.

Both Amy and her father watched him until he was out of sight, and they did not know what to say.

5

After her father and Amy drove out Carol went back to the house, but it was only for appearance's sake. From her bedroom window she watched the corrals until she saw Cap Willis finish saddling up and ride out, and then she went out to the corrals again.

Ted Elser was closing the door of the wagon shed, and he came over to her.

Carol tried to make her voice sound indifferent. "I think I'll take Monte out, Ted. Maybe he's not as bad as I think he is."

Ted nodded slowly and took his rope off the corral post. He roped the big black and saddled him there in the corral, but he did not lead him out. Finished with Monte, he turned his head toward the horses remaining in the corral. They had finished their milling and were bunched to one side, watching him with a wary suspicion.

Ted whistled, and a big long-legged grulla horse laid back his ears and slowly broke away from the bunch. He followed Ted over to where Ted's saddle and bridle were on the rail and waited docilely while he was saddled.

Carol, watching Ted, had a sudden suspicion, and she asked, "Are you riding, Ted?"

He looked up at her, mild surprise in his plain face. "With you, Miss Carol."

"I'm afraid I'd rather ride alone," Carol said.

Ted shook his head. "It's orders, Miss Carol, straight from the boss."

Carol was panicked. She must, must get word to Tate some way to call off the night raid. But she couldn't do it if Ted Elser was with her. She looked at his browned, honest face, and for a moment she hated him. A choking anger was in her, and she said viciously, "I don't care what your orders are, Ted. I'm riding out of here alone!"

"No ma'am," Ted said gently, doggedly. "I'm ridin' with you."

It was the same even-tempered, stubborn, iron-willed way he spoke to the horses, Carol thought, and she hated him passionately. But behind her anger she knew this wasn't getting her job done. If she couldn't make him obey her—and she couldn't because John Lufton was the Blockhouse boss—then she must win him over.

She smiled. It was a warm, sweet smile that Ted Elser had never seen before. "Ted, just between us, let's forget this. I won't tell Dad. Cap's gone, and only the cook's around. Nobody will know."

"No ma'am," Ted said stubbornly. He didn't even pause to consider it, and Carol knew it was a hopeless thing to try to persuade him.

"But it's only to Nellie Cavan's, Ted!" she cried.

Nellie Cavan was the schoolteacher; her house was a half mile from the Roan Creek school, some three miles on the road to Sun Dust.

But again Ted shook his head. "If they'll shoot at Miss Amy they'll shoot at you. Besides, it's orders."

Carol knew despair for a moment and tried to keep it from showing in her face. Suddenly she thought of something. "But I'm going to stay all night."

Ted considered. "Then I'd better take the buggy, hadn't I?"

"Oh no," Carol answered quickly. "I'll just put my things in a saddlebag. Do you still want to go?"

"It's orders," Ted reiterated.

"Thank you," Carol said acidly. "It's a comfort to be so well protected you haven't any privacy."

She went back to the house for her things, and Ted led the horses over to the porch. He waited there, sober and unhappy, scuffing leaves with his boot toe and watching the door. When Carol came out with her packed saddlebag Ted stepped over to her horse and offered to help her up. He was refused coldly.

That next half-hour was one of the most uncomfortable Ted Elser had ever spent. He was a man with an inclination to solitude. His work here at the Blockhouse had been humble and lonely enough, and he was less concerned with what went on at the house than any of the other hands. But the times Carol came out to the corral to accept her horse and passed the time of day with him were the times he lived for. He could remember them all, everything about them, down to the slightest detail of Carol's dress. He had never seen a woman so beautiful, so regal and, when she wanted to be, so gracious. His love for her was something he could no more help than the color of his hair. The times she smiled at him were treasured; the times she frowned were pondered and examined and always explained, always with tolerance for her and blame for himself. Until he admitted bleakly that she didn't know he was alive and didn't care. Like today, like now.

Carol neither looked at him nor spoke to him during that ride. He watched her with the hunger of a lost man in his eyes, and he was sorry to see Cavan's place. It was a stone shack under a lone cottonwood tree on the lip of the long slope that led down into Roan Creek Valley. A homesteader had abandoned it, and the county had taken it over for the schoolteacher.

When they rode into the yard Ted saw that Nellie Cavan's corral was empty. Carol saw it, too, but said nothing. She rode over to it, turned her horse inside and strode toward the house.

Ted followed her afoot and didn't speak until Carol had reached the door.

"You want me to wait, Miss Carol?"

Carol turned on him, irony in her voice. "I think I'll be able to lock the doors and hold them off until help comes from town."

Ted looked down at his feet, not wholly satisfied. "I could wait."

Carol stamped her foot. "But why must you be so stupid! Let me alone! Go home!"

Ted touched his hat and walked back to his horse. On his way he heard the door slam viciously. His face was hot with a deep humiliation, and he stepped into the saddle and started back toward the Blockhouse. But an uneasiness was upon him. Lufton had told him never to let Carol or Amy out of his sight away from the Blockhouse. Lufton wouldn't have said it if he hadn't believed they were in danger. And here he was, riding back and leaving Carol alone in a strange house.

Over the ridge he pulled up and considered, but his mind was already made up. Women were reckless, unthinking, willful. Because they were was no reason for him to shirk his orders. He kept behind the ridge until it petered out among the growth along Roan Creek. Once in the shelter of the trees, he made his way upstream and dismounted, turning his horse out on picket. He squatted down in the growth of the far bank, where he could see the schoolteacher's house, and brought out a sack of tobacco, prepared for a long, lonely wait.

He was still rolling it when he looked up, and his fingers were motionless. Carol had left the house and was half walking, half running toward the corral. Ted watched her lead her horse out, mount and put her horse south, crossing the road and disappearing into the scrub-cedar hills beyond.

He dropped the half-made cigarette and rose. It was what he had not allowed himself to suspect: Carol never had any intention of visiting Nellie Cavan.

Ted went back to his horse, already knowing what he must do. He cut her sign at the road and swung in behind her, his pace leisurely. He was both worried and curious, but the memory of Carol's anger kept him from overtaking her. He could watch her in his own fashion without her knowing it.

Carol's trail cut across these hills and finally dropped down and picked up a wagon road through the Orphan Valley that Ted knew led eventually to Chet Avery's homestead. That didn't make sense, since Chet Avery's wife was no friend of Blockhouse. Ted lost the trail once where the road crossed a shale upthrust of a mile's hard going. He came back and found it, but it took him an hour, and now he was convinced that Carol wanted to cover her trail. She had abandoned the road now and was headed west, following the shale until it petered out, and then she pointed southwest. There was nothing that way except a nester's place, for the land began to tilt away into the Long Reach Desert beyond, through which the first nesters had entered.

He came to a stretch of malpais and saw where Carol had picked up a trail that crossed it and wound into the canyon country that was almost the south edge of the Basin's proper grazing country. He went more cautiously now, for they were close to one of these nester outfits. Finally he came to the lip of a canyon and paused, thrusting back into memory. The trail beyond was a series of switchbacks that led down to the canyon floor, where there was a house, he recalled.

Ted dismounted and approached the canyon edge cautiously. The whole wedge of the canyon opened out onto the amber grass beyond, but close, almost below him, was the log shack. Carol's horse was in the yard, and she was sitting on the porch. Ted Elser groped in his memory for a long moment, trying to place this shack, and then he had it. It was Bice Fales's place— or used to be, that is. It was Tate Riling's now.

He sat down, cross legged, and sifted gravel through his fingers, his mind seeking a way to interpret this. It just didn't make sense—Carol Lufton, daughter of the Blockhouse owner, camped on the porch of her father's bitterest enemy. He refused to try to fathom it finally; he watched and listened, and the sun heeled over as he waited.

Carol's patience had long since worn thin; he could tell. She was pacing the yard now, looking up every so often at the trail above. Finally, toward sundown, she mounted her horse. Ted drew back a little, waiting to move until she hit the lower switchbacks on the trail up. But she didn't take the trail; she left the canyon and lined out west.

Ted came down the trail, not liking this. Over west was the crossed herd, where trouble would be. It was no safe country for anyone connected with Blockhouse. Besides that, it was getting dark. It wasn't impossible that a half-dozen men had seen her entry into this country. Ted Elser had a bad few minutes then as he lost sight of Carol ahead of him across the flats in the twilight.

Finally he came to his decision and didn't like it, but he stuck to it. He touched spurs to his horse and lined out in a long lope after Carol. It was almost dark when he saw her pull up, hearing a horseman behind her, and wait.

He put his horse into a walk and came up to her, watching her face in the dusk and unable to see it.

"Is it—Ted?" she asked.

"We better turn back, Miss Carol," Ted said.

Carol sat utterly motionless in the saddle; he could get no clue to her temper.

"How long have you been following me?" she asked. Her voice was unsure, frightened.

"All afternoon."

"Then—you saw me at Riling's place."

"Yes'm."

Carol tried to laugh and failed, and Elser weighed its meaning and was curious.

"What do you think of it?" Carol asked slowly.

Ted shifted uncomfortably in his saddle. "That's your business, I reckon."

Carol didn't speak, and Elser waited out his time and then said doggedly, "I think we better ride back."

Carol didn't object, didn't speak. Docilely she pulled her horse around, and they started back for the canyon. They reached it and made the long climb up the switchbacks and at dark crossed through the malpais. Still Carol hadn't spoken. There was something wrong, Elser knew, and he kept silent and wondered.

The pressure on Carol broke finally. She reached out and seized the bridle of Ted's horse in the dark and hauled him up savagely.

"This can't go on," Carol said in a tight voice. "I've got to know."

Ted didn't answer her, didn't help her.

Carol said impatiently, swiftly, "Ted, you're in love with me, aren't you?"

The shock in his face wasn't visible to Carol, nor the slow readjustment as he tried to stop his hands trembling. He said in a reluctant, miserable voice, "Yes."

"You'd do anything in the world to save me from hurt, wouldn't you?" Carol went on brutally. "I know you would because you've done it today. It's in your eyes, in the way you talk. Isn't that true?"

Ted nodded now, unable to speak.

Carol moved her horse closer to him and reached out and laid a hand on his. "I thank you for that, Ted. I need your help terribly." She paused and she could feel the muscles in his hand iron-hard and trembling beneath her own.

"I want you to forget this afternoon," Carol said, her voice hard. "I don't care what you think, but I don't want anyone ever to know. No one, Ted—*no one!* Do you love me enough to promise that?"

"More," Ted said. He said it in a dry, ironic voice that surprised Carol. Coming from this stubborn, dull man, it was a revelation. She had always supposed him incapable of irony, of understanding.

"Then I have your word, your promise?" she asked.

"Till death do us part," Ted murmured. He moved away from her then, waiting for her to move. She had won his promise, Carol knew, but in an obscure way she knew she had lost something else. And strangely enough this troubled her as she touched spurs to her horse and they rode on into the chill night.

Cap Willis reached the north herd across the Massacre before dark, gave his orders to the five men there without dismounting and then pushed on to Ferg Daniels' herd, arriving late.

A night herder took him into camp and stirred up the fire, then left, and the crew came out of blankets. As soon as Willis told them they'd move tonight the horse wrangler drifted off in the dark and the rest of the crew pulled on boots. The fire was built up, and Cap Willis squatted beside it, conferring with Ferg Daniels as to the best route for the drive. The herd was bedded down in a shallow valley that fingered off among the pines to the south and west and was on the short plateau that lay between the mountains and the river flats.

Cap Willis knew this country as he knew the lines of his face, and tonight, for the first time in weeks, he felt as if he was counting for something. Up to now Lufton had figured, and rightly so, that his lowliest punchers could ride the brush and gather his herds. Cap had been kept at Blockhouse because it was in the Basin that Lufton had figured the trouble would start. It hadn't, and Cap had been a general without any army. Tonight he was in command again, and it suited him. He was an abrupt man, sure of himself, shrewd in the ways of his work. At times he had the deceptive appearance of a cow-town banker gone to belly; his quick and authoritative manner of speech and the saddle of thin hair that he plastered across his skull heightened the impression. But his ability to size up cattle —count, weight, condition, age, asking and selling price—had been acquired in a half a hundred trail camps and towns where a man was never far from violence. He was a formidable barroom brawler who went about it in businesslike unconcern, and to him this fight had the earmarks of a barroom brawl.

He asked Ferg Daniels now, "Added anything to your count?"

"Cruver came in with jag he found in a box canyon yesterday. Makes eight hundred and fifteen."

Cap Willis nodded. He had six men here, counting himself. Once they got the stuff shoved off the plateau into the canyons they could drive them fast, and the tallow be damned. He rose, and Ferg rose with him. Out in the rope corral beyond the chuck wagon, where the remuda was corraled, the horse wrangler was swearing mildly. A puncher had built a second fire on the other side of the chuck wagon to help the light from the lone lantern swinging from the wagon top.

Cap started toward it, and Ferg fell in beside him and was saying, "You must be pretty sure of Riling if you make this—"

He paused, and so did Cap. A lone gunshot had sounded off to the southwest. And as they were looking at each other, wondering, a wave of gunfire broke out. It rolled out like an artillery salvo.

Cap wheeled and ran for his horse, yelling, "Head 'em toward the river."

Already he had sized up that this was a raid, that there would be a stampede and that at all costs they must head them toward the river.

When he swung onto his horse he heard the sound. It was one he hated, one that still held fear for him. It was the mute thunder of cattle roused from sleep to terror and running. And these cattle were close. Their frightened bawling rose above the thunder of their running. Now, facing away from the fire, he could see the flashes of the guns spaced like fireflies beyond the herd. They were to the east and south, and they were driving the cattle this way.

And then, riding out, Cap met the herd leaders. He pulled his gun, angling toward the west, and began shooting at the ground, trying to turn them. He tried to hold his horse at them, but the horse was panicked. He turned now with the leaders, and they were headed straight for the camp. Cursing wildly, Cap put his horse against the leader and shot right beside the steer. But even the weight of the horse and the surprise of the shot didn't alter the steer's course. He was headed straight for the camp.

Cap had two shots left. He rose in the saddle and looked across the back of the herd and then saw what he was waiting for. A strange rider at the opposite side of the herd and a little behind him let go with a volley intended to counteract Cap's shooting. Cap raised his gun and sent two snap shots at the man, and he heard a wild howl above the stampeding of the herd. And now his attention was turned to camp.

The crew, afoot and with no time to get their horses, saw the oncoming rush of cattle and broke for the timber behind the camp. The horse wrangler yanked down the last of the remuda ropes and was running. Only Ferg Daniels had stuck, and he was fighting a spooked horse with only a hackamore. Cap yelled to him to run, and then the whole camp lay spread out before him, abandoned by the men.

Cap was almost in the vanguard when the herd hit the camp. The leaders split to dodge the fire, throwing themselves against the others. The drive of their change of direction was communicated over to Cap's horse. The leaders charged against his pony, and too late Cap saw the chuck wagon. His horse staggered, lost footing and crashed into the chuck wagon. Then the force of a hundred fear-driven beeves slammed into his horse. The near wheels of the wagon lifted and tilted, and Cap kicked free of his screaming horse and lunged. The wagon went over on its side, and Cap clawed out of the saddle, grabbing for the sideboard. He pulled himself over it and fell to the ground on the other side, and then the wagon came all the way over on him, resting on its high chuck box in the rear, wheels in the air.

In that small space left between the bed and the ground Cap lay and watched the camp go. He saw Ferg Daniels, who had been too stubborn to leave. The cattle hit him, bowling him down out of sight. His horse was rearing in fright, and the impact of the fear-maddened herd sent him over on his back, neighing wildly, and then he was lost too. The fires were trampled out as if some giant hand had smothered them. The wagon

rocked under the glancing impact of the cattle who hit it, and
Cap felt the ground under him quivering as if alive.

In a few minutes the last of the herd had passed into the
timber, crashing into that darkness where they would run in a
thousand directions until they dropped with exhaustion.

Cap wearily climbed out from under the wagon. The remuda, of course, was taken away in the stampede too. It was
blacker than soot now, and Cap stood there helplessly. It was
useless to shout yet, for the cattle were making too much noise
out in the brush. It was, in fact, useless to do a damned thing,
Cap thought bitterly. Automatically he set about looking for
wood with which to build a fire and survey the damage. The
sideboards had fallen from the wagon and had been splintered
by the trampling herd. Cap gathered up an armload and then
got a fire going.

By the time the blaze had taken hold the crew came strag-
gling in from the timber. Someone hallooed out in the night,
announcing himself, and then came into camp on horseback.
He was a night herder, his horse lathered and trembling from
the run. The rest of the crew was cursing bitterly, or else they
were glum and afraid to look at Cap.

Cap counted noses. Daniels was missing. He reluctantly left
the fire and made his way over to where he had seen Daniels go
down. Presently he returned and salvaged a tarp out of the
tangle of bedrolls and took it out to Daniels and covered what
was on the ground there.

When he came back nobody spoke. Cap said, "How'd it
start?" to the night herder.

"I couldn't stop it, Cap. They waited till I was on the other
side of the herd and began shootin'. I didn't even see one."

Cap grunted and stared bitterly into the fire. "Nine days to
make the deadline. Hell, it'll take two weeks to round up that
stuff in this brush."

"What about horses?"

Cap grunted and said to the night herder, "You come back
with me and bring out a new string."

They nodded, and still they said nothing about Daniels. It

was what they were thinking about and not talking about. There wasn't a man here but who imagined that death, had imagined it many times. It was the old trail death and it had come into their midst again tonight.

One of the punchers said softly, "By God, I'll make Riling remember this."

Cap wasn't looking at him. Far out from the circle of firelight he had seen the shining eyes of a horse with the fire reflected in them. He walked out toward it, approaching slowly, talking softly. The horse shied a couple of times, and then Cap caught him.

Immediately he saw the man on the ground, one foot caught in the stirrup. Still holding the reins, Cap knelt and struck a match. It was young Fred Barden, and Cap knew dismally that it was his own shot that had knocked Barden out of the saddle. It had caught him in the chest, and the horse had apparently swerved wide of the herd and stopped immediately.

Now the others came up and looked down at young Barden. A month ago they had been at dances with Barden, had drunk with him and laughed at his jokes and liked him. The whole bitter folly of this fight was expressed in this scene, and they all felt it and it made them angry. They had traded Daniels' death for this Barden's, and the exchange pleased none of them.

Cap quietly led the horse back to the firelight and looked around the camp. It was utterly wrecked. Some grub that had been locked in the chuck wagon's box remained. But the basin, plates, fry pans and the coffeepots had been lost when the wagon overturned. They were tramped into shapeless masses of tin bedded in the torn turf. The bedrolls were rags, parts of them festooned in the brush back in the timber.

It had been an expert job, Cap thought. The herd had been stampeded up the valley and then turned directly at the camp by the pressure of riders on the swing. Cap hunkered down by the fire now, warming his hands, eyes musing and bitter. The cook was rummaging around salvaging tin cups, while the rest of the crew righted the wagon.

When the coffee was made and shared out of two bent cups Cap Willis rose.

"I'll be back tomorrow," he said. To the night herder he said, "You come back with me."

They reached the river before daybreak, and Cap sent the man on ahead. He traveled the wagon road that followed the banks of the Massacre for a couple of miles and then swung away. A low, rounded river bluff backed away from the river here, and in the bare dawn he paused and looked toward the base of it. Soon he would be able to make out the shack and he wondered if he should wait.

But he went on instead. The road meandered through a big stand of cottonwoods, and presently, in that half-light, he pulled into the yard. The shack had been made of giant cottonwood trunks, three logs to a side. It made the place squat and low, so that when Anse Barden stepped out he had to duck his head to avoid the door. He was carrying a rifle, which he held carelessly in his left hand, not bothering to point it.

The sun was touching the Braves now, reflecting a little light into the deep, dawn half-light by the shack. Cap saw Anse Barden's face, and he felt sick.

"He's over there, Anse. I didn't have a team to bring him home."

"Thanks, Cap," Anse said in a dead voice.

Cap felt closer to Anse Barden than any of these other men. Anse was an old Blockhouse hand who kept his wife and boy in town while he'd worked for the small single man's wages that Blockhouse paid its punchers. He'd been frugal and quiet and dependable, and John Lufton had let him run his own herd on the side. Anse had sold in a good year and with the proceeds had quit to set himself up here. Neither Lufton nor Cap would ever have bothered him, but Anse had never asked for favors and never accepted them. He had joined the small ranchers because he had considered their fight his fight. Cap wondered bleakly if any range Anse ever got, however big, would compensate for last night.

He said, "I'm sorry, Anse. Believe that if you want to."

"Sure," Anse said numbly. "Sure."

There was a long pause, and Cap went to knee his horse around. Anse cleared his throat and said softly, "I figured that's what happened. We scattered and was supposed to meet here. But he didn't come."

Cap didn't say anything, and Anse went on in a tired voice, "That's a hell of a price to pay for a little peace. Does Lufton know that?"

"Ferg Daniels was tromped to jelly last night," Cap said quietly.

Barden looked up at him with a searching glance, and then his gaze fell. Cap said gently, "Quit it, Anse. You've paid up more than Riling ever can pay."

Anse shook his head. He kept shaking it a long time, as if repetition would prove the point of his thoughts. Then he looked off across at the Braves and said bitterly, "No, by God. Lufton pays for this as long as I'm alive."

Cap rode out then, leaving Anse standing there. "We're all fools," Cap Willis thought dispiritedly. Men get stubborn, so their sons are killed off, and they're lost. He thought about Anse's threat to Lufton and knew it was not to be ignored. But maybe after last night Lufton was beaten. If the loss of a third of the reservation herd could sink him, then John Lufton was lost. Because they'd never round up that spooked herd before the deadline, and after that the army had them. It was a thought that he hated, that turned the day and the future gray.

6

When Cap Willis left, Anse Barden set his rifle up against the doorjamb and went back into the shack. He sat down at the table Sweet and Big Nels and Chet Avery had vacated only a half-hour before. He was glad it was over, glad he knew for sure now. Between the time he suspected it and now, he had made his bitter acknowledgment. Once before, when his wife died, he'd had to do it, and he could do it again. It was simple; you can't raise the dead, so you don't have hope. Time, enough of it, would cure everything, people said, and Anse knew they lied.

He rose and made himself breakfast and ate it, and then there was the day to think about. He went out into the clean dawn, walking toward the woodpile, thinking about Cap Willis and John Lufton. Strangely enough he found that he'd lied to Willis this morning. He didn't hate John Lufton and he wasn't going to get even with him. He didn't hate anyone. His threat had been a reaction prescribed by custom and was untrue. He just felt empty, deprived of all feeling.

He chopped wood for a while, and when there was enough he stopped. About to lug it back to the house, he paused and regarded it bleakly. This, too, was one of the small gestures of living, a voicing of the belief that you would be in your house that night to burn the wood. Anse wasn't sure about that. He went over to the grindstone and sat on its seat and packed his pipe with thick steady fingers. Looking around him, he discovered that something had happened to this place in the night. Nothing was physically changed, but it was different. It looked like the frowsty, hard-scrabble outfit of a dirt-poor man. Affection for it had left him; even the memory of how he'd worked for it had no power to move him.

Forgetting to light his pipe, he went into the house again, curious. He looked at everything there: the stove his wife had been so proud of, the few pieces of gay china, the pots, pans, beds, pictures and the excellent clock on its shelf. Seen now in this new mood, they provoked an obscure irony in him. This house, its surroundings and the possessions it contained represented sixty years of a man's life, all he owned. It made a man want to smile and it was after this that Anse knew what he was going to do.

He went to the shelf above the stove and took down the

cracked brown teapot. On the table he dumped out the coins it had held and, without counting them, put them in his pocket. Afterward he went out to the corral and saddled a horse and turned the other one out, leaving the gate open.

He rode out of the place without looking back, believing it was forever and not even sorry about it.

An hour later he rode into the Blockhouse. There was activity out by the corral, and when he approached he saw that Ted Elser and Cap Willis were shoving some horses into the corral from the horse pasture.

Cap spied him and came over, and they faced each other on horseback across the fence. Cap pulled down his dusty neckerchief from across his mouth and looked sharply at Anse.

"Anything I can do, Anse?"

"Yes," Anse replied after a pause. "You can bury him, Cap. Over there, wherever it's handy."

This, too, was against the rules, Anse thought. A man buries his dead and mourns them in decent gravity, just as he fights for what is his and acquires property and a good name, so he might die in bed. Anse watched to see if Cap Willis would be shocked at his request, but Cap only nodded and said, "Sure."

Anse said, "I won't be back."

"Why would you be?"

There was one more thing Anse wanted to say. "You tell Amy good-by for me, will you, Cap?"

Cap nodded, and Anse rode out and on to Sun Dust. He knew every man in this town and he was hailed a dozen times. To the women he knew he spoke and lifted his Stetson, revealing his stiff ruff of iron-gray hair. There was nothing in his seamed face or in his eyes with their wind-puckered skin at the corners to show he was a changed man. He rarely stopped to gossip, nor did he today. Riding on through town, he took the dug road up to the rim and, once on top, reined up and turned in the saddle, putting a bracing hand on his horse's rump. He had his look.

From here a good part of Massacre Basin was visible, stretching out in tawny unbroken reaches to the far lift of the

Braves. Anse had one moment of bitterness when he realized that more than half his life had been lived with a wife and son between this rim and those mountains. That was done and he rode on.

The Bench was roughly that country that lay between the rim and the far distant Raft Mountains to the east. It was a dry country whose lower hills to the south melted imperceptibly into the Long Reach Desert. Anse crossed it that day and at night was almost into the desert. He could see the few lights of Commissary a long way off. It lay on the edge of Long Reach, abutting the low round hills that were the beginning of the Bench. Up there beyond the hills there was grama grass for forage. On the Long Reach there was nothing, and the army had dug a well here at the borderline hills. That was a decade ago, during the campaign when the Indians were pushed back to their reservation. The army wagon trains supplying the campaign had crossed the Long Reach to deposit supplies here, take on water and return across the desert.

But even after the army left and hotel, saloon, blacksmith shop and store had risen by the well, it was still called Commissary. The place had faded while the buildings were still new, and the store was abandoned. The hotel was seldom used, and line riders for the Bench outfits avoided the saloon because of its name. It had turned into a furtive place, where a dozen dim trails out of the hills and the Long Reach met and scattered again. When a Bench rancher missed some horses he came here first and asked questions that weren't answered and found nothing. Afterward he rode the trails until he lost them and was obscurely angry.

It was the hotel's light Anse saw from afar, and then he lost it as he snaked down through the bare hills. Presently he was in Commissary's only street.

The lamp in the hotel and adjoining saloon threw long rectangles of silver light out into the weed-stippled dust of the street. A big cottonwood by the hotel rose thick and motionless into the higher darkness, and a vagrant breeze clattered its dead leaves in a dry whisper. It made Anse feel old and tired, and he walked his horse to the trough by the dark blacksmith shop opposite the hotel. There were a couple of horses at the hotel's tie rail. Beyond it the ruin of the abandoned store hulked lonely on its bare lot, framed against the night sky.

Anse walked across the street to the hotel's tie rail and left his horse, afterward mounting the porch steps. Down at the far end of the porch he saw the coal of a cigarette come alight and die. A man stepped into the doorway, hands on hips, and Anse paused and said, "Where can a man eat?"

"It's pretty late," the man said. Then, as if relenting, he went on, "The old lady will fix up something. Be a half-hour maybe."

Anse nodded, and the man shuffled off across the cheerless lobby. He was in his sock feet, and there was a long rip the length of his vest in back.

Anse came back to the steps, suddenly lonely. Someone in the saloon next door laughed, and Anse went down the steps, past the man on the porch, toward the saloon's light.

When he entered the talk between the bartender and a customer ceased abruptly. It was a small barroom and let onto the hotel lobby through a door at the far end of the bar.

Anse came up and asked for whisky. He saw the bartender look at the customer, and the man went out the back door.

"He'll look at the brand on my horse," Anse thought wearily, and he didn't care. He wanted to be let alone—forever.

The night silence settled on the saloon. The thin bartender picked his teeth placidly, eyes blank. It was so quiet that Anse actually heard the man on the porch rise from a creaking chair, pause on the steps, come down them and turn toward the saloon.

He was looking in the back-bar mirror when Jim Garry stepped in. Garry didn't look at him but came toward the far end of the bar, put his elbows on it and said, "Whisky."

Anse watched him in the back mirror, and he had his moment of wondering if Jim Garry had followed him. He tried to remember if he'd seen Garry since Ripple Ford and couldn't, and suddenly he didn't care. Since this morning he'd broken every other rule, so why not break the rule of worrying about what a man would do to you?

Garry finished his drink and then turned to him and said quietly, "Would you be looking for me?"

"No."

"I'll only ask you that once," Garry murmured.

"It better be just once," Anse replied in a voice touched with truculence.

Garry paid for his drink and went out, and Anse bought another. He took a second drink because he'd made it a rule all his life to take just one. The compulsion to change everything in the old life was on him now. For sixty years he'd clung to that way of thinking and acting, and it had got him nothing. "Maybe," he thought wryly, "a different way is better."

Jim Garry turned to his seat on the porch and sank into the creaky chair again, his mind at rest. Barden wasn't looking for trouble: he just wanted to be let alone. The dry rattle of the cottonwood leaves came to him, and he smelled the bitter, pungent odor of desert brush that came off the Long Reach with the stirring of wind. He let the night settle on him, and it was like a healing.

He'd shod his horse that morning, working with the blacksmith across the way. In the afternoon he settled into this chair and had only left it to eat. During those hours of indolence he had sat in slow judgment of himself and he knew now that his old life was finished. The end of it began that moment in Sun Dust while he stood there on the porch of the Basin House listening to Lufton order him out of town and watched Shotten and Riordan move toward the kill. What had prompted him to do what he did wasn't clear yet. Even what he was going to do now and where he was going didn't make much difference. The point was, he was through with the other.

Back of thought he heard two horsemen coming down out of the hills at the end of the street. Leaning forward in his chair, he listened again, and now it seemed only one horseman.

Barden's good night to the bartender was plainly audible

from the saloon, and then the swing door droned on its hinges and Barden's thick body blocked the light.

Barden now heard the horseman, too, and he looked out into the darkness.

"Anse," the horseman called.

It was Tate Riling.

Barden paused, and Riling rode up to him. Only his horse and his legs were visible in the light coming through the saloon window.

"I heard about Fred," Riling said quietly. "I'll kill Lufton for that."

"He's dead. What good'll it do?"

"Some. It'll make me feel better."

Barden was silent, and in his silence he contrived to communicate a defiance and dislike for Riling that didn't escape Jim, who was watching this from the darkness.

"You come all the way over here to tell me that?"

Riling said, "No. I missed you this morning, but I didn't know you were here. Why are you?"

"I'm leavin' the country."

Riling hesitated and then said mildly, "But, man, the fight's almost won. Both Lufton's herds are stampeded halfway up the Three Braves."

"Who cares?" Anse said bitterly. "God damn you! Do you?"

Riling didn't answer, and Barden turned toward the porch. Riling called, "Is Garry here?"

"Find him yourself," Barden growled, not even turning. Jim was watching Riling now. He saw him turn in his saddle and look back in the direction from which he had come. Then he raised a hand and moved it away from him in a flat-palmed gesture, afterward riding on to the hotel tie rail. He came up the steps and went into the lobby.

Jim sat peering out into the darkness by the hills, watching and listening. Once he thought he heard a movement out there and was satisfied. There was another man out there; he must remember that.

He rose and walked into the lobby and found Riling standing

in the doorway, surveying the empty dining room. Riling heard him and turned and smiled swiftly. "Jim. Where you been? I've hunted the country for you."

"How'd you find me?"

"Settlemeir said you took the Commissary road. I took a chance." He spoke as he came over, and now he stopped in front of Jim. The restlessness of the big man was on him; he looked around the dreary lobby and made a wry face and asked mildly, "What's the answer? Running out on me?"

He looked at Jim and grinned and put a hand on his arm and said, "Let's get a drink. I've got news."

Jim led him through the lobby door and was down the three steps into the saloon, his face expressionless. Riling paused at the bar and said to the bartender, "Give me a bottle and a handful of cigars and then get out."

Jim took a rear corner table and put his back to the door. It was a foolish thing to do, but he wanted no suspicion on Riling's part to mar what was coming. A cold, passionless curiosity was in him as he watched Riling come over with the bottle and the glasses. Riling tossed the cigars on the table and then sank into a chair. His clothes were powdered with a fine dust that sifted out of the creases in his shirt as he moved his thick upper body. He had ridden from the Massacre this morning, but Jim knew he wouldn't be tired.

Riling poured two drinks, and they lifted their glasses, nodded to each other and drank. Afterward Riling took one of the cigars, lighted it, inhaled its tip to a glow and clenched it in his teeth. All the while his face was bland, but Jim knew he was studying his approach.

In other times Jim had had to steel himself against the breezy persuasiveness in Tate; it had been a hard thing to be stubborn in the face of his reason. All that was gone now; he knew his man.

Jim sat indolently in his chair, eyes veiled, amused and watchful and faintly excited. He had never been further from anger, never more certain of what this night would bring. It was this last that he looked to with a deep pleasure.

Tate leaned back in his chair and began: "On the level, Jim, what are you doin' here?"

"Runnin' out," Jim murmured.

Riling frowned. "You must have a pretty good reason."

"Two. Their names are Shotten and Riordan."

Riling grinned swiftly. "I heard about that. I never saw you take water from a pair like that."

"No, you never did."

"Then why?"

Jim moved his glass in a circle, looking steadily at Riling and talking slowly. "Those lovelies were primed to kill Lufton, Tate, when I stepped in."

"I'm glad you did."

Jim smiled faintly. "Are you? When I told Shotten to drift he mentioned that you'd told him to go through with it."

They stared at each other a long moment. If Riling was cornered it didn't show on his face. He said finally, "When I hired Shotten and explained the layout I told him the wage I'd pay. He was surprised at the amount. I said it was big because sooner or later he'd likely face a shoot-out with Lufton, and I didn't expect any man to take that on for fifty dollars a month." He paused. "He remembered that and saw his chance. That answer your question?"

"I guess you think so," Jim murmured.

Riling leaned forward and gestured sharply with his hand. "Jim, what the hell's eatin' you? We've got more than a box of marbles at stake."

"You have, you mean."

"That means you quit?"

"That means I have quit," Jim corrected.

Riling settled back slowly in his chair, his troubled gaze on Jim. He shook his head in puzzled disbelief and then he sat up again. "Look, let me talk. Lufton's not dead; he's not even hurt. Last night we ran off his two herds, scattered them from hell to breakfast. He can round 'em up before the deadline only if he uses his whole crew and we let this crossed herd alone. We've got him over a barrel."

"You've swung it then," Jim said. "Why bother about me?"

"I need you. Now's the time I've got to have you. Can't you see that?"

Jim shook his head, and Riling leaned forward, talking in a low, earnest voice. "Even if I could ride into Blockhouse, you think Lufton would deal with me? You think he'd sell me his herd? You think he wouldn't get word to Sweet and Big Nels and the others that I'd used them to blackmail him into a giveaway deal?"

"He'd rather lose the herd than deal with you," Jim said.

Riling's palm came down on the table. "Exactly. But yesterday you stepped in and made a live man out of one that was as good as dead. Lufton won't forget that. When you ride up and speak your piece he'll listen. Tell him the way you look at the layout. He can't get his stuff off the reservation before the deadline unless we let him alone. His cattle are lost. But you'll offer him a fifth of what his herd's worth. The nesters will let you alone as long as you take the cattle out of the country. So he can beat the deadline, make delivery at the Massacre, and you'll have men to take them out of the country. What about it?"

Jim picked up a cigar, studied it idly and said, "No dice."

"Why not?"

Jim looked at him, and his gray eyes were smoky. "It's something you wouldn't understand."

"Try me."

"No, you wouldn't understand it unless I made it pretty simple."

"All right, make it simple."

Jim said gently, "It starts with your double cross of some poor jug-headed nesters. It goes on to your hirin' gun hands, Tate—me along with the others. It leads up to your try for Lufton yesterday. It goes past that to the death of Anse Barden's son. It winds up right here, Tate, with a man outside that window waitin' to see if I'll go back with you or he'll shoot me in the back." He leaned forward a little. "It all adds up to this," he murmured quietly. "I've seen dogs that wouldn't claim you for a son, Riling."

Riling sat erect. He looked briefly at Jim, bitter judgment in his eyes, and then he reached for his glass. He was smiling as he knocked it off the table onto the floor and put his feet under him to rise.

Jim knew the glass was the signal, and he put both hands on the edge of the table and shoved it against Riling's belly. Tate went over backward, clutching at the table, and Jim lunged for him just as the sound of pounding feet in the street came to him. Jim landed on Riling's chest and slashed down at the gun Riling was dragging from its holster. Riling grunted with pain, and the gun slipped out of his fingers. Jim palmed it up, came off Riling and shot first at the overhead kerosene lamp. It blinked out, and he turned the gun on the doorway and emptied it, the shots clattering into the wood and moving the doors. Then he threw the gun through the door and backed against the rear wall, waiting in the sudden dark.

He saw Riling, framed in the front window, come to his feet, and Jim smashed into him, sinking a blow into his belly and sending him crashing on top of the table. He moved back against the side wall now, watching both the door and the spot where Riling went down. The gunman outside was held there by uncertainty. He heard Riling come erect again and he picked up a chair and hurled it at him. The rungs cracked like kindling as they broke against Riling, and he swore in a wild, anguished voice. Jim picked up another chair and hurled it, into the stacked glasses behind. They fell with a musical, crashing cascade, and then Jim saw the light approaching from the lobby. It framed the door dimly, and he knew that as soon as there was light in the saloon the man outside would have a target. He moved down the wall and caught Riling's silhouette in the doorway. He was standing there like a wary bull, head down, thick shoulders hunched, listening, not even intending to run.

Jim smiled at that and came at him. Riling heard him and whirled and lashed out with a blow that caught Jim on the head and seemed to split it. But his momentum carried him into Riling, shoulder first, and they both slammed into the bar with a wall-shaking crash. The picture of the unclad woman above the bar fell unheard into the bottles. The small bar tilted against the combined weight of them and then overturned into the back bar, bringing down all the bottles with a booming jangle that continued for seconds.

Riling's back was pinned against the bar with Jim's weight, and Jim slugged wildly at his face. Riling raised a knee in his groin and flung him away, spinning him against the uptilted bar. Jim stepped on a bottle, and it rolled under his foot and he went down, and his bracing hand fell on the jagged edge of a broken glass. The pain of it shocked up his arm, and he came to his feet, crouched, barely ready to meet Riling's rush. The impact shook the breath out of him, and now Jim was dimly aware that there was light in the room. He even heard the man with the lamp clatter down the stairs, and then Riling wrapped his thick arms around him and bent him backward.

Jim strained every muscle to break that hold, hearing Riling's savage grunting, the shifting of their feet. The room began to go dim again, and Jim struggled against Riling's bone-crushing bear hug. His arms were pinned against his chest, useless, and the pressure that Riling kept increasing seemed ready to break them at the elbows. Slowly Jim's back was arching. Riling had his chin in the V of Jim's throat and was bearing down, bending his back. They fumbled for a footing then, and the room pinwheeled before Jim's eyes. A kind of panic seized him, and he stomped savagely on Riling's feet. He felt Riling's foot grind under his heel, and then the pressure lessened, and Jim raised a knee into Riling's groin and twisted away, pushing against Riling's chest with his numbed arms.

And then they were parted, both sucking in great gagging breaths of air. It was then Jim looked beyond Riling's shoulder and saw Riordan standing just inside the swing doors. His small shadowed face, thin and wicked, was almost smiling. His gun was trained on the bartender in the doorway.

Riling tramped in again now, swinging great slogging blows

that Jim couldn't smother. He took them on the chest and face, and they jarred him clear to the base of his spine, and always he kept remembering to keep Riling's back to Riordan.

He felt his own back against the wall now. Bracing himself, he drove a smashing blow into Riling's face. It raked his cheekbone and skidded and ripped his ear, and then Jim fell into him, hugging his arms, dead weary and searching for air at the very depths of his lungs. They rested that way a moment, too exhausted to move, drawing deep within them for some strength. A kind of stubborn, killing anger was in Jim now; he didn't care about Riordan or about the bartender or about any of them during that exhausted pause.

Then he raised his shoulder suddenly and he heard Riling's teeth clack, and he lifted the whole weight of his weary body into a shove. It caught Riling off balance, and he went over backward and dragged Jim with him, and they fell with a thundering crash among the strewn chairs. Jim sensed what Riling's next maneuver would be and spread his legs so that when Riling tried to pull him off with a great heaving twist he failed. Jim crawled full astride him, taking Riling's punishing, awkward blows, and he was hammering wildly at Riling's face with the side of his hand, as if he were driving nails. Riling gathered himself for one great heave, and Jim felt it coming. He grabbed Riling's ears and alternately lifted and pounded Riling's head against the floor until he did not have strength to do it longer. Riling has ceased struggling now. Jim fell forward, dead-beat. Riling's battered face was under his chest, and Jim lay there on top of him, breathing great shuddering gasps of air that would not fill his lungs.

Behind the dead weariness he knew that Riordan was waiting for him to sit up and he cared now, but he could not move. Then he heard Riordan's voice, close, felt the kick in his ribs.

"All right, get off him." After the words came that slow, grinding wheeze that was like gears meshing. It was Riordan's cough.

Jim put both hands on the floor and raised his head. He was

looking at Riordan's legs. Between them he saw the swing door begin to inch open, and then Riordan kicked him.

He caught Jim in the side, and the force of his kick lifted Jim off Riling and rolled him over on his back onto the sawdust. Jim had one bitterly hating moment when he saw Riordan's gun rise and level down at him, and he even heard the shout of protest from the bartender.

Then a gun hammered deafeningly in the room, and before Jim understood Riordan had fallen on him. His light, sick body dropped across Jim's feet and then rolled off, turned completely over and was still. Jim came to his knees.

He knelt there a moment on all fours, looking at Riordan without comprehension. Then he grabbed the edge of a table and tried to haul himself to his feet and fell back, taking the table with him. It was the bartender who dragged him to his feet, and then Jim looked, saw and understood.

There, just inside the door, gun at side, stood Anse Barden. It was his shot that had downed Riordan.

Jim dropped into a chair and folded his arms on the table and put his head there, letting the sickness of exhaustion and violence ride him.

Barden spoke sharply from the door, an order to the others. "Hold it. Give him time."

Slowly Jim raised his head and fought to his feet, steadying himself. Riling lay on his back, his battered, bloody face turned toward Riordan, who lay small and shapeless on his face ten feet away.

Barden said dryly, "Can you make your horse?"

Jim nodded, and Barden moved his head. "Get out."

Jim picked up his hat off the floor and tramped slowly toward the door. He felt beaten and caved in and gutted, and yet in spite of it there was something he had to say to Barden.

He stopped beside him and put a hand on the doorframe to steady himself and said, "Why'd you do it?"

Barden spat and laid his unfriendly glance on Jim. "I've always wanted to shoot one of you, and he was the handiest. Get out!"

Jim went out through the door and wondered if he could make it to the stable behind the blacksmith shop where his horse was.

Barden stayed there in the doorway, gun at his side, watching the bartender and the man with the split vest. The lamp on a table laid a bright wedge of light on the floor that included Tate Riling. The sight of his battered, bloody face gave Anse Barden an obscure satisfaction. It was something he could treasure, a satisfying memory.

When he heard Jim Garry's horse vanish into the night moments later, he said, "I don't want to be followed," and backed out the door.

Then he broke and ran for his horse, and once on him he turned south toward the Long Reach. Nobody followed him.

7

From his post atop the limestone outcrop above the Blockhouse, Ted Elser saw the rider approaching from the east. Ted considered him for a moment and then slipped down to his horse below, mounted and put him past the Blockhouse.

He met the rider at the edge of the cottonwoods, his rifle slacked easily across the saddle. There was a moment before recognition when Elser dumbly marveled at the man's appearance. His bloody shirt was in ribbons, and great livid bruises showed on his broad chest and flat belly. His lean face was swollen oddly on one cheekbone, and his lips were thickened at one corner of his mouth. The hands atop the saddle horn were clumsily folded, and Elser noted that they were raw across the knuckles. But it was the gray eyes, defiant still through their weariness, that Elser remembered, and his face hardened.

"Ain't you Jim Garry?"

"Yes. I want to see Lufton."

Elser shook his head. "You damned saddle tramp," he said quietly. "Get out of here—and quick."

Jim Garry didn't move, only said, "Let him kick me off. Take me to him."

"I don't even need orders from him to cut down on you. Get out!" He swung his rifle hip high and cocked it, and still Garry didn't move. Elser was baffled and angry too. He'd meant what he said, and still Garry acted as if he didn't believe the threat was serious.

"Do I have to blow you out of the saddle?" Elser asked softly.

"I reckon you do."

Elser debated with himself a moment. Garry had a six-gun, but Ted doubted if his hands were in any shape to unlimber it in a hurry.

"Lufton's gone," he said finally.

"I'll wait for him. You can take my gun."

"Maybe I'd better," Elser said pointedly. "Both the girls are home."

He saw Garry flush under that gibe. He pulled his horse around, lifted Jim's gun out and then gestured toward the house.

Jim put his tired horse in motion, riding under the cottonwoods past the long veranda. When he was beyond the kitchen door he heard it open, and Amy Lufton stepped out.

Jim nodded to her and touched his hat, and Elser said, "He wants to see your dad, Miss Amy. I'll keep him in the bunkhouse."

Jim rode on to the bunkhouse and reined up. For a moment he made no move to dismount, for he doubted if his legs would hold him. Summoning up the decision, he swung out of the saddle, holding onto the horn. His knees gave way, and he hung there for a few seconds and then braced himself and stood up.

Elser watched all this with silent curiosity. When Jim looked at him inquiringly Elser gestured with Jim's gun to the bunkhouse. He followed Jim in and watched him sink wearily onto the stump bench that sat by the table in the middle of the bunk-lined room. Leaning up against the doorjamb, he watched Garry look around, finally put his elbows on his knees and lace his fingers together. Garry was looking out the window, utterly patient.

Ted said, "It wasn't one of our boys mussed you up, was it?"

Garry looked at him. Every time Elser saw those eyes he got mad again. That day when Miss Amy almost shot him Garry's eyes held the same expression. It was a kind of insolence, as if the man didn't have the grace or understanding to be ashamed or afraid, and Elser believed it was so.

"No," Garry said slowly. "No, that was somebody else."

Ted heard a step behind him and looked around and then stepped out of the doorway. Amy Lufton came in. Garry stood up and took off his hat. Elser saw a deep ugly cut in the palm of his hand as it rose to his hat. Garry's dark hair, once uncovered, was matted with sweat and blood.

Amy said, "Sit down. You've been in a fight."

"I'm lookin' for your father," Jim said. He sat down gratefully.

"He's—"

"Careful, Miss Amy," Ted warned. "I don't trust him or anything about him. It doesn't matter to him where your father is."

Amy looked annoyed. "But what difference can it make?"

"He shot at you once."

"He also saved my life once," Amy said evenly. "I'd like to talk to him, Ted."

Still looking suspicious, Ted Elser stepped outside, and Amy came over to Jim. She was wearing a faded blue cotton house dress, and her sleeves were pushed up to her elbows, revealing the golden brown of her arms. Her hair was a little awry, as if she had been interrupted in the middle of work and forgotten to push it off her forehead.

Her scrutiny of Jim was quicker than Ted's. She said, "He's all right. He didn't know about that in town."

"Sure," Jim said.

"That's a bad cut on your hand," Amy observed. "I'll fix it. Have you eaten?"

"Yes'm," Jim lied.

Amy went out, and Jim was suddenly grateful for the solitude. He'd ridden last night until he had fallen off his horse. When he awoke in the morning he was lying under a scrub piñon somewhere south of the Commissary road. Later that morning he'd stopped to wash at a creek where he'd scrubbed the blood from his face. There was nothing he could do about his shirt or the cut, and he'd come on, not stopping again, wanting to beat Riling back into Massacre Basin. That was important; it was about the only important thing in his life now, and he did not think he was too late.

Carol returned with Amy. She nodded to him when she came in and stood in the doorway, having no part in this. Amy had a basin and hot water and salve and rags, and she bathed Jim's hand, afterward wrapping it up. Jim submitted in silence, not watching her. Presently Carol went out. Amy tied the bandage and then put the cap on the salve.

"Tate Riling?" she asked.

Jim nodded. "Has it got here already?"

"I heard just what you heard from the gunman on the sidewalk there in town. I thought that would be it."

Jim said nothing, and Amy asked reluctantly, "Is he dead?"

Jim shook his head. Amy sat down on the bench now, putting an arm on the table. There was a friendliness in her eyes that surprised Jim. "I keep remembering what you said there in Sun Dust. Was this a whim, too—this business with Riling?"

"It was a pleasure," Jim said. Amy laughed then, and Jim smiled slowly, raising a hand to his cheekbone and touching it gingerly.

He heard horses outside now and some low talk. Amy rose, collecting her gear, and was on her way out the door when John Lufton and Cap Willis stepped in. Lufton looked inquiringly at Amy and then at Jim.

"Hello, Garry," he said in an utterly neutral voice. "What brings you back?"

Cap Willis recognized him now, and there was immediate dislike in his face. He said, "Gall, for one thing, John."

"No. Let him talk." To Jim he said, "Been in a scrap, it looks like."

Jim nodded. He thought a moment, gauging how much of what he would tell would be believed. All he could do was to tell it and let Lufton take his choice. He was going to tell it all too.

"I got in a jangle with Riling over at Commissary last night," he explained. "I'm through. I was through there at Sun Dust when I left you, but he didn't want it that way."

"Well?"

"Comin' from a man who hired out blind to Riling for any dirty work he had in mind, you may not want to believe this, Lufton. But I hate a killer, and Riling's a killer."

"I know that since yesterday. I reckon I knew it before, for that matter." He paused. "What do you want to tell me?"

"I want to tell you what you're up against, and then you can do what you have to," Jim said slowly.

"I already know that."

"Not all of it. You don't know, for instance, that Pindalest aims to buy your herd, do you?"

"Buy my herd?" Lufton echoed. "He rejected it."

"He won't reject it when Riling offers it to him."

Willis looked at Lufton, baffled, and then Willis said, "Riling hasn't got the herd."

"He will have. That's something else you didn't know, did you?"

Lufton was mute, puzzled. Jim spoke bluntly now. "Hell, Lufton, it goes back further than you think. Pindalest and Riling planned it. Pindalest rejected your herd and ordered you off the reservation. You didn't have any grass but in Massacre Basin, and Riling had the nesters primed to keep you out. Do you figure you can round up your stuff and cross it before the deadline with Riling's outfit sharpshootin' at you day and night?"

Lufton looked at him steadily and then he shook his head. "No."

"And rather than let the army take it, you'd sell right now and take a loss, wouldn't you?"

"Not to Riling."

"But to a stranger like me with cash in his pocket?"

Lufton nodded slowly, and Jim shrugged. "There's your deal. Riling's countin' on it. I was in it. I was supposed to make the offer with Riling's money."

Cap Willis cut in. "He'd still have the deadline to beat."

"Oh no," Jim said. "You'd round up the stuff and you could do it if the nesters let you alone. And they would because all they want is for your cattle to stay out of Massacre Basin."

"When Riling's got the herd," Cap Willis said, "then what?"

"Pindalest buys it. He's already got the money from the government to meet your bid. But Riling will sell the herd to Pindalest for two thirds of what it's worth. Riling has paid you a dime for them; he sells them to Pindalest for sixty cents, and Pindalest keeps the forty cents of the dollar the government gave him. Multiply that by forty-five on twenty-five hundred head of cattle and you've got a piece of money for Riling and Pindalest."

There was a long pause, and Cap Willis finally said, "I don't believe it."

Jim smiled thinly. "Then you'd have a hard time believin' the rest of it. Because Pindalest is loanin' Riling the government's money for him to buy the herd."

Lufton sank down on the bench, put elbows on knees, folded his hands together and touched his lips with thumbs. Willis only looked baffled, watching Lufton's face.

"It's true," Lufton said in a dry and beaten voice. "He can't fail unless I refuse to sell. And I'd be a fool not to."

Jim rose then and said, "Well, I'll drift. I just wanted you to know."

Amy Lufton spoke from the door then. She hadn't left the

room during the talk. She said, "Wait a minute, Jim. Sit down again."

She came straight to her father. "Think a minute, Dad," she said in a matter-of-fact way. "You aren't going to let him go, are you?"

Lufton was puzzled. He glanced at Jim and then at Amy and said, "Why, yes—with my thanks."

"But, Dad," Amy said swiftly, "there's something more. He didn't come here to tell you only this. You don't go tell a dead man he's dead." She turned to Jim then, who was standing beside Willis. "Jim, what is it? You came here for something else, too, didn't you?"

Jim's face flushed darkly. She had gone to the heart of it with an unerring sharpness. She had asked what he had hoped Lufton would have sense enough to ask, because the answer was something he couldn't volunteer.

"Yes, I had a kind of idea," Jim said quietly. "Maybe it's not what you like."

"Let me hear it," Lufton said eagerly.

The three of them—Willis and Lufton and Amy—were watching him searchingly, and Jim was aware of their hope and he was appalled. It was the risk of the thing that he was afraid of.

He said now, speaking to Lufton, "Sure Riling's got you. But he wouldn't have you if that deadline was lifted."

"But Pindalest set it!" Lufton said irritably.

"Then he can lift it," Jim said softly.

He saw a new hard awareness come into Cap Willis' eyes and then die out. But that encouraged him.

Jim put a leg on the bench and gestured clumsily with his bandaged hand. "Listen to me, Lufton. Pindalest has got to have that beef, or those Utes starve this winter. He's so sure of getting it that he's lost his chance to get more. It's too late for a drive from the Nations now."

"Of course, of course," Lufton said impatiently.

"Then what if the deadline is set ahead two weeks? You can round up your herds. You can hire punchers from the Bench outfits and you can cross your herds and scatter them in every damned canyon and wash in Massacre Basin. Nobody can round them up and shove them back with your men ridin' line."

"That's true!" Amy said.

Lufton looked sharply at her. "Of course it's true. But the deadline isn't lifted."

"It can be," Jim said gently.

"How can it? Pindalest would laugh at me when I ask him."

"He won't laugh at me and he won't laugh at my gun," Jim murmured.

Again he saw the light come into Willis' eye.

And then Lufton spoke angrily, flatly. "No! I'm not hiring gunmen, Garry, to save my money or anything else."

Jim Garry's face went pale with swift, blind rage. He wheeled and tramped out the door to his horse. Amy Lufton ran after him, and before he reached his horse she put a hand on his arm.

"Jim, Jim! He didn't mean it! You can't go!"

Jim didn't even look at her. He shook off her arm and stepped into his saddle.

Amy grabbed his horse's bridle and said pleadingly, "But, Jim, he didn't understand what you were saying! Please don't leave until he does!"

"He understood," Jim said dismally. "Now step back."

Amy let go and stepped back and said, "I'll follow you."

Jim didn't even answer.

8

Amy watched him for some seconds, and then she looked around her. There by the door was Ted Elser's saddled horse. Amy ran to him, untied the reins and swung up on him, adjusting her full skirt as she pulled him around and took out after Jim.

He was beyond the corrals, headed in the direction of the Massacre, when she came up beside him and reined her horse into a walk.

"I told you I'd follow you," she said.

Jim glanced at her, his eyes without humor. "You've got a long ride," he said. "I'm headed for Texas."

"All right," Amy said.

They didn't speak, and yet within ten minutes both of them knew that this was a battle of wills between two stubborn people. It was late afternoon now; the sun heeled far over the Three Braves, and a chill was creeping into the air. Jim ignored Amy, and she ignored him. Not once in the four miles to the river, where they arrived at dusk, did she speak.

Jim put his horse down into the bottom lands and picked out a camp among the trees close to the river. He took his horse down and watered him, and Amy took hers. He staked out his horse below camp in a patch of coarse bunch grass; Amy followed him and staked out Elser's horse.

Jim lugged both their saddles back to camp and began to collect wood, and Amy went out in the opposite direction and did likewise. Jim built a fire and then unlashed his bedroll from behind his saddle. He had a small coffeepot and a sack of coffee and a can of tomatoes there. Amy quietly took the coffeepot and went down to the river and filled it and came back and put it on the fire. It was full dark now.

Jim noticed when she came back to the fire that she stood close to it, hugging her arms against her breasts. He took his coat from his saddle roll and held it out to her.

"Wait," she said. She went over to Elser's saddle and unlashed the saddle roll. There, rolled up in a slicker, was Elser's coat. She rolled up six inches of the sleeves and shrugged into it, smiling a little at the picture she made.

Jim squatted by the fire, watching the coffee. He appreciated the absurdity of this scene and understood that Amy's point was strengthened the longer it continued. But a stubborn pride in him would not allow him to speak first.

He lifted out his sack of tobacco and papers and was fingering the mouth of the sack open when he remembered and put the tobacco back in his shirt pocket. Amy saw it and came over and held out her hand. "I can roll one for you, Jim."

Jim gave her the tobacco, and she rolled the cigarette he'd been longing for all this day, and he thanked her politely. His fingers were so swollen and raw and stiff that he had been unable to build anything he could smoke.

Amy watched him light up and drag the smoke deep into his lungs. She was sitting a little ways from him, her face pensive, watching the fire.

Jim said, "What about blankets?"

Amy raised her head and smiled faintly. "I've slept without them before."

The coffee water boiled now, and Amy deftly hauled the pot off the fire and put in the coffee. Jim's clasp knife served to open the can of tomatoes, after which he handed her the knife.

"We'll take turns," she said. "I'll eat a tomato and you drink your coffee out of the pot."

They ate that way, using Jim's knife as a fork and drinking from opposite sides of the coffeepot, straining the grounds through their teeth. It was the crudest kind of way to satisfy hunger, Jim knew, but he made no apology, and Amy made no complaint.

Afterward she rolled another cigarette for him and they watched the fire, both silent. The strain of it was wearing off now, and Jim was quietly amused and a little angry too. There was a tough streak in this girl, a stubbornness that matched his own. The whole thing was farcical now, but Jim had no intention of giving in.

He watched her covertly as she stared at the fire. There was a fleeting sadness in her face, and Jim studied it. Amy was staring at the fire, content with that small hypnosis that warm food eaten in front of a blazing fire at night brings to everyone. She had the finest eyes he'd ever seen, Jim thought suddenly; the eyebrows were sunburned lighter than her skin, and they had a high arch that gave her a strange sadness. Her face was in utter repose, serene. Jim discovered that during the times he'd seen her the word serene was what he had thought of. But that didn't make sense, he knew, because he had never seen her unless she was angry or frightened. Except when he parted from her in Sun Dust. It was that image of her standing by the arch of Settlemeir's stable that had come to his mind last night in the dark on the porch of Commissary's hotel. And now he pondered the strangeness of this, that he should have been leaving a country and thinking of a girl who held him in contempt. He knew truly that this girl was why he had returned.

He moved his shoulders as if unconsciously trying to shrug off the thought. A resentment welled up in him, and he flipped the cigarette into the fire. This must end, and now.

He said quietly, "Maybe we better quit this."

Amy roused and glanced at him. "You'll come back with me and give Dad a chance to apologize?"

"No. But you'd better go. They'll be looking for you, and when they find you I'll be in trouble again."

Amy shook her head. "I won't go until you go with me."

Jim stared speculatively at her and said, "I think you will."

He came to his feet, and Amy rose too. There was a faint threat in his tone that made her uneasy.

"I'll give you one more chance," Jim said quietly.

"No."

He stepped over to her and took her in his arms and kissed her roughly. She submitted without moving a hand in protest.

Jim felt the sweet warmth of her lips, smelled her hair, and then he stepped away from her. He felt a strange excitement in himself, a kind of shock. For one moment the truth was naked in his eyes, a kind of bewilderment.

Then he said harshly, with more brutality than he had intended, "You'll go now unless you want more of that."

Amy said placidly, "I don't want more of it, Jim. But I won't go."

Jim stood there, a high, flat figure in the bright firelight, and there was bafflement on his face. His glance held hers for three seconds, and then he turned away. He sat down again, arms folded on his knees, and scowled at the fire. Occasionally he looked up at her and each time found her watching him.

Presently he said without looking at her, "You meant it, didn't you?"

"Yes."

"Enough to let a man do that," Jim murmured. "Yes, you meant it. I'm sorry about that—that kiss."

Amy was smiling gently, though Jim didn't see her. She came over and sat beside him.

"You're a proud man, aren't you, Jim?" She spoke in a low voice, and Jim could hear no trace of irony in it. "I think I understand you better than you know."

Jim stared doggedly at the fire, but his heart was oddly hammering.

"You've been in hard luck and you've made mistakes. Your pride has made you hate those mistakes, but it's kept you from admitting them, except to yourself. That day at the river when we met, when you shot at me. I had no right to do it, and you had no right to shoot back. Both of us were wrong, weren't we?"

Jim nodded.

Amy went on. "This mess with Riling. I don't know what went before, Jim, and I don't care. But you didn't like it. You've never liked your part in it. That afternoon in Sun Dust with those two killers, you made your choice, and it wasn't Riling's way. I saw it on your face when Dad was talking to you. I saw the decision forced and I saw what you chose, and you acted on it."

She picked up a handful of leaves and idly felt them, and Jim was quiet, almost holding his breath.

"This afternoon you did the thing you had to do, the thing that would wipe out all the past that's been hurting you. And Dad threw it back in your face. He thought you were proposing to kill Pindalest."

Still Jim didn't speak.

"I didn't think so, Jim," Amy said. "I knew, you see. I knew you did it because you felt it would wipe out all the rest—the part that's gone before and that you don't like. Is—am I right, Jim?"

Jim nodded mutely, staring somberly into the fire.

"You're a proud man, Jim—but this is the wrong kind of pride now. If you ride on back to Texas you're lost. Forever."

She was silent, and Jim didn't move. Presently Amy rose, and Jim looked up at her.

"Shall we go?" Amy said.

"Yes," Jim said. He rose and went out into the darkness for the horses, and in Amy's eyes were unashamed tears.

Jim rose long before daylight. Taking his boots and blanket and coat, he went outside the bunkhouse. The morning was cold, and he slipped into his coat, keening the air and almost smelling winter coming. When he sat down to pull on his boots every muscle creaked with stiffness, but he knew that would go. He heard a movement behind him and murmured, "Who's that?"

"Elser. Thought I'd give you a hand."

They washed up at the bench outside the door, breaking a thin film of ice on the water in the bucket. The cold shocked Jim awake, and he found that he was wolf-hungry. A light in the cookshack told Jim breakfast was not far off. He rolled his blankets and then he and Elser headed across for the veranda in the darkness. Against one corner of the porch were stacked Jim's pack and grub that had been made up for him last night.

There was a lamp lighted in the house kitchen, and Jim knew it would be Amy. She had promised last night after the talk with Lufton to see him off in the morning.

He and Elser picked up the gear and headed for the barn. Elser got a lantern and hung it on the corral pole, and the three horses inside, their breaths steaming in the cold morning air and their eyes bright and dark, whickered softly. There was a paper-thin sheet of ice on the watering trough, too, Jim noticed, and it reminded him again that it was the passage of time he was bucking now.

His own bay, Elser's horse and a short-legged sorrel mare that was Jim's pack horse were the only horses in the corral; Jim's two had been kept in and grained last night while the other horses were turned out to pasture.

Jim saddled his gelding and then helped Elser put the pack on the sorrel. Elser's presence here told Jim that he had been accepted provisionally by the Blockhouse crew. In his quiet and unsmiling way Elser was letting him know that if the boss had passed him he was home. Jim found himself beginning to like Elser; he liked the way he worked with horses and the thorough, methodical way he distributed the pack and secured the diamond hitch and afterward tested it. He was unhurried and mild-spoken, without a trace of the stubborn fight he had shown Jim yesterday.

They led the horses out of the corral and tied them to the hitch rack at the corner of the bunkhouse and went into the cookshack.

The long table looked even longer with all the places set and empty. The Chinese cook brought them their breakfast, and the two of them ate in silence. Jim was ravenous; he had not really eaten in thirty-six hours, and it might be another thirty-six before he ate again.

Finished, he rolled a smoke and went back over the plans to discover what he'd missed. Last night Lufton, Amy, Carol and Cap Willis had planned this with him, plotting each move with care. None had pretended it would be easy to hide a man for weeks in this country. When the discovery was finally made

Jim could count on their searching for him. The odds were heavily against him, for the men who would hunt him knew every canyon and ridge of the Three Braves, and he did not. It was this ignorance that Cap Willis had tried to dispel last night. Alternate hideouts were chosen and directions to them given, and then Cap had explained the rough geography of the range. It was this last that Jim had listened to most carefully, for he knew that when his luck played out this would be all important. His luck, he knew, would be short, for he had not forgotten Carol Lufton's note that night in Sun Dust. If she had betrayed her father once to Riling she would betray his plans again—and Jim with them.

The sound of footsteps outside the cookshack made him turn his head, and then Amy and Carol entered.

Carol was dressed in her riding habit. Amy was wearing a dark blue belted wrapper and slippers, and her pale hair was gathered at her neck in a knot. Carol gave him an indifferent good morning and went around the table to Elser.

Amy came up and said, "With this start, Jim, you'll be over the pass before dark."

Jim nodded, but he didn't hear her. Instead he heard Carol say, "Ted, I think I'll ride this morning. Will you get me Monte?" She'd paused and said, "I'll ride alone, too, please." It had been spoken in a low voice intended only for Elser, but Jim heard. Elser nodded and went out, and Carol wandered into the kitchen.

Jim went outside with Amy. It was still hours till daylight, and the blackness seemed more profound than before, the silence deeper. His horses moved restlessly at the corner of the bunkhouse. Above their stirring he heard the faint sound of someone running behind the bunkhouse. That, he knew bleakly, would be Carol heading for the corral and then for Riling.

He heard Amy say, "Jim, I've been talking to you."

Jim pulled himself up. "I was thinking about this," Jim said.

Amy turned to him in the cold dark. "Jim, tell me the truth. What are your chances of getting away with it?"

"Good—with luck."

"Dad doesn't think so."

"No, I don't suppose he does," Jim answered. "When you're not a young man any more you quit countin' on luck. He's quit."

Amy shivered. "I wish it wasn't like this, Jim. I wish you weren't going to do it."

"Do you?" Jim murmured.

"Not really," Amy said quickly. "Only, you're so alone. We can't help you—nobody can."

"I don't need help," Jim said quietly.

Amy murmured, "No, I don't think you do, Jim. You want to do it yourself, don't you?"

"Yes."

"And you will. I know you will."

"There's something I want to say to you," Jim said stiffly. "Last night there at the river, I was pretty rough. I was trying to drive you home, Amy. If it hadn't been for that I'd never have done it."

Amy was silent for a long while and then she said, "I see." There was something in the way she spoke, a kind of aloofness and a faint disappointment, that puzzled Jim.

Then she put out her hand and said, "Good luck, Jim. Come back."

He took her hand. It was slim and warm and firm, and then it slipped out of his hand, and she was gone into the night. Jim had a brief, baffled moment of knowing that something was wrong. "Come back," she'd said. He put that away from his mind and turned toward his horses.

Once there, he did not mount. He stood there in the dark, turning over in his mind what he had to do.

Then he stepped into his saddle, left the pack horse and cut back toward the corral.

He dismounted by the lantern and went into the corral. Carol was at the pasture gate, holding it open. Jim could hear the distant rumble of the horseherd approaching, could hear Elser's sharp, hazing whistle.

Jim went on through the corral, and as Carol watched him approach her face grew tense. Once at the gate, Jim gently disengaged her hand from the bar and swung the gate shut. The horses were so close now that he didn't speak but waited there. The lead horses saw the gate closed and swung off to the right, the others following. Elser's whistle stopped suddenly, and he rode up to Jim and Carol.

The light from the far lantern barely lighted Carol's face. Jim's was shadowed by his Stetson, and Elser looked from one to the other, puzzled.

"Anything wrong?" he asked.

Carol tried to speak imperiously. "I don't know, Ted. He pulled the gate out of my hands and shut it."

They both looked at Jim now. He said quietly, "She doesn't ride today or for the next two days, Elser. Don't give her a horse."

"Why not?"

"Ask her," Jim said briefly.

Both men looked at Carol, waiting for her to speak. Jim wasn't going to say that by keeping Carol home today he was insuring himself against Riling and his crew overtaking him before his job was done. He was going to let Carol do any talking that was done.

A blazing anger mounted in Carol's eyes now. She came over to Jim, facing him. "I don't think you're hired by Blockhouse, are you?"

"No."

"So you haven't even a puncher's authority around here?"

"No."

Carol's anger lashed out at him. "How dare you tell me if I can ride or not. Get away from that gate!"

"No."

She lashed out at Jim, slapping him across the face with the palm of her hand. Jim didn't move, didn't speak. Elser was held motionless by the scene.

"Will you get away from that gate?" Carol raged.

Jim said softly, "No. I could tell you why I won't, but maybe you wouldn't want to hear it."

Carol stared at him. The anger slowly washed out of her face, and in its place was alarm, and behind that fear. She said uncertainly, "I don't know what you mean."

"You know," Jim said quietly.

She held his gaze for seconds, then wheeled and ran off into the darkness toward the house.

Elser watched her go, and then his sober glance shuttled to Jim. "So you know too."

Jim's head came up. Slowly he tramped over to Elser. "How did you know?"

"I followed her to Riling's."

Jim's voice held a hint of anger as he asked, "Then why do you let her ride?"

"If a man's own daughter isn't loyal, I'm no man to tell him so," Elser said quietly.

Jim fought down his impulse to anger, but there was a bitter soberness in his speech as he said, "I don't give a damn who you tell, Elser. But you keep her off a horse for three days or I'll have a bullet in my back before sundown."

"All right."

"I mean that," Jim said harshly. "I'll take my chances with a man, but with a sweet redheaded beauty cutting my throat, I've got to know."

"Careful what you name her," Elser said quickly, quietly. Plain warning was in his voice.

Jim's eyes narrowed and he murmured, "So that's the way it is?"

"That's the way it is," Elser replied. "Any comments?"

Jim smiled faintly. "None I haven't made already—and none I didn't mean."

Elser nodded. "She won't ride for three days. That's a promise."

Jim believed him. He went back to his horse, picked up the pack horse at the bunkhouse and rode out into the dark morning toward the Three Braves.

A fair wagon road from Sun Dust to the agency cut across the upper part of Massacre Basin and slanted a little south for the pass in the Three Braves. Jim picked it up sometime after daylight. The dawn broke cold with a low scud of clouds blotting out the peaks, and Jim knew snow was not far off. It gave an urgency to his business and made him quietly impatient. By noon he was in the steep canyons below the pass, and a fine snow was sifting down and disappearing immediately.

Soon after midday Jim left the road and cut up a small canyon whose slopes of red rock were stained purple in places with the snow water. He left the road where he forded the canyon's stream and he kept to the stream for a mile or so, his eyes watching for a likely place. He found it soon, a pocket in the canyon slope where wind had eroded out a cave of sorts. Dismounting, he stowed the load from his pack horse in the shelter of this rock overhang, then turned and retraced his steps, leading the pack horse in the stream. His provisions were deposited now, and he could travel faster.

Once on the road again, he drove the pack horse ahead of him as he had been doing, so that nobody but a sharp tracker following him could spot his cache by the absence of the pack horse's tracks. Three miles beyond he circled the pack horse and drove him back down the road.

He had planned last night to camp this side of the pass but he knew now that he couldn't chance a deep snow in the night cutting him off from the other slope. He hunched down in the Mackinaw he had borrowed from Lufton and let the dismal afternoon thread on as he climbed. Before dark he came to the old snow, which was almost ice and had been rutted deeply with the broad tires of the wagons freighting to the agency. The steep slopes up to the peaks were blotted out by whirling snow, and a cold wind funneled down the canyon he was winding through. A scattering of aspen and an occasional pine interrupted the dismal gray of the landscape when the walls broke away for a high meadow.

He remembered the last time he had crossed these mountains, avoiding the pass and skulking into the country like something hunted. When the time came for him to leave he might go out the same way, but it would be with the satisfaction that he had made up for many things in the past.

Darkness came on him in the pass, and with it a steady-flowing, bitter wind from the west. Presently the trees grew denser, and he knew he was over the pass and on the other slope of a country that was new to him.

He camped late that night in the pines, grained his horse and threw his blankets under the wide spread of a tall spruce that the wet snow had not reached.

His supper eaten, he wrapped a blanket around him and sat cross legged before the fire, again returning to his plans. His lean face held a kind of sober peace; occasionally a faint smile would light his eyes and shape his face anew, and he would rise then and poke the fire and sometimes lose himself in contemplation of it.

The snow would make a difference, depending on how much of it there was, he knew. A heavy snow would shut him off from the other slope and drive him down out of the high country to avoid leaving a wide-open trail. He wanted badly to make it back to the other slope, the Massacre slope. Besides having his food cached there, he felt more familiar with it. There was another important reason too. On that slope there would be few Indians. On this, once the alarm was raised, the Indians would be on his trail, not for the judgment they would place on his crime but for the sheer fun of finding him. Beyond this he couldn't plan, and he turned in his blankets and was asleep before his fire was coals.

He was traveling before sunrise again next morning. The clouds had lifted from the peaks, revealing them in their new white, but the sky was still overcast. It was a raw day, and Jim knew this wasn't the end of the snow and he hurried. In mid-morning, slanting into the lower country, he saw his first Ute lodge. A little later he met a Ute buck on the road, his squaw riding some fifteen paces behind him. The Ute hailed him and talked with great dignity for some moments and then asked him for tobacco. Jim left him his sack and rode on, considering the gift a form of toll.

The country, still high, leveled off into a piñon plateau now, and Jim rode it through the long morning and into the afternoon. He saw many meat camps with their drying racks and their poles and an occasional lodge, and once a band of horses crossed the road ahead of him, their tails leveled out and heads high. An Indian boy who was so small he had probably needed a stump to mount his horse was chasing them, lying flat on his horse's neck and riding bareback. At sight of Jim he pulled his horse into the trees and vanished.

In late afternoon the country shelved off in a broad, bare valley bisected by a sizable stream, and here lay the agency.

It sprawled on a grassy shoulder of land free of trees and bare as a stone save for the ragged willows fringing the stream.

The wagon road formed the only street, and in tumultuous disarray on either side of it were the skin-and-canvas lodges of the Utes. A hundred dogs skulked about the camp, which was littered as far as the eye reached with the bleached bones of game and beef. Wide-eyed children dressed in a mixture of ill-fitting store clothes and buckskins watched Jim's entry and did not greet him. Campfires burned in front of most of the tepees, the smoke riding the heavy air barely above the camp. Sprinkled through this army of lodges was an occasional log cabin, ill constructed, roofed with brush or sod, windowless and doorless and its yard littered with refuse. Pole corrals lay among the lodges, and off to the west beyond the camp were log storehouses and a bigger corral where the beef issues took place.

At the far end of the camp, on the brow of the hill, was a long log building comprising the store and quarters of a white trader. Beyond it, close to the far slope of the valley, was the stone house of the agency and office. A picket fence, badly needing paint and repair, enclosed the yard where a garden had died without anybody's caring or noticing. The barns and corrals were separated from it by an orchard of new trees which Jim guessed the former agent had planted.

He tied his horse at the hitch rail by the gate and went up to the house. It was L shaped, the front angle comprising the office, on whose door was painted the legend "Agent."

Jim knocked and, waiting for an answer, looked around the yard. It was as littered as the Indian camp below. The last wind had wedged an open newspaper against the fence, where it was aging unheeded into a rich brown. Bottles, Jim noted dryly, comprised most of the litter.

"Come in, come in!" A voice shouted impatiently from inside.

Jim palmed the knob and stepped inside. The office was gloomy in the fading afternoon light, and he could see nobody at the moment. Then he spotted Pindalest standing in the doorway that let onto the living quarters of the house.

The agent was in shirt sleeves, his galluses trailing down behind him, his sparse hair mussed, his boots off. He stared stupidly at Jim for a moment, small mouth pursed in sleepy truculence.

Then recognition came, and he said, "Why, hello, Garry. Jim Garry, isn't it?"

"That's right. How are you, Mr. Pindalest?" Jim asked affably.

Pindalest shuffled over, and they shook hands.

"Sit down, man, sit down," Pindalest invited. "Been riding all day and was just having a nap. Here, fire up the stove. It's cold in here. I'll be back in a minute." He started back for the other room and said over his shoulder, "Might light the lamp too."

Jim went about these simple chores carefully, rehearsing what was to come. He was in luck that Pindalest recognized him, for what he was about to say would carry more weight now. He threw a chunk of wood in the Franklin stove and raised the draft, though to him it was hot in here now. He lighted the lamp and looked around him. Pindalest's roll-top desk in the corner was littered with papers. The spittoon needed cleaning, and the whole room a thorough sweeping. It had an air of shiftless disinterest about it that seemed to go with petty officialdom, Jim thought.

His judgment of Pindalest at Sun Dust had been accurate enough, even without Riling's contemptuous dismissal of him, but he had no intention of underestimating his man. When Pindalest came in carrying a tray with a pitcher of water, two glasses and a bottle of whisky on it Jim was sitting patiently, almost broodingly, hands folded, like any puncher on an errand to his superiors.

"Here, pour your own," Pindalest said. "Make mine light, very light."

Jim poured the drinks, and Pindalest sank into the swivel chair by his desk. It creaked ominously under his soft bulk, and he tilted it back against the wall.

Pindalest was obviously anxious to hear Jim's news, but he was playing his role of affable host first. He had tidied himself somewhat and put on his boots and smoothed down his hair. Drinking the raw whisky and welcoming its fire, Jim thought suddenly that he had seen this face a thousand times behind bank wickets, in stores, in railroad stations. It was a face of small greeds, transparent and shrewd.

Pindalest gave him time to put his glass down and then he asked with affected unconcern, "Well, how goes it with you and Riling?"

"Fine, Mr. Pindalest, fine," Jim murmured. "I've got the news you've been waiting to hear."

Pindalest shed all pretense of unconcern. He leaned over as far as his paunch would allow and said excitedly, "What is it, Jim? Has Lufton given up?"

Jim nodded. "That's about the way it shakes down. Riling had a parley with him after I pointed out to Lufton that he had to sell. He pounded sand there for a while, but he came around."

Pindalest settled back slowly into his chair, a broad smile on his narrow face. The naked greed in his eyes was not pleasant to see, but Jim's face was expressionless.

"Bravo," Pindalest said. "Bravo." And then, quickly, "Does Lufton suspect anything?"

"Nothing so far."

Pindalest smiled again, and Jim gave him a moment to contemplate his triumph, count his money and spend it in his own mind.

"That's fine," Pindalest mused. "A great piece of work. It went off without a hitch."

Jim looked dubious. "Well, maybe one hitch, you might call it."

Pindalest was immediately wary, donning caution like a coat. "And what's that?" he asked carefully.

Jim decided to let him have it, making it sound grave. When the facts came out Pindalest would swing back to even higher spirits.

"Lufton wanted more money than Riling had," Jim said.

Pindalest scowled, and at the same time his eyes were veiled with a slow suspicion. "I see," he murmured. "That's bad. Riling should have kept to his original estimate." He pursed his lips and said suddenly, "How much more?"

"Three thousand," Jim said. "Riling said his selling price to you still held, so this was just a loan. He'd take the three thousand out of his own cut."

Jim had anticipated Pindalest's reaction, and it came with the simple idiocy of greed. Again Pindalest was beaming, again smug, his good humor restored. Jim decided to let him find out the next move himself.

"Easily done, easily done," Pindalest purred. "If that's all that's holding us up there's nothing to worry about. Here, let's have another drink to celebrate."

He mixed this drink himself, and Jim noticed that this time he did not go light at all. Jim's drink was burning in his belly and he didn't want another immediately, but he accepted it.

"Here's to success," Pindalest toasted. "We can drink to that now without even worrying about it, can't we?"

"We can," Jim said, and Pindalest laughed and drank his whisky neat. Then he looked around the room with a pleased, musing expression and rubbed his soft hands together. "Well, well," he murmured apropos of nothing and sat down again.

"So it's a little matter of three thousand dollars that Lufton's worried about, is it? Well, we can fix that quickly."

A thought occurred to him; Jim could see it start, unfold and come to full flower in Pindalest's mind.

"Let's see," Pindalest said slowly. "Maybe this is going to be a nuisance. I haven't got the cash here at the agency."

Jim said nothing, and he knew how Pindalest's mind was working. Lack of cash meant a check, and he knew that all through this affair Pindalest had been very careful to give Riling cash so none of his moves could be traced through his bank checks. This was what Jim was counting on—Pindalest's continued caution even when the deal was a certainty. But he couldn't speak; he was supposed to be a not over-bright puncher who was a minor fellow conspirator.

"Damn!" Pindalest said petulantly. He looked at Jim now. "Does Riling need the money to sign the deal?"

"Lufton said cash."

Pindalest sighed. "Then I'll have to ride over to Sun Dust with you myself to draw out the money."

Jim nodded placidly. "Riling said you likely would."

Pindalest rose now, a deep frown of petulance on his face. He rammed his hands in his pockets and paced once around the room, head down.

"How's the pass? Clear?"

"A little snow," Jim said. "It'll hold off, I reckon."

"Well, I've got to go back with you; that's all there is to it," Pindalest said sternly. He hated the discomfort of the trip, Jim knew, but he wasn't going to let that stand between him and his money. "If we start tomorrow early we can be across by tomorrow night, can't we?"

"That's right."

"Good. That's settled. Where's your bedroll, Garry? I can put you up tonight, and we'll get an early start."

Jim said slowly, "You think that's smart, Mr. Pindalest? I mean, me hangin' around here? They'll be wonderin' who I am and remember me, and maybe that wouldn't be so good in case of trouble later."

"But where'll you sleep?"

"Anywhere out in the brush. When you pass on the road tomorrow I'll pick you up."

Pindalest nodded slowly, glad to accept Jim's suggestion. It had stemmed from a twofold desire on Jim's part: he didn't want to spend the night with Pindalest and he wanted to make what he was about to say final and irrevocable.

He rose now and reached for his hat.

"You're not going?"

"The less time I spend here, the better," Jim said.

Pindalest put out his hand and Jim took it. "Like another drink?"

"Thanks, no," Jim said.

He started for the door, and Pindalest followed him, a hand on his shoulder.

Jim snapped his fingers suddenly and stopped. "I come close to forgettin' it," he said, turning to the agent. "Riling says call off the army. Lufton will likely run over the deadline roundin' up some beef that we stampeded for him. Riling says he don't want to have to explain to the army about it, and a note from you would stop them."

"Of course, of course," Pindalest said. "What day is this? The twenty-eighth." He paused, pinching his lower lip between thumb and forefinger. "It's an easy two days' march from Fort Liggett, so they'd start on the twenty-ninth around noon. Yes, I'll get a message to them by tomorrow morning, in plenty of time. I'll start a man now."

Jim nodded and put on his Stetson, lowering his face so Pindalest couldn't see any expression that might betray his excitement.

He said, "I'll pick you up on the road tomorrow. Better make it early. And bring a coat because it's cold up in the pass."

"Right. Good night, Garry."

Jim went out into the lowering dusk, and he experienced a

quiet, vicious pleasure that surprised him. The deadline was lifted, and tomorrow he'd have Pindalest over the pass. Then the real job would begin.

9

Joe Shotten had had a toothache for three days. The beating he had taken from Jim Garry in Sun Dust started it, and nothing, including whisky and cut-plug tobacco, could stop it. It wasn't a raging kind of toothache that will send a man over the driest deserts or through the deepest snow to get the tooth yanked, but it was one of those dull, persistent aches that raveled a man's temper and got him into trouble.

Joe was headed for trouble now. Riling's crew had been waiting for him at Chet Avery's place for three days now. This last day Milo Sweet was riding patrol on the crossed Blockhouse herd, and he had seen a large Blockhouse crew systematically scattering the beef in every draw and gully from the rim to the Massacre. While he and the others did nothing, of course, because Riling wasn't there. Sweet had put them all in an edgy temper by his fire-eating insistence that they had lost their chance to make trouble for Blockhouse's crossed herd.

His raging before now had broken up the poker game and scattered the men to their bunks. They weren't comfortable bunks either, for Chet Avery was a farmer and used the bunkhouse for a tool shed. Added to that, Avery's womenfolk refused to cook for them, and they had been feeding for three days on a half-cooked mess stewed up by them in a borrowed wash kettle. They were sick of waiting, sick of inaction, sick of Milo Sweet. And Joe Shotten had a toothache.

He prowled through the bunkhouse after the noon meal. The sight of Avery's hand cultivator in a corner irritated him beyond reason. He was used to having these men ignore him as an all-but-convicted gunhand rider for Riling, but their added taciturnity now angered him.

Sweet was playing an impatient game of solitaire at the table. Joe came over and watched him for a moment and said, "Red queen on black king."

Milo looked up at him. Sweet hadn't shaved for a week, and his beard grew just like his hair—in all directions. It gave him a ferocious and half-wild look that wasn't far from missing his true frame of mind.

"Maybe I'm playin' a new game," he snarled. "How do you know?"

"You was tryin' to run a sandy," Shotten sneered.

"All right, I'm cheatin' myself. What have you got to say about that?"

Shotten shrugged. "I don't care."

"Then keep out of it," Sweet said flatly. "The next time you stick your nose in here I'll slap it off."

"Wait a minute," Shotten said softly.

Somebody, Big Nels, drifted out of a bunk and came over and put his shoulder against the top tier of bunks and looked meaningly at Shotten. One of the Paulsen boys joined him, only he wasn't so subtle; he carried a rifle in his hand, and there was plain dislike in his face.

Sweet said, "All right, you hundred-a-month hero, go on and talk."

Shotten shrugged and walked to the door and stood in it, back to them, looking out. In a quarrel they'd gang him, he knew. He would gladly have murdered them, man by man, at that moment. To him they were a bunch of dumb hard-scrabble nesters and two-bit cowmen, not a man among them. He had a sudden longing for the company of Riordan and Riling, who were more like himself and who could keep this rabble respectful. And his tooth ached damnably.

Avery's house lay across a hundred feet of hard-packed yard, a neat long shack backed by a nice stand of half-stripped cottonwoods behind it. The barn and corrals lay off to the right, and between them and the house were the well and chicken house. Shotten vaguely resented the neatness and prosperous look of the place even under this gray fall sky.

While he was watching, Chet Avery's fifteen-year-old daughter came out of the house, carrying a water bucket and a pan of bones.

When she reached the well she deposited her bucket. She went on toward the barn and stopped and then whistled for her dog.

Shotten eyed her attentively. She was a slim girl and was wearing one of her mother's dresses that was too large for her under an old coat of her father's. But there was something young and appealing in the way she walked, her kind of coltish grace, that Shotten noted slyly.

He stepped down into the yard and walked toward her, hands in pockets. She was still whistling as he approached, and then the dog broke from the corrals and ran toward her. He was a big-footed pup, and she was still enough of a child to talk baby talk to him as she set the pan on the ground in front of him.

"That's a mighty fine hound," Shotten observed.

The girl wheeled, startled, to face him. What she saw didn't lessen her uneasiness: Shotten's loose lips were twisted in what he hoped was an engaging smile, but the hunger in his eyes couldn't be disguised.

"Well, he's not much of a dog," the girl said shyly. "He's kind of nice though."

Shotten stared at her, and in that stare was the whole history of his association with women. The girl felt this and her face flushed, but she was not going to move. This was her father's place, and she had a right here, her expression seemed to say.

"I ain't seen you around," Joe said. "A pretty girl like you ain't goin' to get any prettier sittin' in the house all day."

"I—I've been working," the girl said. She was furiously embarrassed.

Joe came closer to her, still smiling. "You ought to get out and see the country, show yourself. Don't you ever go to dances?"

"Yes."

"I ain't seen you at any," Joe went on. "I'd sure have fought some of these young kids for a dance with you too."

The girl's gaze dropped, but she held her ground stubbornly and did not answer.

Joe grinned with amusement. "I got the prettiest bay horse with white socks you ever seen, gentle with women too. You figure sometime you could—"

That was as far as he got. He felt himself whirled around by his collar and then something smashed into his jaw with a ton weight. He sprawled on his back in the dust, and his first instinctive reaction was to streak for the gun at his hip. He heard the girl scream, and then a bony, snarling fury hit his chest. Joe knew it was the pup, and he raised his hands to his throat and struck out savagely. The dog slashed at his hand, and Joe rolled over and came to his feet. He kicked out at the dog and missed him and then saw Chet Avery standing there.

Behind Avery, racing for them, were half a dozen men.

Shotten forgot his gun then and looked at Avery. Solid, stocky, his face blazing with fury, Chet Avery faced him, and there was murder in his eyes.

"Damn you, Shotten, get off this place!" Avery said in a thick voice.

"What did I do?" Shotten protested.

Sweet was the first to arrive. He hauled up, looking at Avery and then at the girl, who was kneeling by the dog, holding him and crying.

"What'd he do?" Sweet demanded.

Avery didn't hear him. He kept looking at Shotten, and his face was contorted with rage. "If you ever speak to her again, Shotten, I'll kill you. Get off this place now and stay off!"

Sweet said thinly, "Can't even let a decent girl alone, can you, Shotten?"

"I never—" Shotten began.

Sweet stepped up to him and slapped his face once with his

palm, once with the back of his hand. "I don't know why we don't string you, you damned cheap tin-horn killer. Listen to me. Are you listening?"

Shotten didn't answer, didn't dare to. He knew these men hated him and he knew it would take very little to make them do just what Sweet had threatened.

"You get on your horse," Sweet said slowly, "and ride out of this country. Get out! If we see you here again we'll hunt you down like we would a sheepherder. Get out!"

Shotten stooped and picked up his greasy Stetson and put it on without dusting it off. He was too afraid to be angry, and beyond his fear was the dull throb of his aching tooth. Avery's blow hadn't helped it.

He went out to the corral, followed by the others. In silence they watched him saddle his horse and mount.

Sweet said thinly, "You got till sundown."

Shotten rode north out of the place, past the bunkhouse and the shack. The farther away from Sweet he got, the more his sullen fury mounted. So they'd kick him out of the country! Wait till Riling heard that, and they'd sing a different tune.

And then his tooth began to ache in earnest. Avery's blow had caught him on the side of the jaw with near bone-smashing force, and it seemed to fan into fire the spark that Garry's blow had lighted. It was a real ache now, crowding out all other thoughts, all other awareness, even anger, except at it. He'd have to have it pulled and after that he could find Riling.

He lined out for Sun Dust on the wagon road, and pure and exquisite misery rode with him. It was near dusk when he came in off the flats to Sun Dust, pressing a chew of sodden tobacco against his tooth with his hand. His eyes were bleak, misery filled, and he stopped the first man he saw and asked, "Where can I get a tooth pulled?"

"Doc Hogan, above Miller's saddle shop."

Shotten put his horse downstreet. Passing the sheriff's office, he saw a horse that he thought he recognized. The pain was rioting through his jaw now, but he pulled up, having a hard time concentrating. And then it came to him. It was Riling's pony.

But he went on. Not even a session with Riling was more important than this tooth. He dismounted at the saddle shop and climbed the outside stairs that lifted to the second story. He entered a musty waiting room and knocked on the inner door. A gray-haired, roly-poly little man listened to his story and waved him in.

Joe Shotten then spent fifteen of the worst minutes of his life and proved to himself and several people down on the street that he was not a stoic. Doc Hogan found that the tooth was broken, and its extraction necessitated a minor operation. Shotten first groaned, then yelled, and when the actual extraction took place he came close to screaming.

Afterward he sat limp in the straight chair that Doc had pulled to the window for the last light and gazed stupidly down at the street. He was wet with sweat and shaking like a foundered horse, but the pain had stopped. He didn't mind the even hurting now; it was gentle compared with the skull-lifting throb that had been with him all afternoon.

Presently he paid the doctor off and went out, holding a dirty neckerchief to his mouth. At the top of the steps he found that he'd have to pause a moment for rest if his knees weren't going to buckle.

He was standing there, overlooking the street, when he saw Lufton pass. The Blockhouse owner was riding leisurely down the street abreast another rider. A pair of punchers followed them, and still another brace followed the pair. They looked dusty, and since they were heading downstreet, Shotten assumed they had just come off the rim from the Bench.

Curiosity replaced self-pity now. He descended the steps and tramped down the plank sidewalk a little behind the last rider, trying to see the horse's brand in that fading light.

And then he saw Lufton pull into the tie rail in front of the sheriff's office. Lufton sat his seat a moment, regarding the horse next to his own. That horse, Shotten could see, was still Riling's.

Shotten felt a swift lift of excitement. Lufton and Riling in the same room would spell shooting anywhere—except in a sheriff's office. It occurred to him that a sheriff's office might not make any difference.

He had a swift moment of judgment as he saw Lufton dismount stiffly and tie his reins to the rack. The others dismounted but didn't go in. Shotten decided to chance it, so he cut across the street, coming in behind one of the rider's horses. He saw the brand Star 88 and identified it as a Bench outfit. The fact that these weren't Blockhouse horses encouraged him to go on.

His entrance into Les Manker's office was only ten seconds behind Lufton's. When he stepped quietly inside the door he found all three men standing. The lamp on Manker's desk against the back wall was lighted. Riling had just come off a chair back-tilted against the side wall under the gunrack. Shotten wasn't prepared for Riling's altered appearance. Riling's nose looked oversize and somehow different, and his right eye was a mixture of green-and-purple-tinted swelling that left only a slit to peer through. There was a barely healed scar running from the corner of his mouth almost to his ear, which was bandaged.

Riling saw Shotten and nodded and returned his gaze to Lufton. Manker looked uncomfortable and apprehensive. He gestured toward his desk chair and said, "Here, John, take a seat."

Riling tried to smile. "I'll see you later, Sheriff."

"You might as well stay," Lufton said dryly. "This includes you, Riling. I won't sit down, Les. This won't take long."

Lufton didn't even look at Shotten, although Shotten was sure he was aware of his presence.

Lufton said matter-of-factly, "I'm moving my herds off the reservation into the Basin this coming week, Les. I'm claiming all the range between the rim and the river and south of the agency road down to the Long Reach hills. Whatever stock is left there after this week will be pushed across the line and kept there."

"Your ambition's shrunk," Riling remarked.

Lufton shook his head. "No, that's all I ever wanted. But I want it."

"Gettin' it is something different," Riling murmured.

"I've got one herd across and scattered," Lufton said easily. "This week I'll get the other two."

"There's a little matter of a deadline you must have heard about," Riling observed.

Lufton's answer was placid. "I did hear something about it. Better let me worry, hadn't you, Riling?"

Manker cleared his throat. "John, there's folks already south of the road. Riling here, for one. Avery too."

"They'll move."

"They won't," Riling said flatly.

Lufton regarded him with indifference and spoke to Manker. "I'm just telling you what I aim to do, Les. If you want to stop me bring plenty men and plenty guns."

Manker said bluntly, "You try and move any of them out that don't want to go and you're in real trouble, John."

Lufton snorted softly. He stood there with his hands on his hips, a kind of lean-faced arrogance about him that answered both Riling and Manker.

Lufton said, "When I get my range stocked I'm goin' to put out line riders with orders to shoot the first man they see across the line. Better tell them that, Manker. You're sheriff."

Lufton nodded to them and turned to go. He had a hand out to brush Joe Shotten aside when Riling said, "Just a minute, Lufton."

John Lufton paused and looked sharply at Riling.

Riling said with easy good humor, "Why don't you admit you're licked, Lufton? You really think you can round up two big herds like that and push 'em across the Massacre with us ridin' your tail, all in the time you got left?"

"What if I can't?"

"The army seizes your beef if you can't, don't they?"

"So they say."

"And what'll you get out of it—outside a fight with the army if you try to stop 'em?"

"I'm surprised you should care," Lufton said slowly.

Riling essayed a grin, which was hard enough to do. "Hell, I'm not all Injun, Lufton. You'll lose your herds and you can't move us even if you claim you can. Then why not use your head and not cut your own throat from ear to ear?"

"Cut my throat?" Lufton drawled.

"Sell your herd," Riling pointed out. "Get money for the beef instead of lettin' the army grab it for nothing. You'll wait ten years for your claim for the beef to be honored by Washington. On the other hand, if you sell the stuff we'll let you alone and not bother you, so you can clean 'em off the reservation. Just so they don't end up in Massacre Basin is all we ask. We don't aim to strap you."

Lufton's forehead wrinkled. "You know," he said, "that's interesting. You're suggesting I sell my herd to you nesters, are you?"

Riling laughed. "And we'd pay you with what for money? No, all we want is for your cattle to stay out of Massacre. But a Bench outfit might buy the stuff if your price was right."

"You handling the sale?" Lufton asked insultingly.

Riling flushed. "To hell with you, mister. I was just showing you a way to settle this and still come out of it with money. It's nothing to me, though, what you do. Anyway you figure it you lose."

"Do I?" Lufton said, and he was smiling so that his dark mustache lifted a little at the corners.

He shouldered past Shotten and went out. The three men left in the sheriff's office looked at each other in puzzlement.

"What did he mean by that?" Manker asked.

"Bluff," Riling said in sharp anger. "He can't beat the deadline and he knows it."

"Seems like he don't care either," Manker said in a puzzled voice.

Riling moved impatiently. "There's no use fighting over a dead horse. Lufton's done. About that other at Commissary,

Manker. I admit I jumped the county before the inquest. If
they come asking for me stall them off. I've got to be here in
Massacre now, not at an inquest in Commissary."

"Whose inquest?" Shotten said.

Riling looked at him and said curtly, "Riordan's."

Shotten had an uncomfortable moment of not knowing what
this was about. Riling was marked up as though he'd been in a
tough fight; Riordan was dead. And Riordan, like Shotten, was
one of Riling's hired gunmen.

Riling nodded curtly to the sheriff and went out, Shotten
following him. Shotten couldn't shake the conviction that Riling had killed Riordan. He made up his mind to ask, but when
he came up to Riling, who was facing the tie rail, and saw his
face his question died unasked.

Riling's face was ugly with anger. In his one good eye Shotten saw a murdering rage as he watched Lufton riding out with
his crew. Something had gone wrong, plenty wrong, Shotten
thought.

He held his silence for long minutes until Riling turned to
him. The anger was gone now as Riling asked curtly, "Where
are the others?"

"Avery's."

"Let's ride," Riling said.

Shotten shook his head uneasily, for he didn't know what
Riling would do at the news he was going to tell him. "Not me,
Riling. I been run out by that bunch. For plumb good and all."

"For what?" Riling said after a pause.

Shotten grinned sheepishly and recklessly told the truth. "I
took a long look at Avery's girl. They didn't like it."

"And they ran you out?"

Shotten nodded, watching Riling. Trouble was, with Riling's
face marked up the way it was, you couldn't tell soon enough if
he was mad or not. Shotten was glad, for once, that he was
standing in front of the sheriff's office with the street filled with
people.

But he soon saw that Riling wasn't angry. He accepted it as
something done, something that was inevitable.

Riling said finally, "But I need you, Joe."

Shotten said nothing, and Riling stood there, looking out at the dark street, musing.

Presently he turned on his heel and said to Shotten, "Come along, Joe," and went back in the sheriff's office.

Manker had seated himself at his desk, but now he reared back and looked over his shoulder.

Riling said in an even voice, without excitement in it, but with a tone of authority, "Manker, I want you to deputize Joe."

10

Jim didn't like the looks of things the night he and Pindalest camped in the snow beneath the pass. The snow was a couple of inches deeper down here than it had been yesterday, which meant it would be more than that in the pass, but he said nothing to the agent.

He made the camp as comfortable as he could, even cutting brush for Pindalest's bed. The agent was dead-beat from the day's ride. He groaned softly as he sat on his blankets by the fire, watching Jim make camp, and Jim knew the man probably hadn't been on a horse since his last trip to Sun Dust. Pindalest had a flask of brandy in his war bag, and several drinks from it, which he did not share with Jim, seemed to revive his spirits.

They were both hungry for the supper Jim fixed up, and afterward Pindalest seemed content. There was even a sparkle in his dull eye and a flush that wasn't a whisky one in his cheeks from the cold night air. Jim built the fire up and then settled down to conversation with Pindalest, but all the time he was wondering about the pass. The agent wanted to know the full details of Riling's success, and Jim lied blandly. There was little he had to invent; according to his story, the stampeding of the two herds on the reservation had turned the trick. Lufton had chosen to salvage a little money from his herds instead of letting the army seize them.

When they turned in Pindalest was in high humor. He was asleep almost as soon as he hit the blankets, but Jim lay awake. He turned his head so he could see Pindalest and the small mountain of flesh under the blankets. What did he have to fear from the man during these next days? Certainly not physical violence or bravery. But the man had a certain cunning that he would be a fool to ignore. Jim felt plain contempt as he regarded Pindalest, whose face was even softer in sleep than in life. A cheap politician, one of The Looters, making a fortune on graft.

Next morning it was snowing in earnest. Jim broke camp in haste, but he did not let Pindalest glimpse his near panic.

When they reached the road Jim anxiously noted the depth of snow as it measured on his horse. It came between fetlock and knee, and Jim felt a sudden gloom. What would it be near the peaks, where it had probably snowed all night? It was close to eight miles of this travel and worse before they were safely on the other side.

Jim hunched down in the saddle and ordered Pindalest behind him. The agent's horse was carrying an added weight, and Jim hoped the pony had the bottom he was sure to need.

The snow held on, steady and implacable, all through the morning, and as they climbed the snow got deeper. Caution told Jim to turn back, but he was stubborn now, and nothing in his life had seemed so important as getting through the pass.

At the end of four hours they were in the pass, and here it was bad. The snow was almost belly-deep to their horses. The only luck they had lay in the fact that the wind was at their backs.

Jim reined up and turned in the saddle, waiting for Pindalest to catch up with him. They had been taking turns breaking trail, but Jim saw that even that wouldn't save their horses.

Pindalest's lips were almost blue when he came up to Jim, and there was fright in his eyes.

"We'll have to take turns breakin' trail on foot," Jim said. "It's too much for the horses."

"I think we ought to turn back," Pindalest said, shaking his head. "I really do, Garry. We can't hope to make it."

Jim smothered a sharp reply and drawled easily, "Whatever you say. It's your money we're losin'."

Pindalest was tormented by the choice, and he asked piteously, "But can we make it, Jim?"

"We'll bull it through, but it'll be work." He paused and then added, "Every minute we sit here chewin' leather the snow gets deeper."

Pindalest was silent for several agonizing seconds while he chose.

"Then let's get on," he said finally.

Jim dismounted and led his horse, glad of the exercise to warm his numb legs. An hour of it creeping at snail's pace, however, exhausted him, but he stuck to it until he could scarcely lift his legs.

Then he leaned against his horse and motioned Pindalest around him. The snow was coming on a long slant now, plastering white the rumps of the horses and blowing their tails between their legs. It held a sustained, steady howl that rode Jim's nerves like a file.

Pindalest pulled up on the other side of him, wanting to talk, but Jim waved him on. The agent was wholly in his hands now, and Jim pitied him.

He mounted and followed in the trail made by Pindalest and left by his horse. Jim knew it was agony for the agent with his short legs, his slack paunch and his indoor living. Pindalest wallowed ahead a few hundred yards and then stopped, dragging great guttering breaths of wind into his lungs, and then plunged on again. Jim was merciless. Pindalest's pace was slow, but it was eating up ground. When he turned around to Jim, pleading wordlessly to be allowed to ride awhile, Jim waved him on. When Pindalest fell Jim put his horse around him and went on, leaving him to pick himself up. It went on for hours like this, hours in which Jim wondered dismally if they would ever get through. Pindalest's help soon dwindled to nothing, a quarter of a mile and he lay face down in the snow, sobbing to get his breath. Jim kept doggedly at it, not even stopping to eat, because he knew he couldn't start the agent again.

And then in late afternoon the snow slacked off and Jim saw that it was less deep. His legs were wooden now, and each time he lifted them clear of the snow and put them down he was certain it was the last time he could.

It was then that he called on the strength of his horse, which he had been husbanding for a half day. He mounted, shaky with exhaustion, and let the horse break his own trail. And slowly the snow slackened and the depth of it lessened, until dark, when his horse could go no farther, the snow was knee-deep. The slope of land was to the east now, and Jim knew that they were on the other side of the pass.

He headed into a stand of pine among which was a lone lightning-shattered tree. He chose this stand because it meant wood for fire and because he had seen something else too. There was a windfall among the stand, a big pine whose needles were brown but still clung to the branches, even though it lay on the ground.

In the half-light Jim dismounted behind the windfall, putting it between himself and the wind. He off-saddled and rubbed his horse dry and then unrolled his bedroll and from it separated a blanket. He put this on his big bay and grained him and then went back to the edge of the timber.

Pindalest was sitting on the ground, his back against a tree, his head hung in exhaustion.

Jim said wearily, "There'll be stuff for a fire under the snow by that dead pine, Pindalest."

He didn't answer, and Jim took his horse and led it back to his own. He tended to the agent's horse, even to using part of Pindalest's bedroll for a horse blanket. When he was sure that their horses were taken care of and out of the wind he tramped back to Pindalest. The agent had a small fire lighted, but Jim could see he was so beaten he could scarcely move.

Both of them were too tired to eat. Pindalest tried, but he

gave up and wordlessly tumbled into his blankets. His face was gray with weariness as he mumbled good night to Jim and Jim almost smiled. Tomorrow would be time enough to break the news.

Jim was up first next morning, a day that dawned cloudy but without snow. He silently pulled on his boots and his coat and then rose and went over to look at Pindalest. The agent was still dead asleep. Jim went over to the tree against which Pindalest's war bag was leaning. He dumped the contents out on the ground, and there, where he had expected to find it, was Pindalest's gun. It was a small one, a belly gun. Jim threw it far out into the snow and then replaced the contents of the war bag.

He built a fire afterward and went over to look at the horses and grain them. They seemed little the worse for yesterday, and Jim was thankful. When he came back to the fire Pindalest was sitting up in his blankets, staring stupidly at the fire and the morning.

"Morning," Jim said.

Pindalest growled good morning and pulled on his boots. Jim heard his labored breath as he bent over and knew every muscle and bone in the agent's body was sore. Hearing it gave him a kind of shamefaced pleasure.

Jim served up breakfast, and the hot coffee seemed to thaw Pindalest out. Finished, there was that small lull after breakfast that a man likes to take before starting the day's work. Jim rolled his first cigarette of the day, and Pindalest lighted a cigar.

Some of the grouchiness was gone from the agent's wind-ruddied face.

Jim said idly, "Feel kind of stiff, don't you?"

Pindalest groaned. "When we get to Sun Dust tonight I'm going to sleep for a week."

Jim eyed him speculatively, and in his gray eyes was a sly humor. "That so?" he asked gently and then decided he might as well get it over with. "What if we don't reach Sun Dust though?"

"Nonsense. We'll travel till we do."

"A whole week, maybe?" Jim drawled.

Pindalest, finding a sly irony in the tone of Jim's voice, looked sharply at him. "What are you talking about, Garry?"

"I'm talkin' about you and Sun Dust," Jim murmured. "You won't see each other for a week at the outside."

Pindalest just stared at him. "Why not?"

"Because you and me have got a lot of country to travel—a lot of country. Some of it will likely be ahead of a posse too."

Pindalest continued to stare but with suspicion in his eyes. "Posse?"

Jim told him then. "You've been suckered, Pindalest. Riling never sent me over here. He never made a deal with Lufton either. I come to take you and hide you—also, to get a note from you to the army calling off the deadline."

Pindalest came to his knees now, alarm in his small eyes "You mean Lufton hasn't agreed to sell?"

"Not ever. Right now he's rounding up his stuff on the reservation with a big crew. He'll take his time and make sure about getting them across—because there won't be any army to bother him."

He could see Pindalest was figuring this swiftly, trying to get it straight in his mind.

"Then you're not one of Riling's men?"

"Was. I'm Lufton's now."

"Oh."

For a whole minute Pindalest was silent, staring at Jim, taking in this news. He was a man stunned. Several times he began to speak, and only his lower lip quivered. Then he lunged to his feet, the full impact of the thing understood now.

"You can't get away with that, Garry!" he shouted. "They'll jail you for life."

"You wrote the note and sent the messenger," Jim pointed out.

"But you've kidnaped me!" he cried. "I'm a government employee. They'll put you in jail for years for this!"

"If they know it," Jim murmured.

"Know it! I'll tell them; you can be damned sure!"

"I don't reckon you will," Jim murmured. "I'll show you why. By the time I let you go, Pindalest, Lufton's herd will be in Massacre Basin, scattered from hell to breakfast, and his range under guard. Riling isn't going to sell you Lufton's beef because he won't have it." He paused. "How you goin' to feed your Utes this winter?"

Pindalest didn't answer.

"At best, you can't get five hundred head from these Bench outfits, and when they know they've got you over a barrel they'll charge you eight kinds of prices."

Pindalest was listening now, listening hard. Jim went on implacably: "Winter's comin'; it's here. And you with no beef, and the season too late to drive any from the Nations. What do you figure to do when hungry Utes kick to Washington?"

The agent's lips moved slowly, but he did not speak.

Jim said bluntly, "You'll buy Lufton's herd for the price you contracted for; that's what you'll do. There won't be any business about short count and short weight. You'll take his beef and you'll pay contract price, and once that's done you can't squawk to anybody without givin' your own scheme away."

Pindalest suddenly found his voice. "How can Lufton move his herds into Massacre Basin if Riling won't let him? He hasn't so far."

Jim smiled because he admired the point. "Time," he said dryly. "Time and men. With enough time and enough men, he can cross his herds and scatter them because he won't be rushed by any deadline backed up by the army."

"Riling will be warned when the army doesn't show up!" Pindalest said angrily. "He's not a fool!"

"Let him. If Riling suspects what's happened he'll pull his men off to hunt you, and that'll make it all the easier for Lufton." He added dryly, "That's what I meant when I mentioned the posse."

Pindalest's slack face loosened with despair, and it seemed to fall apart. It was crushing news for a man who had thought his scheme had already worked, who almost had his money in the bank. He stared down at the fire and he was shivering. Soon now, Jim knew, Pindalest would discover his only chance lay in escape, and all his thoughts would be directed toward that one goal.

Jim came off his bedroll and flicked his cigarette into the fire. "Time to get goin'," he said.

He knelt by the fire and reached for the coffeepot and dumped the grounds on the fire. He heard but didn't see Pindalest move cautiously away from the fire and he smiled. He gave the man two minutes and then called without turning around, "I threw it out in the snow, Pindalest."

When he looked over his shoulder Pindalest was kneeling in the snow with his arm clear to the shoulder in his war bag. The expression on his face was one of utter and beaten dismay that was close to tears.

Carol learned in those three days exactly how stubborn a man can be. The night of the day Jim Garry left, Carol went out into the horse pasture with a rope and spent a futile hour trying to corner and rope a horse by herself. Even if she hadn't forgotten the tricks her father had taught her when she was young she couldn't have done it anyway, let alone in pitch-black night. She had the miserable conviction that everybody and everything, including the horses, were against her, all conspiring to prevent her from leaving this place to warn Tate of Jim's scheme. The horses circled easily out of rope's throw, evading her at one corner of the pasture after the other. She could see nothing; she made her casts blindly, futilely. When she was so tired she could have dropped she gave it up and came back to the corral.

And there, sitting on the top pole in the darkness, watching her and waiting for her, was Ted Elser. She heard him whistling softly to himself as she headed for the gate and she came over and identified him.

"That's dangerous," Ted said gently. "Spook 'em in the dark and they're liable to run you down."

"It's nice you're worried about me," Carol said with weary sarcasm.

Ted didn't reply. Carol didn't feel like fighting now. You couldn't fight with this man; he agreed blandly with you and then did what he wanted, and right now he wanted to keep Carol off a horse.

The night was chill and smelled of distant snows in the Three Braves. Carol wondered about Jim and then she asked the question she had been wanting to ask all day.

"Ted, how did Jim Garry know about me and—about Riling? Did you tell him?"

Elser said quietly, "No ma'am. I promised you I wouldn't, didn't I?"

"Then how did he know?"

"He worked for Riling; don't forget."

Carol shuddered a little with distaste. Ted Elser had put into words the thought that had been in Carol's mind this whole long day. If Jim Garry knew about her and Tate, then Tate had told him. The thought of that outraged Carol and made her feel soiled. But what if it were true that Tate would boast of his conquests to his hired gunman? If it were, then mightn't the preposterous story be true that Jim Garry had told and that her father, Amy and Willis had swallowed last night? Carol couldn't believe it, wouldn't believe that Tate would use these nesters as his army to impose a cheap blackmail on her father. Garry had fought with Riling, Amy had said. Then this lie was Garry's way of getting even with Tate for beating him. Only, was it? Garry knew about her and Tate, so mightn't he know Tate's true plans? Carol didn't know, but she had to find out.

If Ted would let her go she wasn't going to tell Tate about Jim Garry. From now on, since the death of Ferg Daniels, she had sworn that she would give no more information on Blockhouse's activities to Tate. She hadn't been to blame for Ferg Daniels' and Fred Barden's deaths, thanks to luck in not finding Tate home, but it had shown her that another time she might be to blame for other deaths. No, it wasn't to carry information that she wanted out of her prison; it was to see

Tate, to hear him deny this story of Garry's, to have him tell again that it was because he was too proud to take charity for himself and his wife that he was fighting her father.

And Ted Elser, even if she told him, wouldn't believe her, she knew.

"Ted," Carol said quietly in the dark, "I think I'll tell Dad you're keeping me here against my wishes."

"All right."

Carol looked up at him, surprised. "He'll fire you."

"Not before I speak my piece, he won't."

"He won't believe you."

Ted considered that and then said quietly, "I'll take my chance. He'll get to thinkin' and Miss Amy will get to thinkin', and then they'll find out I'm right."

That was true, Carol thought wearily. But she couldn't give up so easily. She said, "Ted, if I give you my word of honor that I won't mention Jim Garry to Tate Riling will you let me ride over to see him?"

"No." Ted's answer was flat and immediate.

"You don't trust my word of honor?"

Ted cleared his throat and then said without any censure in his voice, "No ma'am. That's a word you don't rightly understand. If you did you'd be loyal to your dad, not to the man that's trying to ruin him."

Carol thought then that Ted Elser could see her shame, even in the darkness. His words cut deeply, and their truth wasn't open to question. She left him then without saying good night and walked through the dark corral and up to the house, where she went to bed.

But her talk with Ted settled nothing. It even made her desire to see Tate more urgent. Next day she schemed anew. If she could get to town on a legitimate errand with Amy, then she might be able to shake Ted. But Amy didn't want to go to town, and Carol had to give up the idea. After dark her father and Cap Willis returned with the new men, and there was planning and discussion about the drive. Already most of the Blockhouse crew was on the reservation roundup. The new men would give them a great numerical preponderance over Riling's men, enough to handle any trouble that would come. In all their thoughts, and frequently voiced that evening, was speculation on Jim Garry's luck. They wouldn't know until on the day of the deadline whether they would or wouldn't meet the cavalry from Fort Liggett.

Lufton and his additional men left before daylight. A long gray day faced Carol, and by midmorning she was wild with impatience. Ted Elser was puttering around in the blacksmith shop, his eye forever on the corral. This was the last day, the third day, and tomorrow she could ride out. She wondered bitterly if she could live through it.

In midmorning a stranger rode into the yard. Carol and Amy, who left her bread baking to come out, asked him to dismount while Ted hovered at the corner of the veranda, watching. The stranger demurred politely. He looked like a city man, prosperous and a little ill at ease on his livery horse.

"Is your father in, ladies?" he asked.

"He left this morning for the reservation," Amy said.

The man's face showed dismay. "Can I catch him?"

"I wouldn't know where to tell you to look for him," Amy said. "If you're a fast tracker you might catch him."

The stranger sighed. "I have information that he's looking for à buyer for a large herd of cattle," the stranger said. "I've got to find him, and that's all there is to it."

Amy said dryly, "I think I can save you some trouble."

The stranger was attentive, and Amy went on, "He's not selling a single head of beef. You've been misinformed."

The stranger looked politely skeptical. "My information leads me to think otherwise."

"Then it leads you on a wild-goose chase," Amy said. "Where did you get the information?"

"It's—around Sun Dust."

Amy smiled and gestured with a flour-whitened hand toward the Three Braves. "Dad's out there. Find him and ask him."

The man thanked them and pulled his horse around and rode

out. He was a whisky drummer that Riling, in his desperation, had paid to serve as his dummy buyer.

Amy looked after the man and then laughed and looked at Carol. "If Jim's story needed any more proof, there it is."

"How do you mean?" Carol asked cautiously.

"There's Riling's man. He tried to buy from Dad last night and now he's sending out men to buy for him."

"Nonsense," Carol said sharply.

Amy looked at her queerly and said, "I'm going in. I'm cold."

She and Carol both went in. Amy returned to her bread baking, and Carol nervously paced the kitchen. Amy watched her covertly and presently, since she was a frank person, said, "Is there anything wrong, Red?"

Carol stopped, caution coming into her face. "What do you mean by that?"

"Nothing. Only you've been like a caged lion for days now."

Anger flashed in Carol's eyes now, and she spoke quickly. "Maybe I have. It seems we're staking our whole fortunes and upsetting our lives just because Jim Garry sold us a wild, lying scheme."

Amy was dumbfounded. She stared open mouthed at Carol. "Lying? You don't believe what Jim told us?"

"So it's Jim now," Carol gibed angrily.

"Garry, then. Don't you?"

"No. Why should I?" She stared angrily at Amy, and the sight of her sister's surprise seemed to burst the dam of her anger and impatience.

"He's a cheap gunman," Carol said angrily. "A killer. He tried to kill you. You saw him with that nester crew. And now he comes back here with a trumped-up story that hasn't a word of truth in it. How do you know these nesters didn't send him? Even if they didn't, why should we believe him? What's he ever done to make us think he ever told the truth to anyone?"

"That's not so!" Amy cried. "That man that was just here proves Jim's story!"

"Jim again," Carol taunted.

"Yes, Jim! What's the matter with calling him Jim? He saved Dad's life! He's no more of a gunman than I am!"

Carol paused in her anger. "Why, baby!" she exclaimed softly. She came across the room to Amy, who was watching her defiantly. The tan on Amy's cheeks was deepening now, but her gaze didn't falter.

"What's this?" Carol asked gently.

"You haven't any right to say that about him!" Amy blazed. "He's trying to help us, and I'll stick up for him to you or Dad or anyone!"

"This sounds a little stronger than sticking up for him."

"Maybe it is," Amy said challengingly.

The two sisters regarded each other for long seconds, and into Carol's green eyes crept a dismay that she couldn't hide. "Amy," she said, "tell me the truth. Are you in love with Jim Garry?"

"I—I think I am," Amy answered in a low voice.

Carol was speechless. Her protest, when it came, wasn't angry. There was kindness and concern and reasonableness in her tone. "But a gunman, baby! A saddle tramp. A man that would shoot at you, that will go up against hired killers because he's better than they are. How did he get that expert? Have you thought about that?"

"Longer than you think," Amy said, and she was serene again. "I know what he was and I don't care. What counts is what he is now. Nobody made him come back and help us—"

"Except wanting to get even with Riling."

"It wasn't that either. You don't understand him. He's really decent. Dad sees it. He—"

"Does he love you?" Carol asked.

"No."

A sudden bitterness crept into Carol's eyes. "I pity you, baby. You don't know men, and if you love Jim Garry you never will. You'll know how many pieces your heart can be broken into though. You're a fool."

"A happy one, anyway," Amy said dryly.

Carol turned and left the room.

* * *

Next morning Carol had breakfasted and was out at the corral by sunup. Inside the corral was her horse, saddled and ready to ride. Ted loafed in the barn door, smoking. His hands were blue with cold. When he greeted Carol his face was expressionless, though Carol knew that Ted, despising what she was going to do, had got up early to bring in her horse.

His impassiveness that seemed to her to border on smugness made her want to hurt him.

She looked around the corral, switching her quirt against the legs of her levis, and then turned to him. "Where's your horse?"

"I turned him out."

"Then I'm allowed to ride this morning all by myself?" she asked, not troubling to smother the sarcasm.

Ted shrugged and flipped his cigarette away. "Why not? You can't do any harm now, I reckon. Besides, you'll be safe enough with him." He stepped back into the barn before Carol could answer.

When she was out of sight of the Blockhouse she put her horse into a long lope. It was cold this morning, with the definite promise of the snow that had been hanging off these last few days.

Twenty minutes later Carol dismounted at the limestone outcrop where Tate and she always left their exchange of notes. There was one there, scribbled on the margin of a piece of newspaper and unsigned.

For the third time, I've got to see you. Where have you been? I'll be at home till noon and in town tonight.

Carol pocketed the note and set out across country for Riling's place. An hour or so later she was on the switchbacks that let down into Riling's canyon, and it had begun to snow big flakes that fell gently and slowly and melted immediately.

Nobody was home at Riling's, but Carol went in. The stove

was still warm and she stoked it. The single cabin was in disorder and the breakfast dishes on the table.

She took off her coat and started to clean up, and midway through it she heard a horse outside. She ran to the back door in time to see Riling hazing a pair of horses into the corral. He waved to her and dismounted, shut the gate, put his horse in the sod-roofed shed next to the corral and hurried to the house.

He took Carol in his arms and kissed her hungrily, and Carol clung to him. It was all right now. All the doubts that had been in her mind were dissolved.

Afterward she leaned back in his arms and looked at him. "Tate, what's happened to you? You've got a scar on your face, and your eye is purple."

"Fight," Riling said laconically and grinned. "Where you been?"

"Fight with whom?" Carol persisted.

"A man," Tate evaded. He let her go now. "I've been looking for you for two days."

"I couldn't get out," Carol said simply. Tate pulled up a chair for her and then peeled off his coat and shook the melted snow off it. Carol watched him hungrily, noting his every movement, and she felt herself growing tense. She was going to ask him now, ask him everything, and hear him tell her the truth.

"I know who you fought with," Carol said. "It was Jim Garry."

Riling paused, holding his coat in both hands, and stared at her. "Who told you?"

"He's been at the ranch," Carol said. "Tate, I want to ask you something. Come over here." She stood up. Riling threw his coat on the bunk and came over to her, scowling.

Carol tried to make her voice light and gay and humorous now. "Garry had a story, and it went something like this. I want you to tell me if it's true. He said that you and Jacob Pindalest had cooked up this fight with Dad long ago. He said you were doing it, hoping to crowd Dad off the range so he'd sell his cattle cheap to you, and you could sell them back to Pindalest. Is that true?"

Riling's slow grin was a hard one. "So Garry told you that, did he?"

"Is it true?"

"What else did he tell you? This sounds good."

"That you wanted him to make the offer to Dad. Is it true?"

"Did he tell your father that?" Riling asked swiftly.

"Yes."

Riling's face was ugly now. He turned on his heel and walked to the door and stood in it, looking out at the slowly falling snow.

"Tate!" Carol said sharply, alarm in her voice.

Riling turned and looked at her.

"You haven't answered me. Is it true?"

"Of course," Riling said carelessly.

Carol was shocked, stunned. She put a hand on the table to steady herself and she saw Riling turn his head again, looking outside. Was he crazy? Carol ran over to him and grabbed his elbow and yanked him around.

"Tate, listen to me! Answer me! You mean that you didn't buy this place because you wanted it? You mean you've been swindling these nesters into thinking it's their rights you're fighting for?"

Riling smiled and took hold of Carol's arms. "Sweetheart, I want money for us. That was a way to get money, a lot of it, money your dad could spare."

Carol shook his hands away savagely, but when she spoke it was coolly. "And you did try to talk Dad into selling there in town the other night?"

Riling nodded.

"And sent a man out yesterday to see him?"

Riling nodded impatiently, his eyes almost unfriendly. "What do you care, honey? It was for us."

Carol's face was a dead white, and she looked at Riling with unblinking gravity. "Tate, look me in the eye. Do you love me? Have you ever loved me?"

Riling did as he was bid and looked at her and then he laughed softly. "What do you want me to say? Of course."

"You lie! You're a liar!"

Riling's smile faded, and Carol spoke wildly, heedlessly, bitterly. "You've used me to beat Dad! You've used me just like you've used these nesters! I've lied for you and betrayed Dad for you, and that's all you ever wanted! It's all you ever counted on, isn't it?"

Riling put his shoulder against the door and regarded her thoughtfully. "I wouldn't say that," he murmured.

"Will you marry me now? Will you go in town with me this minute and marry me, like you promised?"

Riling was silent a moment and then shook his head. "Not until I can support you."

Carol laughed then, laughed wildly. She was still laughing when she went over to her coat and put it on. She picked up her gloves and her quirt and her hat and came over to him again. He was standing by the door, watching her with a puzzled look on his face.

"What's funny?" he asked.

Carol smothered her laughter and said, "I was thinking of something I told Amy this morning about men."

Riling only scowled, watching her. Carol took a deep breath and got control of herself. She kept looking at him, and as she did he could see a passionate hatred in her eyes.

"I'd like to leave something with you besides memories," Carol said gently. She raised her quirt and lashed him across the face with it.

His reaction was instinctive, immediate. He slapped her across the face hard with the palm of his hand. Carol staggered back against the wall, righted herself and calmly walked across the room and out the front door, her back ramrod straight.

She swung into the saddle and didn't even look back or down as she climbed the switchbacks. But once she was out of sight she couldn't pretend any longer.

She dismounted and sat on a rock and cried. The slow snow

fell silently around her as she sobbed, her face buried in her hands.

She didn't know how long it was before she was aware that there was someone with her.

She looked up and saw Ted Elser, his face sober and troubled, standing in front of her. He was holding out a freshly laundered neckerchief.

"Maybe you could use this," he said gently.

11

When Riling rode into Big Nels's line camp that afternoon he was wet and cold and as close to being scared as he could get. The thing he feared was Jim Garry, and not the man alone but also the things he could do. What were they? All during that ride he had cast about for a clue to Jim's actions. They were concerned someway with Lufton's refusal to sell his herd. Where was Jim and what was he doing? He simply didn't know and couldn't guess.

Big Nels's camp lay between the Chimney Breaks and the Massacre and was nothing but a cabin measuring scarcely eight by ten, with a brush lean-to for horse shelter, set alone on the clay flats that were now greasy mud.

The snow had held on all through the day, melting as soon as it fell. To Riling it held the reminder that the end of his gamble was approaching, and not the way he planned it. When he rode into the yard nobody greeted him, although there was smoke coming from the chimney. This was one camp for his men who were patrolling the Massacre these last three days until the deadline was here.

Riling rode around to the lean-to, reined up and sat there in the snow, regarding the lone horse under the brush. It was Milo

Sweet's roan. Riling grimaced at sight of it. The prospect of spending the remaining hours of this day in a tiny cabin with only Sweet for company wasn't inviting. But he was wet and cold, and there was a stove inside.

He dismounted, put up his horse and tramped across the greasy clay toward the cabin. He'd had to be careful with Sweet since Shotten got in that trouble at Avery's. That near mutiny ended by putting the men out on patrol, giving them something to do, but Sweet was the least tractable of them all.

Riling had to stoop for the low door of the sod-roofed shack, and when he stepped inside he could see nothing for a moment. Then his eyes accustomed themselves to the gloom, and he saw Sweet lying on the lower of the double tier of bunks that extended across the rear of the shack. Sweet hadn't shaved yet; he lay there with his fingers laced behind his head, and when Riling entered he didn't move, only observed, "Wet, ain't it?"

Riling said it was and peeled off his coat and hung it on a nail to dry. The rusty stove gave out a welcome warmth, and Riling held his hands above it and looked around the shack. It was about as plain and small as a line shack could be and still have any value. It was dirt-floored, and a couple of boards shoved into the cracks between the logs formed the table. The lone chair was a section of cottonwood stump that did double duty as a chopping block. A rusty ax was sunk in it now, and Riling pulled it out and leaned it against the wall and sat down. The door had to remain open since the place was windowless. A stack of wood took up most of the front corner.

Riling unbuckled his wet chaps and hung them and his gun belt by his coat and then sat back to roll a smoke. Sweet was watching him, he knew, but Riling was in no mood for talk. When he'd finished his cigarette there was nothing to do except sit on his stump and warm himself or sleep.

He went to the bunk and swung into the top one and lay down on the hay. Near the roof it was warm and comfortable, and he found himself doing as Sweet had done, lacing his fingers behind his head and staring absently at the ceiling.

His thoughts returned to what had been bothering him all

day. It wasn't Carol; he had forgotten her utterly and completely as he had forgotten other pretty women whom he had used and discarded. It was Lufton that was bothering him. Was the man crazy, that he'd take a total loss on his herds rather than sell them for what he could get? It was the first time Riling had ever heard that money can have morals, and he didn't believe it.

His musing was interrupted by Sweet's voice from the lower bunk. "I hear Manker deputized Shotten."

"That's right."

Sweet was silent a moment. "I told him I'd cut down on him if I saw him in this country again. I'll do it too."

"He ain't in your hair in Sun Dust, is he?"

"No."

"Then let it ride. We may need him," Riling said lazily. Purposely he kept any argument out of his voice and was relieved when Sweet subsided.

Riling returned to his thoughts. Jim Garry, damn him, had spilled the scheme to Lufton, and now Lufton was merely being stubborn. How long would he hold out? And Jim Garry was back. Riling didn't deceive himself; this was the worst of bad news. He had no illusions about Garry. He knew Garry could hate like an Indian and, once aroused from his indifference into anger, could be as wild as hell. And he'd be mad now, Riling knew. The course his anger would take was another thing that troubled Riling, but not so much as Lufton's stubbornness. What was Jim doing? That question ran like a refrain through his mind.

Again Sweet's voice broke into his reverie. "What's Lufton doin', Riling?"

"Rounding up the stuff we stampeded, ain't he?" Riling said patiently.

"Yeah, but why? He won't have it rounded up in time to drive across ahead of the army."

"That ain't our worry," Riling said indifferently. It was though, and he knew it.

"No," Sweet agreed doubtfully, but he said no more.

A stick of wood cracked in the stove, and a fitful gust of wind blew down the chimney and sent a puff of smoke out around the ill-fitting stove lid. Riling heard Sweet yawn and he hoped he was going to sleep. Riling's leg was going to sleep, and he shifted it carefully so that the rustle of the hay wouldn't disturb Sweet. He had it settled comfortably and all was silent when Sweet spoke again.

"Where's Riordan?"

Riling had been waiting for somebody to ask that question, and now it was here. These nesters hadn't paid any attention to Riordan while he was alive except to ignore him; now that he was dead their curiosity wouldn't give him oblivion.

"Dead," Riling said.

He heard the hay move, and then Sweet's head and shoulders appeared above the edge of the bunk. "Who done it?"

"Garry. Cornered him in the saloon in Commissary."

Sweet pondered this, his searching eyes on Riling's face. "Good," Sweet said and added, "That's how come you got marked up, too, ain't it?"

"Is it?"

Sweet grinned faintly and turned and walked over to the stove. He shoved in a chunk of wood and then stood in the doorway, peering out at the slowly falling snow. Presently he put his shoulder against the doorjamb.

"Yes sir, Garry is one smart gunman," he observed idly, dryly. "He knew where to hit for."

Riling was listening hard, and Sweet went on, "He knew damn well the law couldn't touch him on the reservation."

"So that's where he is," Riling thought grimly; "helping Lufton round up his stuff."

Sweet looked out at the snow and laughed softly. "So now it makes sense."

"What does?"

Sweet looked at him, grinning. "Mitch Moten come in yesterday with the news. He'd got it from an old Ute buck on Sulphur Creek that had seen them." He paused. "I guess Garry didn't even want to leave anybody at the agency for the Bench

County sheriff to complain to. He just took the Ute agent huntin' with him."

Riling lay utterly motionless for three seconds and then he came up on his elbow.

"What did you say?"

"A fact. Garry's rammin' around this slope of the Three Braves with Pindalest."

"You're a liar!" Riling said flatly. He vaulted out of the bunk, took the four steps to Sweet, bunched Sweet's vest in his big fist and almost hauled him off his feet.

"Damn you, you lie!" he raged. "Who put you up to that?"

For some seconds Sweet was more surprised than angry, but then his temper that was never far from the surface flared. He batted Riling's hand away with a vicious sweep of his hand and then lashed out at Riling with his fist. His blow landed on Riling's broken nose.

Riling felt an agony of pain that washed a savage rage through him. He struck out blindly at Sweet with a blow that caught Sweet in the chest and sent him backward over the stove. Sweet landed on his back with a breath-jarring impact. And then, wild with anger in his face, he groped for his gun.

Riling saw him move and remembered in a flash that his own gun belt was on the nail above Sweet's head. He grabbed the first thing he could reach, which was the ax. He swung it up with one hand and stepped to the stove. He saw Sweet's gun clearing leather and then he swung blindly with the ax, using both hands, bringing it down with a lashing sweep that caught Sweet full in the chest.

The force of his swing carried him onto the stove and over it, so that he fell across Sweet's leg.

He clawed wildly away from the man on the floor until he was brought up against the far wall. Then he looked. The head of the ax was entirely buried in the dead center of Sweet's chest, the helve angling up toward the door.

Riling huddled there against the wall a moment, holding his face, not because of the sight of Sweet lying there but because of the pain in his nose, which was a throbbing, fiery torture.

Presently, minutes later, it died away and his nose stoppe
bleeding.

He got shakily to his feet and looked down at Sweet, an
then the slow realization of what he had done came to him. H
went over and looked closely at Sweet and saw he was dea
The sight wasn't pleasant, and he stepped to the door. He'
been a fool, he thought meagerly; he'd let his temper get awa
with him. And now Sweet, the man these nesters looked to a
one of themselves, was dead at his hand.

Riling listened carefully for anyone coming and then got
grip on himself. This was bad but it wasn't irremediable. Wha
was worse was that Jim Garry and Pindalest were together. Fo
the first time Riling considered this fact without panic an
without anger. Could Pindalest be double-crossing him? Th
only way he could do it would be to supply Jim with the mone
to buy Lufton's herd. And then he knew Pindalest wouldn't d
it; the agent had already given Riling enough money to buy th
herd to insure loyalty. The only reasonable explanation of Jim
presence with Pindalest was that Jim was blackmailing th
agent in return for silence. That was the most that could b
between them.

When Riling arrived at this conclusion he had a moment o
deep self-contempt. He'd lost his temper and he'd killed Swee
over something that had no importance at all. His rule wa
never to act before he'd thought, but he'd forgotten it this tim
Sweet's blow on his broken nose had destroyed all reason, an
he'd acted with the abandoned rage of a hurt animal.

He brought out his tobacco and rolled and lighted his ciga
rette, considering what to do about Sweet. He could clai
Sweet tried to kill him and probably make his story stick wit
Les Manker. The circumstances of the death were all in h
favor. But even if he made it stick the mere fact that Sweet wa
killed would lose him these nesters that he needed now. The
loyalty right now was a pretty thin thing, and it would nee
only this to destroy it. On the other hand, he needed the
loyalty and help for only two or three more days, until Lufto

could be made to see his foolishness and sell out. After that they could go to hell.

He knew what he was going to do then. It was easy to hide a dead man for a week or a month. He could tell his men that Sweet was fretting about the appearance of the army and had decided to ride over to Fort Liggett to make sure there was no slip. That would cover the three days he needed. After that he wouldn't be here to answer their questions or their doubts.

He could see nothing wrong with that scheme. Turning, he went back into the room for his coat. He stepped over Sweet, not looking at him, put on his coat and chaps and gun belt and went out.

On the way to the brush lean-to he noted the tracks he had made coming in. The snow was like a slow rain, blurring every mark on the ground. He was safe.

Saddling his own and Sweet's horse, he brought them around to the door of the shack. From Sweet's bedroll on the bunk he took out the ground sheet and then considered his next move with distaste. It was all right to say that when a man was dead he was like any other dead thing. It wasn't true. He spread the tarp out beside Sweet and then braced himself.

His face had a cold, shrinking brutality in it when he rolled Sweet onto the tarp. When he couldn't see his face it was better. He wrapped him tightly, lashed him with rope and then picked him up. Sweet's horse wouldn't take the burden at first, spooking away with a wild fright, but Riling finally calmed him.

During those few remaining hours of daylight Riling rode deep into the Chimney Breaks. They were the badlands of the upper Basin, a fantastic wind- and water-eroded series of deep canyons and gaunt ridges that were useless for grazing.

Before dark he found what he was looking for, a steep cut bank with a considerable overhang. On this particular one there was a cedar tree whose roots were exposed on the side of the bank.

Riling led Sweet's pony under the bank, put a gun to his ear and shot him. Afterward, not touching the burden that was lashed to the roan's saddle, he put his rope around the tree, took a dally on his saddle horn and touched spurs to his horse. The tree pulled out, starting a slide of dirt that moiled up in a great cloud of dust. When the dust had cleared away Riling surveyed his work.

There was nothing there but a gentle slope of freshly exposed clay. He pulled his horse around and rode placidly back to the shack.

That same night Jim Garry and Pindalest were camped north of the road, high in the stormy Three Braves. They were leaving tracks; it was still snowing, but Jim, like everyone else, wanted to have his look on the day of the deadline.

12

The first of November, the day of the deadline, found the Blockhouse roundup crew almost cleaned up. The light snow of the past three days had been a help to them. All that morning little bunches of cattle were shoved down to the big holding herd on the flats that was slowly moving south. They were within a few miles of Sand Creek, which was the end of their sweep. Cap Willis' crew had started at Sand Creek and worked south, so that within two days both herds would be made up and ready to move.

John Lufton found loafing intolerable this morning. He had a hunch, which he communicated to none of his crew, that Jim Garry had turned the trick. If the army was going to move in on them by the first it wouldn't wait until that very morning to arrive.

By the middle of the morning nothing had happened, although the crew was expecting it. Punchers hazing small bunches down to the big herd came clear down to swap talk with the boys riding herd. A fine snow was falling so that, ooking up against the foothills of the Braves, Lufton could see and recognize his crew, black against the new snow, as they worked in and out of the timber.

The wagon had gone ahead, leaving its lone track string-straight across the flats. Ahead of the big herd the ground was white; behind it was a sea of churned mud, a great black swath that reached north until it disappeared behind a low ridge.

Lufton was riding point with one of his riders, but this was too slow for him. He touched spurs to his horse and went ahead, determined to see just how much country they had left to clear before Sand Creek.

Several hundred yards ahead of the herd he looked down toward the distant river and saw two riders approaching. He reined up, his heart suddenly heavy. Could this be the army? He pointed his horse toward them and went on.

Approaching closer, he saw that his fears were groundless. It was Cap Willis approaching with a stranger.

Cap greeted Lufton with unaccustomed politeness and said, 'Gent to see you, Lufton. I thought I'd come with him." There was a throttled mirth in his voice.

"Thanks, Cap," Lufton said. He sized up the stranger as a city man who wasn't enjoying himself. The man's clothes were rumpled and muddy; he needed a shave, and his white shirt was days old and grimy. He was riding one of the livery horses branded Dollar, which was Settlemeir's brand. In the man's sallow face was an air of ruffled dignity and outrage.

"What can I do for you?" Lufton asked.

"Are *you* Lufton?" the stranger asked with some acerbity. "I've been introduced to ten John Luftons in the last three days. I'm a little suspicious, and with some reason."

Lufton nodded. "I'm the only John Lufton around here."

"I wish you'd tell your crew then," the stranger said sarcastically.

Lufton frowned, and Cap said innocently, "I think he run into Willis and the boys by mistake."

"I see," Lufton said, his face impassive. "Well, you found me. What's your business, Mr.—?"

"Cable, Matt Cable. I'm a cattle buyer, Mr. Lufton, and came to see you on business. Apparently none of your crew takes business seriously."

Lufton began to see the light now, but his face remained grave. "How's that?"

"I stated my business to one of your punchers south here and he took me to his boss. I was under the illusion he was Lufton. I argued price with him for two days, sleeping in wet blankets and eating garbage. At the end of two days I found he wasn't Lufton at all, but a man named Willis." The man's tone was indignant.

Lufton smiled faintly, but his mustache hid it. "He must have misunderstood you."

"I hardly think so," Cable objected angrily. "He introduced me to another man, and I went through the same thing, only to learn that he wasn't Lufton either."

"That's too bad," Lufton agreed. "But I'm Lufton, at last. What's your business, Mr. Cable?"

Cable took a deep breath and plunged in. "As I told you, I'm a cattle buyer, Mr. Lufton. I've been informed that you want to cut down your herds."

Lufton shook his head. "You've been misinformed."

Cable bit his lip in chagrin. He looked sharply at Lufton and then smiled. "Look here, Mr. Lufton. I know you need a bargaining point and I'll grant it. Only let's meet on common ground. Everyone knows you're being moved off the reservation today and that you have no range for your stock. Why can't we make a deal?"

Lufton folded his arms and leaned on the horn. "I'm being moved off the reservation, you say?"

"By the army, aren't you?"

"When?"

"Today was the deadline, I heard."

Lufton gestured loosely back toward the herd. "See any army, Mr. Cable?"

"No, but they'll be here."

"So I'm rounding up my beef to hand over to them in one package?" Lufton asked dryly.

"What are you rounding them up for then?" Cable asked.

"To drive across the river to my own range."

"But you haven't any range, I understood," Cable objected.

Lufton said gravely, "Then why am I rounding them up?"

Cap Willis turned his face away, shaking with silent laughter. Cable merely stared at Lufton as if he doubted his own sanity. "Mr. Lufton," he said finally, "I have to get this straight. Are you being moved off the reservation by the army?"

"No."

"Have you got range of your own?"

"Yes."

"And you don't want to sell any of your cattle?"

"No."

Cable looked blankly at Lufton and said, "Then why am I here?"

"I was wondering."

Cable began to swear then, and it was too much for Cap. He burst out into shouts of laughter, doubled over in his saddle. Cable was furious, and when he saw Lufton laughing silently he was inarticulate with rage. He yanked his horse around and started back for the river. The horse was tired or else unimpressed by its spurless rider, for it ambled slowly across the flats. Cable was drumming its ribs with his heels, all to no avail.

Cap, watching him ride off, went into new gales of laughter. He tumbled out of the saddle and knelt, shouting with laughter, and Lufton, at long last, joined him.

After noon the nesters, singly or in pairs, began to drift into Big Nels's line shack. They came unbidden, and all for the same reason; from their different points of vantage they had seen that the army hadn't arrived. The wiser of them were inclined to gloom. If the army didn't arrive and seize Lufton's herds, then sooner or later Lufton would try to move his stuff across and there'd be a fight. The less farsighted of them were satisfied, claiming that once Lufton saw he wouldn't be kicked off the reservation he'd leave his cattle there instead of trying the drive into Massacre. If Sweet had been there they would have looked to him for advice, but he was gone and nobody knew where. Riling wasn't there either. There were six of them altogether, and they crowded into the shack and loafed around the door of it, trampling the light snow into greasy mud, waiting for Riling.

In the early afternoon he came, riding in from the south. He rode straight to the shack and dismounted, and his face had an ugly set to it that told the nesters how he felt about it. He swung down in the inch-deep snow and pulled the reins of his horse over its head. The nesters were quiet now, waiting for him to speak, and on some of their faces was a faint dislike.

"Anybody seen 'em?" he asked brusquely.

There was a general shaking of heads, and Riling looked grim. "Well, there'll be hell to pay for us then."

Mitch Moten put his shoulder against the wall of the shack and said, "I don't see it, Riling. If the army don't kick Lufton off he won't move."

"The hell he won't," Riling grunted. "He means business. Some of you don't understand that, it looks like."

"He's just after graze," Moten insisted.

"After his own graze," Riling said grimly. "He's seen he can't depend on an agent always takin' his beef or lettin' him use reservation graze. No sir, he's goin' to move into Massacre."

"Let's wait and see," Big Nels suggested.

Riling looked at him searchingly. "That might be sense except for one thing."

"What?"

"We won't have the army helpin' us next time he tries."

"Help us how?" Mitch said.

Riling pointed out, "This time if we can keep him from crossin' and get the army here he won't have any beef to drive, will he?"

They agreed on that, but Riling was reminded that the army wasn't here.

"Then get it here!" Riling said flatly, angrily.

He looked challengingly from one to another and he was raging inwardly. They were indifferent to him, almost, and it seemed that nothing could rouse them from their damned stupor.

"Listen," he said savagely. "Don't you see how we been tricked? Didn't any of you hear what Moten said the other day?"

"Sure. Garry's quit and is across the river," Big Nels said.

"With Pindalest," Riling added.

"What does that prove?" Moten asked.

"That Garry has forced Pindalest to call the army off long enough for Lufton to round up his stuff and cross it."

Big Nels pondered that and then said, "Sounds pretty wild."

"Then why isn't the army here?" Riling countered brusquely. "Tell me that. Can anybody tell me that? Only one thing could stop them, and that's a note from Pindalest telling them not to come."

That was the strongest he could make it, and it sounded weak. It even sounded weak to him, although he knew that it was true. Jim Garry had stopped the army some way, and the only way he could was through Pindalest, who had no more guts than a mouse. And as long as Jim kept the agent the army would remain at Fort Liggett.

The nesters looked at each other, not excited, dubious. Riling wanted to smash them. Here they were, the men he had to have to find Pindalest and keep Lufton back across the river, and they weren't even angry. The whole scheme was disintegrating before his eyes, and he couldn't stop it.

He moaned softly, and when he spoke it was a savage pleading. "Don't you see it? We've got to hold Lufton where he is and then get the army on him. We can't do it unless we find Pindalest, can we?"

"Where'll we look?" Big Nels said.

Riling smiled. "That's talk I like to hear. I'll find him. Mitch, you know the mountains. Come with me. I want one other man."

He looked them over, and it gave him a sick feeling. He'd started out with a dozen. Riordan was dead; Sweet was dead; Shotten was useless; Garry had deserted; Fred Barden was dead, and Anse Barden had high-tailed it. That left seven, counting himself, and he was taking two of them with him. Four men to hold Lufton—and not one of them mad enough to risk his neck.

He said, "Avery, I'm goin' to leave you to boss this here. Because if Lufton crosses he'll kick you and your whole family out into the snow." To Mitch and Big Nels he said, "Get your horses, you two."

The men broke for their horses, and Riling watched them dismally. Everything had gone wrong. Was it too late to save it? That depended, he knew bleakly, on his ability to get Pindalest and send word to the army before Lufton was ready to cross his herds. For he felt with absolute certainty that once Lufton knew the army was to seize his stuff he would sell. The only reason he hadn't sold already was Jim Garry. He saw Garry's hand in all this, saw how Garry had put his finger on the weak spot in Riling's plan. A slow, murdering wrath rose in him when he remembered that he had missed Jim Garry over at Commissary. The only way to save this was to find Pindalest, get word to the army, hold Lufton from crossing, and then, when Lufton saw he was about to lose, he'd sell.

But find Pindalest first of all. Riling had a hunch, which he kept to himself. When Moten and Big Nels joined him Riling put his horse out in a southeasterly direction.

"This ain't toward the Three Braves," Moten observed presently.

"It's toward Blockhouse," Riling said and explained. "Garry don't know the Three Braves. We do. He'll more likely hide right under our noses. That'll be at Blockhouse."

When Amy was finished with her work in the kitchen she turned down the lamp and started down the corridor to the living room. Outside Carol's door she paused and listened. Something was wrong with Carol, really wrong, Amy knew. A little after noon three days ago she had returned with Ted Elser and gone straight to her room, locking the door. Amy had caught only a glimpse of her, and Carol looked like death. She had remained in her room most of the time since and had refused to eat or to answer questions.

Amy saw the crack of light under the door and knew Carol was awake. She knocked, and Carol answered in a dull voice, "What is it?"

"Will you drink some tea, Red?" Amy asked through the door.

"No, thanks."

Amy was about to say more and then thought better of it. If Carol didn't want to tell her what was wrong she wouldn't ask. There was enough of her father in her for that. She went on into the parlor and lighted the lamp. It seemed big and empty, and Amy knew suddenly it was useless to try to do anything. She was worried about Carol and knew she wouldn't know any peace until she found out what was the matter.

She went back to the kitchen, slipped a coat on and stepped outside. There was a lamp lighted in the bunkhouse, and Amy headed for it. At the door she knocked, and presently it was opened by the Chinese cook. Beyond him, at the big table, Ted Elser and Tim Minder, the blacksmith, were playing checkers.

"May I come in?" Amy said.

Both Ted and the blacksmith came to their feet, and Amy said, "I'd like to talk to you, Ted."

The blacksmith and the cook retired through the door into the mess shack, and Amy sat down on the bench. Ted settled down beside her, his lean face impassive and his glance evasive.

Amy put it bluntly. "Ted, what's wrong with Carol?"

"Wrong?"

"Don't pretend, Ted. Anybody could see it when she came back the other day. What happened?"

"You better ask her," Ted said, not looking at her.

"Where were you?"

"Maybe she better tell you that too," Ted said, staring at the lamp in front of him.

"But I'm just trying to help her," Amy said, exasperation in her voice.

"Nobody can," Ted said gloomily. "Nobody—" He ceased talking. The lamp flame was guttering, the way it always did when the door was opened.

He looked over his shoulder, and Amy, watching him, looked too. There, standing in the doorway, was Tate Riling, a gun held loosely in his hand. There was a sudden commotion in the mess shack and voices, and then Tim Minder and the cook, their hands over their heads, came into the bunkhouse followed by Mitch Moten.

Big Nels Titterton stepped in behind Riling, nodded sheepishly to Amy and said to Elser, "Stand up. I'll take your gun."

Ted came to his feet slowly, and Amy did likewise. Nels took Ted's gun.

Amy said calmly, "Somehow, I didn't think you'd come to this, Nels. I knew Riling would want to when the army didn't show up, but I didn't think you'd let him."

Big Nels flushed clear to the roots of his hair. "We don't aim to hurt anybody or do anything, Miss Amy. We're lookin' for somebody."

"Jim Garry and Pindalest?"

"Then they're here?" Nels said.

"No."

Riling had a trace of a smile on his face as Amy answered. "You have the word of a lady," Riling sneered. "Myself. I'll look."

"Careful with your tongue!" Elser said sharply.

Riling raised his gun lazily. "My friend, unless you want to see this thing go off you'd better take your own advice."

"Keep quiet, Ted!" Amy said sharply. If Ted hadn't seen it she had: Riling meant business as he had never meant it before. Amy knew he'd calmly shoot down anybody who crossed him now in this mood.

"You're welcome to look for him," Amy said.

Riling bowed mockingly, but there was no humor in his eyes. He said to Big Nels, "Take the cook and look around the bunkhouse here. Mitch, take the old man and look around the barn and sheds. I'll take these two over to the house." He stepped aside and said, "I don't think I'll need a light, but I warn you, I'm nervous in the dark."

Amy ignored him and walked out, Ted behind her. The three of them tramped over to the house and into the kitchen in silence. Amy said, "Where do you want to begin?"

"Anywhere. You"—and he waved his gun at Elser—"keep ahead of her, and she'll carry the lamp."

They went through the storerooms and the lean-to and then Lufton's bedroom, the parlor, Amy's room and finally arrived at Carol's locked door.

Ted tried the door and then looked at Amy.

"That's my sister's room, and she's in it," Amy said to Riling.

"Get out of the way," Riling order. They backed a way down the corridor, and he lifted his foot and kicked the door. It opened with a crash, and Riling nodded his head toward it. "Get in there, both of you."

Carol came out of her chair when the door crashed open, and when Riling walked into the room she went dead white. She put out a hand to steady herself and clutched the top of her dressing gown.

"Such modesty from you, sweetheart," Riling gibed.

Carol tried to speak, and the words wouldn't come. Riling circled toward her, keeping his gun pointed in the direction of Amy and Ted. Carol backed away until she was against the wall.

"Afraid of me, darling?" Riling taunted. "You weren't the other day. You wanted me to marry you. Remember?"

He looked obliquely at Amy, who was staring blankly at Carol. Elser's face was taut, his eyes wild and dangerous.

Riling put out a hand and said mockingly, "Come to Papa, dear, and have a good cry."

"Keep your hands off her!" Ted Elser said. His voice was thick and choked with rage. Amy put a hand on his arm.

And then Riling laughed. "Why? That's where they belong. She use to like them once, didn't you, honey?"

Elser lunged for him then, but he didn't have a chance. He was the whole width of the room away, and before he had taken two steps Riling shot. To Amy it was as if Ted had run into some invisible barrier; he stopped, raised his arms, and then his knees folded and he fell on his face.

Carol screamed. Amy looked down at Ted with horror and then at Riling.

"Good-by, girls," he said placidly, a kind of amused malice in his tone. "I'll marry you both after I find Garry."

He kicked out the window that opened on to the veranda, stepped out and was gone.

Amy knelt by Ted and turned him over. He'd been shot high in the chest, and his wound was bleeding fast.

"Help me get him on the bed," Amy said.

Wordlessly Carol helped her. They lifted him onto the bed, and Amy looked at him. Then she looked at Carol, who was watching her.

"Now you know," Carol said bleakly. "Ted knew too. That's why he did it." Carol came over to her, and Amy folded her in her arms. Carol was fighting tears, trembling like a frightened colt.

"I *won't* cry," Carol said. "Oh, baby, I've done everything wrong—everything. Help me to make up for it! What can I do?"

"You can help the man who loves you," Amy said quietly. "Red, he's hurt badly. We've got to get a doctor."

And then for the first time in her life Carol forgot herself and thought of someone else. "What are we standing here for?" she said abruptly. "Let's get help."

13

The manhunt was on. Jim knew it the day after the deadline when, around dusk, he and Pindalest slipped down into a canyon they had camped in three days ago. Pindalest was riding ahead, sunk in a gloomy stupor which had lasted since the morning in the pass. Jim had kept him in the saddle long and punishing hours, so that at their evening camp the agent was so weary he could scarcely finish eating before rolling into his blankets.

He was weary now, Jim knew, for he had passed the ashes of their old camp and saw nothing there worth stopping for.

Jim did. He slipped out of the saddle and looked at the fresh tracks in the light snow. They'd been made today by four horses, three of them shod and one barefoot. They had come up the canyon, paused at the old fire and then slanted off to the north, following the tracks Jim and Pindalest had made three days ago.

When he rose he had read all he could. Three whites, with an Indian guide on the barefoot horse, were on his trail. That would likely be Riling, probably with Shotten and a man who knew the mountains.

Jim whistled sharply to Pindalest down canyon and then set about gathering wood. He left camp with perfect assurance, knowing that Pindalest would have no surprises for him on his return. Jim had spent long hours planning this and he knew his man. He'd made two concessions to Pindalest's guile: he had no gun of any kind with him and he slept close to the horses. The first precaution was only sense. If he'd brought a gun it meant that his sleep would be fitful and uneasy, with the threat always hanging over him that sooner or later the agent might steal the gun. The second precaution wasn't so necessary, but he took it just the same. Somehow, he couldn't picture Pindalest rousing in the night, stealthily saddling his horse and slipping out without waking the camp. And whenever it became necessary to use force Jim had concluded that his fists would do.

He came back and built the fire and started the meal. As always, Pindalest didn't help. Jim went about his business, whistling cheerfully, occasionally looking at the agent.

These last days had done something to Pindalest. With several days' growth of sandy beard stubble on his ruddy cheeks he had lost his air of dandified pomposity. His eyes were glassy with weariness, and Jim could almost pity the look in them. Exhaustion didn't account for it entirely, Jim knew; he was watching a drinking man suddenly deprived of liquor and he could imagine the hell Pindalest had lived through these last days. The man had lost weight; his pouting lips were drawn tightly across his teeth now. But more than anything else, he was hungry.

Jim regretted that part. His grub was in the high canyons. He could get to it, but it meant traveling the deep snow, and once he was cornered in the high reaches he was done for. The heavy snow had made the difference, forcing him down into the lower slopes where he might go hungry but where he had freedom of movement.

He dished out their thin rations, and Pindalest wolfed his down in silence, afterward lying down on his bedroll close to the fire.

Jim piled wood on the fire and sat close to it, staring into it. This week had gaunted him, too, but in a different way. His senses were sharper and his eyes brighter, and sometimes Pindalest, who would watch him at night with baleful eyes, thought he was part wolf.

Tonight Jim smoked placidly and took stock of his situation. It was good. Finding these tracks so early was a piece of luck. He wondered idly how the roundup was coming. He judged it was coming along fine, else Riling would have spared more men to hunt him.

Pindalest's voice, which Jim had not heard all day, suddenly broke the silence.

"Garry, I'm through," he said. He cleared his throat afterward, trying for his normal voice, and looked at Jim.

"That so?"

"I won't move out of here tomorrow."

Jim smiled and said nothing. Pindalest waited for him to say more, and when he didn't the agent pulled off his boots and rolled into his blankets. Jim finished his smoke, picked up his bedroll and moved up-canyon to where the horses were picketed. This was the first trouble he had had with Pindalest. He didn't think it would be serious.

Before he went to sleep that night he thought of Lufton and then, inevitably, of Amy. She had been right, dead right, that night he'd lined out for Texas. If he'd kept on he would have regretted it until his dying day. Somehow, what he was doing now was making up for a lot of the other. If he succeeded in this, if he made it stick until Lufton's herds were safely shoved off the reservation, he could face himself again. He wondered, before he slept, how Amy Lufton had known it would be like this.

Next morning after breakfast Jim brought the horses into camp. Pindalest watched him warily, challenge in his weak face. Jim saddled both horses and then went over to the fire where he rolled a smoke, picked up a coal and lighted his cigarette.

He squatted there on his haunches, worn Mackinaw unbuttoned, and shoved his hat back off his forehead. The fire was welcome in this bitter dawn, and he held his hands out over it and began to talk.

"We hit it lucky," he said. "I don't know if you noticed it last night, Pindalest, but there's three whites and a Ute on our old trail, starting from this camp."

He looked at the agent, who said nothing.

"We'll follow their tracks," Jim said placidly. "That ought to keep them off our trail for two more days before that Indian thinks of it."

Still Pindalest said nothing.

"Ready to go?"

"You know I'm not."

Jim smiled. "If I take your horse, the grub and the bedroll, then what?"

"I'll try and make it afoot to the Basin."

Jim said gently, "I'm givin' you your chance to change your mind. Will you?"

"No."

Jim rose and walked over to him. "Stand up," he said gently.

"No."

Jim reached down, bunched Pindalest's sheepskin in his fist and hauled him to his knees. The agent's arms flailed wildly, ineffectively. Jim clipped him across his receding chin. Pindalest went limp, and Jim gently rolled him off his blankets.

Then he rolled Pindalest's bedroll, lashed it to the saddle and cleaned up camp. By the time he was finished Pindalest had come to. He was standing up, weaving on his feet.

Jim came over to him and asked mildly, "Ready to go?"

"No, damn you!"

Jim hit him again, this time at the base of his ear, and Pindalest went down again. Jim hoisted him onto his saddle, tied his feet together under the horse's belly and started out, leading Pindalest's horse.

A half mile beyond camp Jim saw Pindalest rouse. He pulled his horse around and said, "The only trouble is, Pindalest, I can lick you, and you know it." He grinned disarmingly. "If you want to keep this up all day you'll get a damn sore jaw out of it, and that's all. Suit yourself."

"You win," Pindalest muttered. "Untie my feet. They're cold."

That was Pindalest's first revolt, and he was quiet that day. Jim clung steadily to the trail of the four riders, not pushing fast because his old trail was obscure and the Ute would need time to read it. That night he figured that he had played this out as long as he dared. Tomorrow, still following his old trail, Riling and the others would swing up the slopes, and when the

Indian saw the trail swing back south again he would be too smart to follow it. He would understand then that all Jim's old tracks in the light snow had been made to throw him off. The four of them would split up then and do what they should have done at first: strike downslope until they came across fresher tracks. Inevitably they would come across the tracks Jim had made today.

Lying in his blankets that night, Jim was satisfied. By the time they found his fresh sign they would have lost two precious days. He thought he had a way to make them lose two more.

Next morning he and Pindalest rose before daylight and traveled hard, heading north and downslope, careless of the trail they left. Around midday he moved into the country where Cap Willis was rounding up the south herd. During that afternoon he clung faithfully in the tracks of the punchers who were rounding up the beef.

When he came to a stream he waited for Pindalest. The agent came up, face sullen and dispirited.

"See what I'm trying to do?" Jim asked.

Pindalest nodded. "Then get ahead of me and you try to do it," Jim said. "I'll be watching you. For a start we'll drop downstream until we pick up fresh tracks. Line out."

They spent hours at it, Jim watching the agent to see that he followed closely the tracks, any tracks, that Willis' crew had made. And during those hours they wove a maze of tracks that crossed and recrossed, always clinging to the trail already made by the puncher before them. Toward dark Jim dropped back to the creek and ordered Pindalest to head up it. They traveled five hours of darkness then, never leaving the stream, and when the horses began to tire Jim called a halt in a thick stand of spruce.

Both of them were so saddle weary that night that they didn't eat, tumbling into their blankets without even bothering with a fire.

That night it snowed. When Jim woke next morning and

shook the two inches of snow off his blanket and looked around
he almost laughed aloud at his luck.

They spent two days in this camp, not stirring from it, never
building a fire except when darkness came. On the third day
they heard a gunshot downslope and to the south, and Jim
pondered it a long time. It came from above the roundup
ground, and Jim guessed it would be the Ute, summoning help
to unravel the riddle of tracks.

He made a quick decision then. "Saddle up," he said to
Pindalest. "We're hitting for our grub cache."

The agent was too dispirited to argue. He had made his stand
and it had failed, and now he reminded Jim of a sulky school-
boy, cowed and sullen.

That day they worked their way up into the higher slopes,
bucking a depth of snow that was hard on the horses. Jim's
main reason for returning to the cache was that both grub and
his grain had given out, and the snow made it difficult foraging
for the horses.

At dark they camped in one of the shallow red-rock canyons
in the high country, and it was bitter cold. Jim fixed the last of
their grub because tomorrow they would reach the cache. For
the first night in six he felt utterly safe, convinced that Riling
and his men were still down below.

He counted the days and was satisfied. Already Lufton
should have moved his herds across. Whatever trouble he had
had was past now, and Jim wondered if he had made it. As for
himself, if he could hang on three more days with Pindalest,
then he would have done all Lufton could ask and more.

Pindalest sat shivering by the fire, staring at it with bleak,
musing eyes. The dirty collar of his sheepskin was almost the
color of his beard stubble. The riding had done him good, had
worked the alcohol out of his system, the soft flesh from his
waist, the loose sag from his jowls. But Jim knew Pindalest
hated him with a deep and profound passion.

Jim said suddenly, "Three days more, Pindalest."

The agent raised his gaze to Jim's face, spat and looked back
at the fire.

Jim took his bedroll up the canyon a way where the horses were staked out and turned in under a ledge of rock that gave some shelter against the frost.

It was the uneasy nicker of a horse that wakened him. He raised up on an elbow and peered out into the night, senses alert. It was late, for the fire was dead, the camp silent with a winter stillness. He listened until he heard his own blood pounding in his ears and then he came silently out of his blankets, silently drew on his boots.

He rose, standing beside his blankets, back to the ledge. And at that moment a force drove into his back with a ton weight, driving him to his knees. A bare arm lashed around his throat from behind, and then the other arm drove down over his right shoulder across his chest. When it hit, Jim felt an agonizing pain under his ribs as a knife tore into his chest, seared along a rib and then buried itself in his flesh.

Through that pain Jim acted instinctively. He held the arm and hand with the knife tight to him, clamped across his chest, and humped his back. His head smashed into the ground, but he felt the man on his back sail over him, carried by the momentum of his jump. He clamped the arm with a furious grip, felt the arm straighten with the weight of the body pulling against it, and then the man screamed. The elbow bone snapped sickeningly, and Jim let go, not even hearing the body land on its back as the knife was dragged out of him by the clenching fist. Jim clung desperately to the arm, feeling the blood gush hotly out of his side. He clawed frantically at the knife in the nerveless hand, wrenched it free and struck out at the form on the ground before him. Twice he felt the knife sink in flesh and twice he raised it and plunged it in again.

Then he bent over across the still-struggling figure, holding his hand over his wound, listening to the shouting down canyon.

"Stone Bull! Sing out!" It was Riling's voice, calling the dead Ute beneath him, Jim knew.

For a still and dismal moment, bent almost double with pain, Jim knew cold and stark fear. And then the old dark lust of combat rose in him and he staggered to his feet, still holding his side.

Men were running toward him; he could hear them, could hear Pindalest screaming, "He's up there by the horses! The horses!"

Jim stumbled over to his horse and tried to vault astride him. He barely made it, pulling himself up by his pony's mane. Pain seared through his whole side. He reached down then and yanked out the picket pin by a savage wrench of the rope and drove his heels deep into his horse's flanks.

It was the smell of blood and the shouting that sent the horse stampeding off toward the mouth of the canyon.

Jim saw a dark figure before him and he kneed the horse over toward it. The man shot wildly just as the horse hit him, knocking him rolling under its hoofs.

Lying close along the neck of his horse, Jim rode over the dead campfire. He saw Pindalest flattened against the canyon wall, heard him scream, "There he is, Riling! There he is!"

Jim was dragging in the rope with the picket pin on the end of it as a horseman appeared out of the gloom, coming toward him. Jim kneed his horse toward the oncoming rider, and a shot slashed out into the night, so close that it blinded him. Savagely Jim swung the heavy picket pin at the man in the saddle, and he felt it hit. The man howled into the night, and Jim was past him. Over to the right someone opened up frantically with a six-gun. Now Jim was in the timber, his horse crashing through the brush in panic. Jim lay on his neck, giving him his head, gouging him in the flanks with his heels.

Minutes later, deep in the timber, Jim hauled up and listened. He could hear distant shouts and cursing, and off to his right a rider was beating the brush in frenzy.

Jim held his left hand tightly to his side and patted his horse's neck, speaking gently and soothingly. Then he put him on into the timber, and when he judged he was out of hearing he stopped again.

The pain had become something constant now, and Jim sat still, waiting to see if it would quiet. He knew that if it were light enough to see, his immediate world would be pinwheeling. Slowly he explored the wound with his fingers. There was a deep gash along his lowest rib, starting toward the center and flaring out and then diving deep into his side. A steady seep of blood ran out between his fingers, and he breathed lightly, easily, so that his chest wouldn't move, and still he felt the hot, leaden burning deep, deep inside him.

Could he sit his horse, and for how long? he wondered calmly. "I've got to ride and ride hard, and the chances are I won't make it because they'll be hunting me."

He hung his head there in the black night and let pain take him. All he could think of was Blockhouse. Slowly from the dark depths of pain he knew that he was going to try to make it. Try to make the flats and then the river and then Blockhouse, one at a time.

When, still astride his horse, he had fashioned a hackamore from his picket rope and tried to slip it on his horse and failed he set off into the night. At the first jarring step of his horse he clamped his jaw against vomiting.

But he rode.

14

Anse Barden knew if it were daylight he could recognize where he was, but not in the dark. He'd never been a man to do much riding off his own range or the range he'd worked on and he didn't know the Bench very well. But the Bench was where he was. He knew that because this morning he'd come off the Long Reach west of Commissary and was heading homeward in a ramrod-straight line.

When he thought of it now he didn't smile at his old foolishness. It wasn't foolish when he'd done it. At first the change had been like medicine, something new to look at, something to keep him from thinking. But there had been too many desert nights. A man shouldn't be that lonely. He'd never thought of it before, but given a week's solitude, a man can live his whole life over.

It was during that solitude crossing the Long Reach that Anse had made a discovery. It was that he'd had a pretty good life, that his mistakes weren't big ones and that he didn't hate anybody. About that time he got to wondering what he was doing out on the Long Reach and he wondered about it until he caught the first glimpse of Quartzite, a little mining town that broke out of the desert far to the south.

The sight of it made up Anse's mind for him. He didn't know the town and he found himself not wanting to know it. He was a stranger. Days ago that might have appealed to him, but he rejected it now. That was when he turned back, and the relief that he felt when he did it told him he was right. A place where a man has lived retains a part of him when he leaves, and if he's lived there long enough it keeps about all of him. It worked that way with Anse; out here he was nothing, but back there he was Anse Barden. He headed for home, where he'd lost a wife and a son.

Anse was roused from his musing with the awareness that his horse had stopped in the night. Anse cursed him gently and was about to put spurs to him when it occurred to him that this might be the rim and that the horse was considerably smarter than he was. He peered ahead and saw where the piebald patches of snow ended. He reined over then, knowing it was the rim, touched his spurs to his horse and rode on paralleling the rim.

Presently he noticed something ahead, a queer patch of the night sky which was lighter than the rest. As he rode on it grew brighter, and when he smelled smoke minutes later he was sure of it. It was below the rim.

When he finally came closer he could see that it was a big fire. The flames almost came up to the rim, but not quite. And then he rode up to the edge and looked down its almost sheer drop.

Four hundred feet below him was Avery's place, with the barn on fire. It lighted up the whole night so that everything was made plainer than by daylight.

The hay had caught in the barn, and the framework of rafters, a cherry red, were ready to fold on themselves. Anse saw that the corral gate was open and the stock out, and then he saw the women. There were two of them standing by the well house watching the blaze. That would be Mrs. Avery and the girl. Only the girl wasn't watching. She was bent over the sprawled shape of what looked to Anse like a dog.

Anse's immediate reaction was to put his horse in motion to go down. And then he reined up, bethinking himself. There was no trail down the rim here. There was one about six miles back, and the only other one was the dug road at Sun Dust.

At that, he reflected, they couldn't use his help much. It was done. He felt a slow wrath at his helplessness, and then it subsided. The rafters folded now, and a great gout of sparks funneled up into the night. The fire flared brighter now, and Anse watched the place. A movement off behind the brush back of the bunkhouse caught his eye. He could see something moving through the frost-stripped trees and he peered intently.

Presently it moved again. It was a horse and it vanished with its rider into the outer circle of darkness, but not before Anse saw that it had four white stockings. Avery, he knew, had no horse marked like that, and he filed it away in his memory.

Anse waited awhile longer until the fire died down and the women went back into the house. The dog, he noticed, lay there by the well house, and Anse guessed he was dead.

He couldn't help them, couldn't even shout his sympathy from this height, so he went on along the rim toward Sun Dust.

Anse came down the dug road in early morning and left his horse at Settlemeir's for a bait of corn. He got a morning's sleep at the hotel and spent the early afternoon buying a little grub and getting the conversation he was starved for. Afterward he got his ruff of iron-gray hair cut and bought a heavy sheepskin because winter was practically here.

At midafternoon he went back for his horse, a sack of flour over his shoulder. He dumped the sack on a stall partition and went back to the corral with Settlemeir.

There were a half-dozen horses in the big corral, and he looked them over as he stepped inside behind Settlemeir.

And then he stopped, staring. He was looking at a horse with four white stockings, its nose nuzzling impatiently at the board bottom of an empty feed box.

"Four white stockings," he murmured. "Who owns him, Jake?"

"Which?"

"White stockings over there."

"Him? Oh, that's Joe Shotten's gelding. He's the new deputy we got now since Riling's boys kicked him out."

Anse looked sharply at him and he found Settlemeir smiling faintly. "Deputy?" Anse muttered. "Lord God."

"How do you like that?" Settlemeir grunted and went on.

Anse was thoughtful on the ride home, his big hands resting on the sack of flour across his saddle. Things had happened here, but he wasn't going to ask what.

At the Blockhouse road, after dusk, he reined up, wondering if he should go in and visit as a token of his forgiveness. No, better find out what had happened here since he'd left.

He rode on home, arriving long after dark. As he came into the yard from the river he saw a horse standing in front of the open door of his shack.

Anse dismounted and called, "Hello, the house," feeling foolish because it was his own place.

There was no answer. He stepped inside the door, careful to scrape the snow and mud from his boots on the sill.

He called, "Anybody in?" from the door.

No answer. He started across the room, feeling in his pocket for a match, and suddenly stumbled over something on the floor. He caught the edge of the table, steadied himself and struck a match.

It was Jim Garry, lying face down on the floor. He had missed making the bed by only three feet.

Anse hauled him to the bed and then built up a roaring fire. Afterward he came back to the bed and looked gravely at Garry. The man looked half dead, his eyes sunken, cheeks stained with color at the cheekbones. His clothes were stiff with blood. Afterward he knelt and looked at Jim's wound, gently peeling away the torn strips of shirt that Jim had used to stanch the flow of blood.

When at last he saw, Anse made a wry face. A knife wound. At the end of a long raking cut that ran along the lower rib there was a neat purple slit in the skin, the lips of it tinged a blue color, the flesh around it angry looking and bruised.

Anse debated on his first move and then judged that he'd better clean the wound before trying to rouse him. With hot water and bandages he washed the wound clean, and Garry lay like a dead man under his ministrations.

Afterward Anse covered him up with blankets and then brought a bottle of whisky. Garry's teeth were clamped shut so tightly that Anse had to spoon the whisky between his lips and let it trickle down his throat. At the fifth spoonful Garry choked and started to cough, and then he groaned and opened pain-filled eyes, pulling his knees up to his chest in an effort to smother the cough that was racking his side.

When the spasm died he looked carefully at the ceiling, and then his gaze settled on Anse. His gray eyes were smoky with pain, and he stared at Anse with puzzled concentration.

Anse knew what he was thinking and said, "Yeah, it's me. You made it to my shack. How do you feel?"

Garry lifted his head and made an effort to rise. Sweat broke out on his forehead, and his head dropped back on the pillow, and he closed his eyes, his face suddenly dead white.

Anse said curtly, "Lie still. What happened to you? Can you talk?"

Jim, eyes closed, heard him and nodded. What *had* happened to him? He couldn't remember, except that he'd been hunted down the slope of the Three Braves for a day and a night while

Riling and Mitch Moten and Big Nels Titterton sought him. He knew they were the ones because at one time or another he'd been close enough to see them. He knew that some protective instinct had again driven him down to the roundup grounds where his tracks would be masked. After that he couldn't remember much, except that the last time he'd tried to mount his horse after passing out in the brush it had taken him an hour to do it. Why he'd ended up here he didn't know. Yes, he did too. When he'd hit the river that night he knew that he couldn't go much farther. He'd clung to the river for more than a mile, his last remembered effort to throw off Riling. The next thing he knew he'd roused, the mane of his horse in his teeth, to find his pony standing here in this dooryard. He'd fallen off and made it inside and then he passed out again.

He couldn't tell Barden all that; he didn't have the strength. He said, "A fight with Riling."

"Him again," Barden grunted. "You should have killed him at Commissary."

Jim shut his eyes again. The pain was with him now, throbbing with every beat of his heart, covering his whole side and beating his breath down to slow, calculated torture. He wanted to say one more thing while he could. "He'll come tomorrow," he whispered. "Watch out."

Barden almost smiled. Garry remembered Commissary, remembered that it was Barden who'd shot Riordan there in the saloon and that Riling wouldn't forgive that.

All right, he'd had his warning. What was he going to do now? He stood there by the bed, watching Garry's fever-cracked lips moving in a whisper that he couldn't hear. Garry needed help, needed more than Anse could give him, but Anse knew he couldn't leave him long enough to get help. But he had to. Outside of the fact that he owed it to any man, he wanted to help Garry. Maybe it was the beating Garry had handed Riling in the face of certain death from Riordan there at Commissary that made him like the man in spite of himself, but there it was.

Anse went over to the stove and put his back to it and pondered. It came to him slowly, and he turned it over in his mind and found nothing but good in it. Yes, he'd get Amy Lufton. Not Carol; she was too flighty. Blockhouse was closest, and Amy would help him, no matter if she hated Garry. There was something else besides his liking for Amy Lufton behind his decision too. If Riling showed up tomorrow as Garry had said he would Amy Lufton's presence would keep Riling from shooting the man in bed. As for the risk to himself if Riling appeared, Anse didn't think of that. He could take care of himself.

Garry had fallen into a light feverish sleep. Anse stoked the fire, put in a couple of green logs to hold it, then loosely tied a blanket around him, lashing him to the bed. It was the best he could do. He blew the light out and went out to his horse.

15

The hand on her shoulder roused Amy, and when she wakened she saw Carol standing beside her.

"Is he worse, Rod?"

"No. Ted's sleeping. Anse Barden is in the kitchen and he wants to speak to you."

Amy sat up, brushing the hair out of her eyes. "Anse? But I thought he'd left the Basin."

Amy slipped on a wrapper and her slippers and went down the corridor. She stopped to look into Carol's room, where Ted lay on the bed. He had been there, almost unmoving, since that nightmare visit of Riling's. For days now it had been doubtful if he would live. Dr. Hogan had come and done what he could and shrugged, leaving it up to Carol and Amy. And Carol, for the first time in her useless life, had taken over a burden. Ted was alive, and that was all, and Carol wanted desperately for him to live.

Anse was sitting at the kitchen table when Amy came out. He smiled a little and stood up, his hair seeming even grayer against the new burn of his skin from the desert sun.

"You're back, Anse," Amy said, shaking hands with him. "I knew you couldn't leave for good."

Anse nodded gravely, "I'm back to stay. And I need your help, Amy. Seems like I haven't any right to ask it, considerin' who it's for."

Amy said curiously, "Who is it for, Anse?"

"You remember that young fella you combed out over there at Ripple Ford? Well, he's hurt."

Amy went deadly pale. "Jim Garry?" she asked swiftly in a voice barely above a whisper.

"Yes, him. I come home tonight and found him on my floor. He got a knife stuck in him."

Amy moaned softly. "Anse, is it bad?"

"I dunno. That's why I come for help. I don't know what to do."

Amy turned and ran out of the kitchen. In her room she dressed swiftly, her hands shaking so that she could scarcely control them. Jim Garry was hurt. She stopped dressing and stared at the wall, a slow horror filling her mind. What if he died? What if— She yanked herself up then, afraid and sick, and afraid to be afraid. She fought her panic under control and finished dressing and went out and told Carol only that there was a wounded man at Anse's and that she was going to help.

Anse saddled her horse for her, and they rode off into the night. When Amy could control her voice she asked Anse about it, and he told her all he could. That was little: simply that he'd said he'd had a fight with Riling.

And then Amy talked because talking would keep her from thinking. She told Anse about Jim's return from Commissary and his disclosure of the real reason for Riling's fight with her father. After that it was easier to explain what Jim had done. They hadn't heard from or seen him in almost two weeks, but the army had not arrived. And that meant that Jim had succeeded in his plan with Pindalest. Yesterday the last Blockhouse herd had crossed and was even now being scattered to the far corners of the range her father had claimed. Jim Garry had done it.

Anse was silent as Amy finished. He was thinking with bitterness of that grave in the mountains, the grave he hadn't even seen. His son had been killed to further a swindle of Tate Riling's. There was cold murder in Anse's heart then, but it passed. He was no better man than his neighbors who had been likewise taken in. Only there was no grave up in the mountains for a son of theirs.

Anse turned his thoughts now to the other implications of Amy's news and saw immediately the way to guard Jim from Riling If he could get hold of Blockhouse before Riling arrived Jim was safe. But he mustn't tell Amy Jim was in danger yet. After she'd seen him there'd be plenty of time. More than ever now, he wanted to see Jim Garry safe; a man like that didn't deserve death.

It was breaking daylight when they rode into Anse's place. Anse went ahead into his shack and lighted the lamp, and Amy went straight to the bed.

Jim was awake, his face turned to the wall and bathed with sweat.

"Jim," Amy said softly.

Jim turned his head, and when he saw Amy his lips parted in protest. "You've got to get out of here," he muttered.

Amy's smile was sweet and tolerant as she shook her head. "Not ever, Jim." She put a cool hand on his forehead and felt his fever. "When did you eat last?" she asked in a calm voice. She was afraid to look at the wound, and this was her way of putting it off.

"I dunno."

"I'll get you something to eat." She steeled herself and said, "Jim, I'm going to change your bandages first."

The sight of his blood-stiff clothes warned her. But her first look at Jim's wound brought terror to her heart. And then she looked again and was encouraged. The cut was bad but more painful than serious. It was the knife stab that was dangerous.

But Amy saw it had missed the lung cavity and angled down into the tight knot of muscles below and into the side of his chest. Nor did the wound seem infected.

Amy rebandaged it and smiled at Jim. "It hurts, doesn't it?"

Jim grinned at that and shook his head, and Amy was suddenly happy. She fixed up some soup for Jim from Anse's groceries and fed him, and he wolfed the food down like a man famished, which he was. Afterward he fell into a deep and untroubled sleep.

Anse ate breakfast with Amy, and then he knew it was time to speak.

"You're goin' on a ride, young lady," Anse said.

Amy looked puzzled.

Anse pointed to Jim. "Riling's on his trail. That's why he told you to get out of here. Sometime today Riling'll be here."

Amy sat motionless, eyes wide.

"We got to get help, get Blockhouse over here. I didn't know until you told me that your dad was working with Garry. I didn't know he'd help him. Now if we can get them here he's safe. Where are they?"

"I—don't know," Amy said hollowly. "Oh, Anse, I don't! I haven't heard from Dad in days!"

"We got to find him. You got to."

"But Jim?"

"I'll stay here. If they come I can stand 'em off forever." He smiled encouragingly. "I got lots of shells, and these cottonwood logs are too heavy to burn. Let 'em come."

Amy protested. "But if I was to stay Riling wouldn't dare—" She ceased talking, looking at Anse.

"He damn well would dare," Anse said bluntly. "You know that, don't you?"

Amy was thinking of Ted Elser. Yes, she knew Riling wouldn't hesitate to shoot Jim. But she hated the thought of leaving him. She wanted to stay by, watching him every minute, helping him when she could and just be near him when she couldn't. But she knew Anse was right. He was worth more to Jim than she was if it came to a fight.

Amy rose and said, "You're right, Anse. I'll go."

"But where?"

"I don't know," Amy said. "Somewhere south. I can pick up he trail of the herd where it crossed and follow it."

Anse helped her into his new sheepskin coat, which was warmer than hers. When she looked at him she saw the rugged, ad and friendly face of a man she trusted.

She said gently, "Anse, take care of him, won't you?"

Anse nodded. "You'll be warm enough. Hurry now."

The morning was clear and cold, and it was tonic to Amy. It rightened her to think that Jim's life might be dependent on whether she could find the Blockhouse crew now. As she rode own through the cottonwoods, her horse rustling the dead eaves beneath the light snow, she tried frantically to think of where her father might be. She couldn't; she didn't know. One Blockhouse rider had drifted into the ranch four days ago for rub, and he'd told her only that they were crossing that day nd that it would be somewhere south.

She clung to the cottonwoods along the river because it was asier riding here, and as she rode she watched for any signs of he crossed herd. She knew how foolish it was to look carefully, or they would leave a swath of churned mud she could see in he dark.

But she looked carefully anyway for the greater part of the morning, riding along among the river cottonwoods. Perhaps it was because of her careful observation that she didn't see the ider until she was almost on him.

Then she looked up and saw Tate Riling ahead, his horse alted, watching her.

Amy reined up, startled, and then she got control of herself, nd her face showed nothing except distaste.

But Riling's appearance frightened her. The ghost of his lack eye was still there, a faded green now. His eyes were loodshot, slitted with weariness and red rimmed. There was lood on his face from the gash on the head Jim had given him wo days ago during the escape, when he swung the picket pin t him. But more than that, there was a mean and savage ugli-

ness about him that told Amy he already knew he'd lost h
gamble and was now only seeking revenge, seeking Jim. Am
was afraid.

"What're you doin' here?" Riling said bluntly.

"I might ask you, since this is Blockhouse range," Amy sai
calmly. "Or had you heard?"

Another rider came toward them through the trees now, an
Amy saw it was Pindalest, the agent. She was shocked by th
change in his appearance. He was thinner, with a kind of burr
ing anger in his face instead of his usual look of oafish pompo
ity. Both men were incredibly dirty, and they looked bor
weary.

"Isn't that Lufton's girl?" Pindalest asked harshly.

"Yeah," Riling answered slowly not ever looking
Pindalest. To Amy he said, "Lookin' for someone?"

Amy said smoothly, immediately, "Why, yes. Dad. Why?"

Riling didn't comment but he looked at her until Amy fe
the blood mounting in her cheeks. She pulled her horse to on
side to go around them, saying, "If you don't mind I'll ric
on."

Pindalest said, "Riling, you goin' to let her go and—"

"Shut up!"

Riling's voice was sharp, final, and still he didn't look at th
agent. He put his horse over next to Amy's and seized he
bridle.

"You're sure," he said slowly, "you're looking for your fa
ther?"

"I told you I was."

Riling said tonelessly, "We're looking for a man too."

Amy knew Riling wasn't satisfied with her answer and sh
also knew he was both suspicious and not the kind to quit unt
he found out the real reason why she was here. She decided
bluff it out, to stake everything on one bold stroke. "I know
Jim Garry, isn't it?"

Riling's jaw set subtly. "Now tell me how you knew."

"He rode into Blockhouse last night. He's in bed with a kni
wound. But he wasn't too sick to mention you."

Riling was watching her ceaselessly. He said, "And you're huntin' the crew?"

Amy smiled. "That was pretty crude, Riling, but I'll put your mind at rest. The crew is there, so there's no chance of paying us a visit."

A smile started on Riling's face, a smile that broadened and made Amy sick at heart. What had she said?

"You're a lovely little liar, my dear, but nevertheless, a liar. I saw the whole Blockhouse crew at work an hour after daylight."

Amy's face was still smiling as she nodded. "Part of them, I grant you. Do you want to ride back to Blockhouse and meet the rest?"

Riling was silent for ten whole seconds and then he said softly, "Why yes, I'd admire to."

Amy laughed shortly. "I can't guarantee you safe conduct over Blockhouse range, but if you want to chance it come along."

She pulled her horse around and started away from the river. Riling said sharply, "Oh no. Not that way. We'll back-track you."

He palmed up his six-gun and shot once into the air and then holstered it. The panic that was within Amy wouldn't go, but she knew she had to fight and do it quickly.

"I don't follow you there," Amy said, putting puzzlement in her voice.

Riling almost smiled again. "I keep remembering a pretty fair gun hand that turned soft in Sun Dust, all on account of a girl, I figured." He paused, watching her. "Maybe the girl liked that enough to help him out of a jam."

"I don't follow you there either."

"You don't have to," Riling said idly. He turned his head toward the river, and soon, from the shore willows, Mitch Moten and Big Nels Titterton and Chet Avery, whom they'd picked up that morning, approached. They touched their hats and Amy nodded.

Riling said, "I'll go ahead. You follow, Miss Lufton."

Despair plucked at Amy's heart. She'd lost her gamble. Her blunder had given them away.

There was nothing to do but fall in behind Riling. They rode Indian file for hours, Riling ahead, following her tracks back to Anse's shack. Each mile Amy felt the burden of blame heavier upon her.

Riling only spoke once during that ride, and his words sunk Amy into deeper gloom. "You kind of took a round-about way didn't you?"

At last in late afternoon they came to Anse Barden's.

Riling paused at the edge of the cottonwoods a hundred yards from the house and regarded it thoughtfully. Amy' tracks, coming away from the door, were plainly visible. Smoke, also, was coming out of the chimney.

He looked at Amy. "Barden home?"

Amy nodded. "He has been for days." She frowned. "Oh, begin to see now. If you'd asked me I would have told you stopped at Anse's."

"I don't think you would have," Riling said. "Chet, let's you and me make a circle and take a look in the corral. Nels, watch her."

They started toward the corral, keeping wide of the house.

And then the silence was broken by the flat, sharp report of a rifle in the shack. Riling's horse began to rear, pitching Riling from the saddle.

Amy knew it was no use pretending further. She sank her spurs into her horse and dashed for the house.

"Hey!" Nels yelled.

Avery was off his horse, helping Riling to his feet. When Riling saw Amy heading for the house he whipped up his six gun, and Amy distinctly heard him cock it. Avery was quick. He saw Riling's intention and clamped down on his arm just as the gun went off.

The slug kicked up a dusting of snow in front of Amy's horse and sang up into the log shack. Amy, leaning far over on her horse's neck, turned the rear corner of the shack, slid out of the saddle and ran for the door. It opened on her, and she stepped inside.

Jim, roused from sleep by the shot, was propped up on both elbows, staring at them.

Barden said from the window, "Lock that door, you hellion, and take this gun. This is it!"

16

The next few minutes with Anse at the front window and Amy at the rear, were bedlam. Riling's outfit scattered, surrounding the house, and it was up to both Anse and Amy to drive them back into the cottonwoods. Anse succeeded on his side and then came over and helped Amy flush Mitch Moten from the protection of the corral to the low bluff behind the house. From now till dark Riling must content himself with throwing shots at the shack from a distance that precluded accuracy.

Amy and Anse sank down against the wall, and Jim, still propped on his elbows, looked at them. "Riling?"

"And Pindalest, Moten and Big Nels and Avery," Amy said bitterly. "Oh, Anse, it's my fault. It didn't have to happen!"

"It was in the cards," Anse growled. "No harm's done."

He went over to the front window and looked out, and Amy went over to Jim. "I'm goin' to get up," Jim announced to her.

"No!" Both Amy and Anse shouted it with a unanimity that made Jim blink.

"But I've had a night's sleep and food," Jim protested. "I'm all right. You can't let—"

"The hell I can't," Anse said grimly. "Amy can shoot and she can stay out of the way. You stay in bed."

Jim settled back into a smoldering silence. Did Barden think this was all in fun that he'd let Amy chance being shot? They didn't know Riling like he knew him. Riling wouldn't hesitate to shoot Amy if by doing it he could get to Jim and Jim knew it. He'd tried to tell them both, and they hadn't listened.

He watched Amy, who was standing at the foot of his bed, flattened against the wall. Occasionally she would peer out through the window, then pull her head back quickly. If anything happened to her, Jim thought—and then he stopped thinking about it. This was the girl who'd laid a slug so close to him on the river that day that she'd nicked his hat. But if Riling succeeded in rushing the shack and taking it her shooting wouldn't do much good. No, there was a way to stop it, and he'd take that way.

Jim said, "Barden, come here."

Anse came over, and Jim talked to him, knowing Amy was listening and watching. "Before this goes any farther tell Riling I'll go with him."

Anse glanced up at Amy and only grinned and shook his head. "These walls are thick. They can't burn us out, and we got plenty of shells."

"But he's an Injun, I tell you!" Jim said hotly. "He won't quit till he's got me and he'll kill you both to do it."

Amy came around the bed and said angrily, "So we should let him take you and shoot you, just to save our own necks!"

Jim glared angrily at her and then spoke to Barden. "Then sing out to them that she's comin' out. They'll let her through."

"No!" Amy said immediately.

"Do it!" Jim said angrily to Barden.

"I won't go," Amy said calmly. "If you put me out I'll stand right out there and shoot at them."

Barden shrugged. "She was out there once and she risked gettin' hurt to come back here." He added dryly, "It looks like this is where she wants to be, don't it?"

He turned and went back to his post. Amy gave Jim a grave, questioning look and went back to the foot of the bed.

Jim turned his face to the wall, raging at his own helplessness. He had to lie there and watch it happen, as it would sooner or later. But he couldn't do it! He had to make Barden understand someway that Riling was desperate, that he knew he'd lost and that he'd risk his life to get the man responsible.

Jim said, "Barden, I want to talk to you alone."

In the dusk he saw Amy turn her head and look at him first and then at Anse.

"The lean-to," Anse said reluctantly.

Amy hesitated a moment, as if knowing they would talk about her, and then she went out. Somebody in the cotton-woods started pumping shots which thumped heavily into the thick logs of the shack.

Anse came over and sat on Jim's bed.

"We got to get her out of here," Jim said.

"She won't go."

"Make her. If you say so she'll go."

Anse regarded him with shrewd dissent in his eyes. "You don't know much about women, do you, Garry?"

"No."

"Why do you think she come back if it wasn't on account of you?"

Jim just stared at him and then he said flatly, "No."

"I'm right."

Jim's hand slowly plucked the blanket as he and Barden eyed each other. Then Jim said, "And why do you think I want to get her out of here?"

"The same reason, I reckon," Anse said.

"You're wrong about her," Jim said steadily. "I've helped her father. Why wouldn't she want to help me?" He paused a moment. "You were right about me though, Anse. That's the way it is. But I've thought it over a lot more than you have. It wouldn't work, Anse, not even if she'd have me. I'm not her kind. Before I got hurt I was plannin' to ride out when this was finished. And I'd still like to finish it my own way."

"How's that?"

"With her not around. I'd like one more crack at Riling—alone. Will you go?"

Anse stood up and called, "All right, Amy," and went back to the window. That was his answer.

Amy came back, and she said to Anse, "Maybe you better go bar the door on the lean-to, Anse."

When he'd gone Amy came up to Jim's bed and knelt beside it. "The walls were pretty thin, Jim. I heard you."

Jim looked at her searchingly in the dusk. He couldn't really see her face, but he didn't need to. He'd carried her image in his mind for weeks now, so that he even knew how the hair curled off her temple and fell to her shoulder in that sleek and beautiful line. He took her hand and said, "Amy, pretend you didn't hear. Because it can't be. I've been fiddle footed and no good all my life; I've even been a gun hand part of it. I'm not askin' any woman to take that."

"I knew that when I came here. I've always known that—and I don't believe it."

"But that's what I am, Amy. That's me!" Jim said flatly.

"That's you, Jim—stubborn, proud and foolish still. Don't you see how useless talk is, Jim? I'm here and I'm staying."

Jim came up on his elbows, mouth open to protest, when all hell cut loose from outside. The glass spattered out of the window above Jim's head, and Barden's clock on the shelf behind the stove seemed to explode in a great racketing whir of the spring before it crashed to the floor.

Anse piled in from the lean-to, grabbing his rifle on the way. Amy broke away from against Jim's grasp and picked up her rifle.

For minutes then the twilight was alive with gunfire. Riling had moved in to the very edge of the cottonwoods and the corral, and now they were sending a withering hail of lead into the door and windows.

But as it grew darker Anse remarked something and spoke about it. "Amy, hold your fire. They'll have to cross this snow if they want to make the shack. And they'll show on it. Watch the snow, and when something black moves against it cut down on it."

Jim lay on the bed, cursing at his own helplessness while Amy and Anse scanned the deepening darkness. It was as Anse said. The snow was a gray against the night's black; the trees looked black, the corral and barn a sooty smudge against the snow.

And then Amy saw something moving. She watched it carefully, and it veered toward her in the night. She could make it out now, a man walking hesitantly and slowly toward the house, curious if he could be seen.

Amy took careful sight on him and then moved the gun to the right and fired. The gun flash blinded her, but she could hear the pounding of the man's feet as he retreated to shelter.

The gloom of the cabin was deep then, and Jim couldn't see Amy any more. He could hear her breathing and her every movement, and her presence was close and dear to him. She was going to stay because of him. Jim hated that thought and was humbled by it. The irony of it, their meeting here when he was helpless to aid in protecting her, was like gall to him.

The firing had ceased entirely now. Anse cocked his head and then murmured, "I can hear 'em talkin' down there in the cottonwoods."

On the heel of his words Riling's voice lifted in the night. "Garry! Oh, Garry! I want to talk to you."

"He ain't here!" Anse yelled back.

"You're lying," Riling said flatly. "He's there. His horse is in the corral."

"I picked it up last night," Anse called. "What do you want with me?"

"Tell Garry something for me," Riling said. His voice was getting an edge of anger now. "Tell him I'll give him a chance to surrender."

Jim said swiftly, "Take him up on it, Anse."

Anse yelled, "He ain't here, I tell you."

Riling called back, "I'll give him three minutes. Then I'm riding into town for Manker and more men."

The three of them were silent, considering this news. Jim said bleakly, "He'll do it too. And Manker will come."

He saw Amy loom up beside his bed. She reached for his hand and took it and then sat down on the bed. "Hush, Jim. Let him go. Manker won't watch a man shot."

Jim knew better. Manker wouldn't have to see it. Riling could wait, but it would come. Jim knew the implacability of the man, and neither Anse nor Amy did.

Riling's voice lifted once more into the night. "Coming out, Garry?"

"No," Anse yelled.

They listened. They heard the soft clop-clop, the rustle of leaves made by Riling's horse as he rode out. He'd kept his word; he was going for reinforcements.

Afterward the man at the corral started to shoot half heartedly at the shack, and someone out in the cottonwoods fired now and then.

Amy and Anse were at the windows again, peering out into the night. It was so dark in the room that Jim could see nothing.

It was then that he made his decision. He held his breath and cautiously pushed himself to a sitting position in bed. The pain of his wound knifed at him, and he waited there, sitting upright until it had subsided. Then gently he swung his feet to the floor and stood up. Again the searing in his side, and he put a hand against the wall to steady himself. He stood there in the dark, waiting for his mind to adjust itself to this pain. It was bearable. His whole side was sore and hurt deep within him, but he could get used to it. That was all he wanted to know.

"Jim." It was Amy. She had heard strange movements from the bed.

"I'm here," Jim said.

The height from which his voice came brought Amy across the room. When she saw the black hulk of him standing she cried out, "Jim! You're out of bed!"

"To stay," Jim growled.

Anse stepped over to him and put a hand on his arm, which Jim gently removed. Something in him hoped Amy wouldn't protest, and he sighed with relief when she said quietly, "What is it, Jim?"

"Riling," Jim said briefly. "Let me talk. He's gone to Sun Dust. I'm going to follow him."

It was Anse who protested sharply, cursing him. Jim said stubbornly, "A half-hour after I'm gone tell Big Nels you'll give up. When they see I'm not here they won't do anything. That's all."

"What about a horse? Have you thought of that?" Anse asked savagely.

"Amy's horse is loose, isn't he? I've been lyin' here in bed and listenin' to him trompin' around off there at the end of the house."

Still Amy didn't speak. Jim knew it would come, probably in the form of a simple request that he not go. And that would be the hardest to refuse, but he would refuse it.

Anse said harshly, "Amy, are you goin' to let him?"

"Yes, she is," Jim said.

"Amy?" Anse insisted.

Amy was long in answering, and Jim listened for it.

"Do you have to go?" she asked finally.

Jim was thankful for that and he wanted her to understand if she could. "I've got to," he said quietly. "It's him or me, Amy. It always will be until one of us is dead. He won't quit and I won't, and if I wait for Manker that would be quitting. No. I'm going to find him—now—because I've got to know."

Amy moaned softly and came into his arms. Jim hugged her close to him, smelling the clean scent of her hair, feeling her fine straight body against him. She was all a man would ever want, and more, and now it seemed more urgent than ever that he go. Amy raised her hands to his face and bent his head down and kissed him on the lips. And then she backed off into the darkness.

When Jim could trust himself to speak he said, "I want a gun."

Anse handed his belt and gun to him, and Jim strapped them on. He put on his coat and Stetson and then walked slowly toward the door, holding his breath against the new throb in his side. Somewhere against the front wall he knew Amy was watching him, but she wouldn't speak again. She knew.

Jim slowly opened the door, and before he stepped out into

the chill night he said to Anse, "When I'm back against the lean-to open up on the corral."

He shut the door behind him. Whoever was in the corral couldn't see him, he knew, until he crossed the snow, and then he would be plainly visible. It was because of this that he had asked Anse to fire, hoping to draw a return fire whose powder flash would blind the man at the trigger.

He moved slowly down toward the end of the shack, crossing the window and then the corner, and finally stood against the dark bulk of the lean-to, looking out toward the cottonwoods where the horse was loose.

Presently Anse opened up at the corral. He put a dozen shots into it before an answering fusillade of hotly returned fire.

It was during this shooting that Jim walked calmly and slowly across to the cottonwoods. If they saw him he could neither run nor well return their fire, and he would be trapped. A kind of narrowing, dismal fatalism was with him then until he reached the first tree without drawing a shot.

The rest was easy. He found the horse deep in the cottonwoods, coaxed him to him and then led him slowly out of hearing of the men surrounding the shack. He mounted then and headed toward Sun Dust.

"There's a dead man," Anse said grimly when Jim had gone. He went moodily to the other window and looked out. Presently he heard Amy's slow, stifled sobbing and regretted that he had spoken. But it was the truth. Jim Garry wouldn't come back, and Anse cursed him for a headstrong, wild fool. And all the time he was praying to his own small gods that he was wrong.

The half-hour dragged out, and then Anse said to Amy, "Ready?"

"Yes."

Anse called out, "We surrender. Nels, can you hear me?" When Nels answered, Anse said, "I'm going to light the lamp and carry it, and we'll both come out on this side. All right?"

He got Nels's affirmative answer and struck a match and lighted the lamp. He smoothed the covers of the bed down, picked up the lamp and walked out into the snow, Amy behind him.

Two men approached them: Nels and Chet Avery.

Nels said, "Stand right there until the boys go through the shack."

Moten and Pindalest came in the other door and thoroughly searched the room and the lean-to.

When they came out Anse said dryly, "Satisfied?"

"He ain't there," Moten said blankly.

"He never was," Anse lied. "Now my arm's gettin' tired holdin' this lamp. I'm goin' back in and put it down."

He turned and went back into the shack ahead of Amy, and the others followed in silence. Once in the shack Anse looked at them, cold contempt in his eyes. "You ought to be mighty proud of the company you run with, boys. Shooting at a woman and an old man all night."

"Where's Garry?" Pindalest demanded hotly.

"Who ever said he was here?" Anse countered. "Riling?"

They nodded, and Anse laughed. "I thought so." He looked at each man carefully, staring him down. "You boys swallowed Riling and his yarns almost as slick as I did. Believed him, let him tell you what to do. Where are you now?"

Somebody shifted his feet uncomfortably, and Anse said, "I'll tell you where I am. I ain't got a son any more. I'll tell you where you are too. You're licked and you know it." His glance settled on Chet Avery. "Been home lately?"

Avery answered warily, "Not in five days."

"Your barn's burned," Anse said bluntly. "Know who done it? Joe Shotten. I seen him from the rim watchin' it burn. He's Riling's man and now, by God, he's a deputy sheriff. A deputy sheriff, appointed by Riling, burnin' barns! You tell me, Chet; what the hell's it all about?"

He made a weary gesture with his hand. "No, don't tell me. Get the hell out. I'm sick of fools; I'm sick of the whole pack of you. Clear out."

He waited until he'd heard them ride out and then he said to Amy, "I've got to know. You comin' to town with me?"

"It may not be too late to bring help for Jim," Amy said quietly. "Let's stop at Blockhouse on the way."

17

It took Jim longer than he'd counted on to reach Sun Dust. When he walked his horse into Sun Dust's street the town was dark, save for the lights in the saloons, the feed stable and the hotel. Jim noticed that Manker's office was dark, and he reined up and looked at it, gray speculation in his mind. Had he ridden too slowly, so that he was late and had missed Riling? He didn't think so, because when Riling arrived with the news he would wake the town and clean out the saloons with his story. He had no way of knowing, of course, that Riling had first detoured to Blockhouse to make sure Lufton wasn't there. Jim rode on at the steady, careful pace he'd held to these last hours, and the pain in his side was something clean-burning and steady and controlled. He'd carefully geared the speed of his travel to that pain, knowing above all things that he couldn't face Riling sick and useless.

He rode on downstreet, and the sight of the ponies at the hitch rail in front of the two saloons reassured him. Abreast of the Bella Union, he reined in at the tie rail and sat his horse a moment. While he rested, a big, infinitely patient man, he looked over these horses. It was too dark to recognize them, and after dismounting he started his search. The neck of the third horse he touched was wet with sweat. Jim spoke soothingly to him and ran his hand down over the left hip. Yes, there was Riling's brand.

Jim turned his head and looked at the Bella Union and then

he came up to the plank walk and strode over toward the saloon. He did not head for the door but for the window. He looked over the frosted lower half of it and could see the whole interior of the Bella Union.

Riling and Shotten were having a drink at the bar with Barney, the barkeep.

Jim backed away and stood motionless, considering the odds. He wasn't afraid of Shotten and Riling together, but it was the bartender, with his inevitable sawed-off shotgun, that troubled him. He hadn't forgotten that it was this bartender who had steered him into trouble the first night in town.

And then he knew he was going in anyway. Let happen what was going to happen.

He turned his head then at the sound of a rider approaching. The rider put his horse in at the Bella Union and dismounted before the horse had stopped. He swung under the tie rail and then, at sight of Jim, he hauled up abruptly.

It was Chet Avery. He looked long at Jim, his slow mind accepting this, and then said slowly: "He in there?"

"Riling? Yes."

"Shotten, I mean."

"He's in there too."

"I'm goin' in," Avery said in a stubborn voice.

"No, you're not," Jim said. "Stay clear of me, Avery." He started to move.

"Wait a minute," Avery said. "Barney likes Riling. That makes three against you."

Jim said nothing, and Avery went on in a musing, almost self-derisory voice, "I'm slow, I reckon, but I've caught up now, Garry. I got a score to settle, like you." He paused. "Riling will come out if I tell him you're here. Then I can hold Barney in there."

As soon as Avery spoke Jim knew this was the way to do it. He trusted Avery. He said, "Tell him if he doesn't come out I'll come in after him."

Avery grunted and put his hand on the doorknob and went in. Riling and Shotten both looked over their shoulders as he entered, and Riling put down his glass. He turned slowly, scowling.

"I thought I told you to stay at Barden's."

Avery said quietly, "He's outside. Garry, I mean."

Riling's face altered, came alert, hardened. "Now?"

"He's out on the street, waiting for you."

A crooked smile twisted Riling's mouth, and he said, "Well, now," and hauled up his belt. Shotten, not even waiting for the word, faded down the bar and headed for the rear door.

Avery stood stock-still and let Riling walk past him to the door, and then he went up to Barney. "Give me your greener," he said.

The bartender, knowing Avery for one of Riling's men, lifted the shotgun onto the bar, and Avery took it. Then he turned and headed swiftly for the rear door.

"Hey," Barney said, uncertainty in his voice.

Chet stepped out into the alley and turned down it. At the place where two stores almost joined each other, leaving a space of three feet or so between them, Avery paused. He looked up this narrow alleyway and saw Shotten making his way toward the plank walk.

Avery waited patiently until he saw Shotten reach the walk, pause, dodge back and then lift his gun.

Smiling, stubborn Chet Avery raised the shotgun to his shoulder and took careful sight, and the memory of his girl, frightened and angry and shamed, kept his arm rock-steady.

Jim had stepped back into the middle of the dusty street, watching the door of the Bella Union. Riling wouldn't dodge, he knew. Too much lay between them for that. This that was happening now was inevitable, the foundation of it laid with a hatred they could no more help than they could help breathing. And Riling wasn't a coward. He feared nothing, and Jim knew this would be welcome to him.

He saw the saloon door open, and Riling, thick shoulders silhouetted against the window, stepped out onto the walk.

Jim felt a cold, sure wrath that was beyond anger at sight of him. He knew that even with a bullet in his brain he would live to kill Riling. He knew this and he hugged the knowledge close to him and was silent, waiting.

Riling said in a dry, hating tone, "This is a pleasure, Jim."

"For me," Jim murmured.

At that moment the raking, booming blast of a shotgun let off in a confined place shattered the silence of the night. On the heels of it Shotten was driven out onto the plank walk. He hit it on his belly and rolled over twice. The second roll carried him off the walk into the dust of the street; he lay there limp and unmoving.

Jim said, "That leaves just you, Tate."

It came sharply to Riling then that the odds had shifted and that whoever held the shotgun was with Jim. He knew then that the time was here and he moved.

He walked toward the tie rail, and his hand streaked for the gun in the holster at his hip. Sudden urgency rode him, hurrying him, pushing him. He pulled his gun and shot blindly, shot fast, angrily.

Jim's hand fell to his holster when Riling moved. He lifted the gun deftly, cocking it in the same movement, and as he swung it up Riling shot. Jim's gun arced up and settled, and Riling shot again, and now Jim saw the black, high sight bisect those wide shoulders at the chest, and when it sank out of sight he fired.

He saw Riling's body jar under the impact of the slug. Riling put back a foot to brace himself and then he staggered forward and lunged into the tie rail with an impact that almost uprooted the post. Leaning against it, holding to it with one big hand, he raised his gun again and he brought all the terrible force of his will into the single concentration of his aim. His gun wavered, and he steadied it in one last, wild effort.

And then his knees folded. As he fell his chin rapped the tie rail, and his head went back, and then he was hanging there by one hand, his chest just off the ground. He made a last stubborn effort to raise his gun hand and couldn't, and then his hold on the tie rail broke. He fell and rolled over on his back and was still.

Jim and Avery met at the tie rail and silently regarded Riling. There was the sound of a man running down the boardwalk, and Jim looked up, aware for the first time in minutes that his side hurt with a stubborn, pounding ache.

Sheriff Manker hauled up on the plank walk now and looked carefully at Riling and then raised his eyes to Jim.

"It was fair," Avery said bluntly. "I saw it. You got a dead deputy too, Manker. I killed him."

Now the late revelers in the other saloon pounded up, and Manker silently took the guns from Jim and Avery. "Come on down to the office," he said, and there was little sympathy in his voice.

After giving orders to some men in the crowd Manker led the way downstreet to the dark office. While he was fumbling with the key to unlock it three riders came in off the flats. Manker went in and lighted the lamp and then said, "All right, step in."

But Jim waited, and so did Avery, so that Manker came to the door. And now Moten, Big Nels and Pindalest headed in to the tie rail, and Nels stepped out of the saddle. He saw the grave faces of the three men and said with a quick interest in his voice, "Where's Riling?"

"Dead," Avery said.

Jim said to them, "Come inside. There's something you'll want to hear."

Moten swung down. Pindalest stayed mounted, staring blankly at Jim. Jim started toward him, swung under the hitch rack and stopped beside his stirrup. "I won't even ask you, Pindalest," he said. He seized the man's belt and yanked him out of the saddle, and he fell heavily into the dust. Jim looked up at the others, his expression wicked and challenging. None spoke, not even Manker, as Pindalest rose, too scared to protest.

Jim said to him, "Get into the office."

Once in the office, Jim waited until Pindalest was seated in the sheriff's chair, and then he said to the others, "Take a good look at him. There's the man you were fighting for."

And then in blunt and harsh language he told them about Riling's deal with Pindalest and how they themselves had been used to the very bitter end when Riling had turned them toward a manhunt for revenge. Jim explained his own part in it, how he'd come at Riling's bidding, how they'd quarreled at Commissary and what he'd done to help Lufton by hiding Pindalest. He told it all, sparing neither himself nor these three nesters nor Manker.

When he was finished Pindalest came out of his chair. "You can't prove it!" he said hotly. "It's lies!" To the men he said, "Make him prove it!"

Jim shook his head. "I don't aim to prove it, Pindalest. I'm telling the truth. They can believe it or not. I don't care."

It was then that Jim caught sight of John Lufton. He'd been standing in the doorway for minutes, listening. His dark eyes were arrogant, faintly amused, as he regarded Pindalest.

Avery was the next to see Lufton, and then Moten and Big Nels. They watched him with hard and hostile doubt.

Lufton walked slowly across to Pindalest, not even looking at the nesters. "You're going to buy some prime Texas beef, Pindalest," he said. "Anyone tell you yet?"

The agent's face was sullen, his eyes wicked with hatred for Lufton.

Lufton said, "I'll rest them for a couple of weeks and then I'll start my drive. I'll skirt the Three Braves and be on the reservation before the heavy snows. I'll take cash for payment, too, as the contract specified. Any objections?"

Pindalest looked at him for a long moment. There was no way out of it, and he knew it, since he couldn't let the Indians starve. But the look of hatred he gave Lufton only brought a faint smile to Lufton's dark face.

"I thought not," Lufton said mildly.

He turned now to the nesters. "Don't think I mean to give up my range to you again," he murmured. "I meant what I said the other day. Everything south of the road is mine." He looked at Avery. "That means you move or I move you. What'll it be?"

Avery said stolidly, "I'll move. It looks like I got to."

Lufton gave one small look of malice to Manker and said, "Good," and walked out. Jim followed him. They were on the walk outside when they heard the scuffle inside the office. They turned just in time to see Pindalest, propelled by the thick plowman's shoes of Avery, explode out of the doorway and sprawl in the street. He scrambled to his feet, vaulted into the saddle and then fled into the night, shrilling curses at them as he vanished into the darkness.

Jim and Lufton walked upstreet in the darkness, and Lufton said, "Amy's in Doc Hogan's office. She said to send you up for a new bandage if you could still walk."

Lufton's voice was oddly stiff, uneasy, and he would not look at Jim.

"All right," Jim said then and started to move away.

"Wait, Garry," Lufton said, and he put a hand on Jim's arm. Jim stopped and faced him, and the two men looked at each other in the darkness.

"When you're old things can happen too fast," Lufton said quietly. He hesitated, feeling for words. "I know Elser and like him, so I know what Carol's man will be like when he's well. I wasn't surprised when they told me tonight. But Amy—" He paused, looking searchingly at Jim.

"Yes."

"She's not like Carol. She's—" He stopped talking, having no words to express his thoughts. Then he said kindly, "I guess you know, son," and walked on.

Jim headed for Doc Hogan's and hurried.

J.T. EDSON

Brings to Life the Fierce and Often Bloody Struggles of the Untamed West